STEP INTO MAGIC

PORTALS TO WHYLAND BOOK I

DAY LEITAO

Ebook ISBN: 978-1-7750637-4-2

Print Book ISBN: 978-1-7750637-5-9

Cover illustration by Xilveroxas

CONTENTS

1

ON FOOT AND SHOES

More than anything, Karina hated to be wrong.

Wait. There was something worse: admitting she was wrong.

Just the thought sent her into a hair-raising shiver. But there she was, giving herself a firm reminder: *never accept invitations to alternate worlds from strangers.*

Quite useless advice, considering the odds of this experience ever being repeated. How could thoughtful, logical Karina have fallen for that? How did it even start? Ah, yes... she was looking for something. Something impressive. Something great. Something meaningful. She found something all right, but she was far from sure it was any of those.

As with any journey, it started with a walk.

~

KARINA LOATHED questions without clear answers. Why couldn't everything be simple, like math? Either the answer's wrong or it's right. No *maybes* or *almosts*. That meant she hated history, especially that last stupid test and the embarrassing grade that came with it.

But did it even matter? She wanted to believe that life could be greater than just projects and school and family and classmates and all that day-to-day sameness. Karina stopped. Her feet had carried her some fifteen blocks from her apartment, and she found herself in a busy commercial street with nice shops, cafes, and restaurants. People passed by and the world moved around her while she tried to figure out where she fit in —and where she didn't, unable to find where that emptiness in her chest had come from. It wasn't just her low social studies grades.

Glittery letters on a cardboard spelled "Yard Sale," without any translation. This was an English neighborhood in a French-speaking city. Curious and having no real direction, she followed the sign.

Junk lay over brown, overgrown grass in front of an ancient, decrepit wooden house. There were coats, small objects, boots, and too many shoes to count. Karina wondered who would want other people's smells. Most shoes were somber: brown or black and slightly worn. One pair stood out, though, as the shoes almost looked like they were made of steel, not really for wearing, just decorative objects shaped like silver flats. Out of curiosity, Karina touched them. The feeling surprised her—they were as soft as fleece.

An old woman with a grey ponytail sat on a rocking chair, behind all the stuff. Karina asked her, "Excuse me, what material is this?"

The woman didn't raise her eyes from a brown leather-bound book she was gripping. "I have no idea."

Karina pretended to take a closer look at the shoes just to check if they had any unwanted smell without being rude or obvious. Thankfully there was none.

"They're ten dollars," the woman said, this time standing next to Karina as if implying she should either buy them or stop touching.

Karina put the shoes back on the chair where she'd found them.

The woman stared at her. "Size seven."

That was Karina's size, but she hadn't asked that question and wasn't planning on buying any of that crap. She turned around and walked away.

As she was getting home, she kept thinking how those silver shoes were curious objects. They felt so different from how they looked, and ten dollars was not a lot of money. But used shoes were a bad idea. Those didn't seem used, but who knew? Ten dollars could go for something more important, like... chocolate —perhaps not *that* important. When would she ever see shoes like those again? A disturbing thought crossed her mind. What if someone else bought them? Those precious shoes were a bargain. Someone would probably notice them. This could not be. Karina ran back as fast as she could.

The silver shoes were still there, shiny as ever, reflecting the sunlight. Panting, she gave the money to the woman and grabbed them. "I wanna take these."

They were Karina's now.

CAYLA CLOSED HER BOOK. She had memorized all the maps of Whyland; every river, every mountain, every major city, and yet, they remained two-dimensional: paintings on paper, still images without much meaning. Beyond the walls of the castle was a world she had yet to see with her own eyes. There was also someone she hadn't seen in over a year. Her chest tightened. She closed her eyes and tried to forget those memories and the pain they brought with them.

Inside, there was still something she wanted to learn. If she pressed her old teacher, sometimes he taught her a little, but only sometimes.

Master Odell raised his eyes. "I see you're finished. We'll pick more books from the library. Any subject you're interested in?"

He seemed to be in a good mood. Cayla's younger sister Ayanna was not in the room, so perhaps that was her chance. "It's not in books. At least not in any we'd find in the main library here. You know much more than you've taught us."

A flash of understanding crossed Odell's face but he sighed. "Some things need to be buried. Forgotten. Or at least that's what your father wants."

"He doesn't need to know."

Odell shook his head. "I serve your father, Cayla."

Cayla gave up and stared at her book. Odell was in a bad mood.

KARINA STARED at the shoes in her hands. Shoes. Right. Hardly an answer to some great question she was yet to ask. But the shoes were pretty—and different from any she'd ever seen. Despite their shiny finish, they were thin and flexible, almost like real ballet flats, but the sole was thicker, like normal shoes. Mysterious and fascinating, they'd become her special secret, a secret she didn't want to share with anyone, not even her friends.

A knock on the door startled her. Karina barely had time to shove her glistening shoes in the closet before Zoe walked in pulling a trolley suitcase. Overkill for a sleepover, but hey, to each their own quirks. For the first time since they'd become friends, Zoe was early, and Karina's mom must have welcomed her in through the front door.

Zoe spread the outfits onto the bed. "I brought clothes. For you and me. You'll look so good you won't even recognize yourself."

Karina stared at her friend. Zoe was pretty and all, and Karina didn't usually mind her enthusiasm for fashion, but sometimes she went too far. Plus, Karina was perfectly comfortable with her own non-supermodel looks, wavy brown hair and eyes, thank you.

Zoe cleared her throat. "I meant... you usually look great. You're cute. It's just, sometimes, it's a matter of mixing and matching, trying different things. Not that you have to lend me anything—"

Karina shrugged. "You can have anything you want."

Zoe smiled. "Thanks."

The idea of Zoe borrowing anything from Karina was rather preposterous, as her clothes were so much plainer than her friend's, but at least she didn't want to make her feel bad about it.

Zoe started picking outfits. "We'll look amazing at the dance."

So that was what it was about. Karina had stopped caring about school dances long ago, but there was something sweet in Zoe's endless enthusiasm for them. At least her friend didn't bring her special eyeshadow for brown eyes or come up with a ridiculous suggestion to tame Karina's hair. But it was worse: she started talking about her crush. Karina had always felt like the least qualified person to give love advice, until she figured out that it wasn't so much about advice as it was about listening and nodding. Karina, for her part, didn't have a crush and was glad not to suffer from any of the illogical behaviors associated with the affliction.

Even with an overflowing suitcase, Zoe had somehow forgotten her pajamas. Karina prepared a bed on the floor and told her friend to get a pair from the top drawer in the closet. Not hearing any sound, she turned around to check on Zoe. "Did you find it?"

The girl stood in silence with her eyes fixated on something in the bottom of the closet. Oh, no. Not only had she seen the silver shoes, she stared at them with the greediest eyes. Karina's heart sped up, without any idea where that fear came from. All she felt was that by no means should her friend even touch those shoes.

She tried to divert her attention. "I'll get you the pajamas. We need to sleep."

Without moving her eyes, Zoe asked, "Where did you get those?"

Perhaps Karina could undervalue the shoes and make her friend lose interest in them. "They're yard sale shoes. Too small."

"Can I try them?"

"No!" Ouch. That sounded desperate. Karina tried to change her tone. "I mean... they won't fit you."

"My feet are smaller than yours."

"Yeah, they'll be too big for you."

Zoe bent to pick up the shoes. "I'll see if they fit."

Karina was faster, sweeping them up in her hands "You can't. They... are not mine. They're a cousin's, and she's going to wear them for a wedding."

Zoe rolled her eyes. "I'm sure *your cousin* won't mind if I just put them on for a second."

Karina sat far on the bed and put the shoes behind her back. "No."

Zoe sat next to her. "Karina, you're being ridiculous. Let me try your shoes. I just want to see how they look. Don't give me this fake cousin talk."

"Fine." Lying was pointless. "I'm sorry. These shoes, they're special to me. I don't know how to explain."

"Are you four or fourteen? Still haven't learned to share?"

"I just like them very much."

Zoe sighed. "You said I could have anything I liked from your closet."

"And you said I didn't need to lend you anything if I didn't want to."

Zoe sat down again, looked away for a moment, and then looked back at Karina. "So you're not lending me the shoes."

Well, no, and it sounded terrible when her friend put it like that, but before Karina could come up with anything to say, Zoe seemed to change her mind.

"Fine, you're right." Her voice was calm and understanding. "You don't have to lend me anything if you don't want to. There's no point arguing." She had a big smile. "You'll see."

BY FRIDAY THE GIRLS' argument had become little more than a distant memory. Karina walked into the school with her friend Tori. With lights down, doors shut, and only the gym illuminated, the school didn't feel like the place she went almost every day. Karina had on a black dress and a small purse, both weighed down by the discomfort she felt in most social situations. But something else was making her feel uneasy. Zoe would be coming around later, but that was normal. The girls found a corner near the entrance stairs and watched people coming in as if on a strange fashion runway surrounded by a handrail.

Karina was debating with herself whether she should nod to people she didn't usually say hi to when a familiar face at the top of the stairs cheered her up.

Zoe.

Karina was about to smile when she noticed what was on her friend's feet: the silver shoes. Zoe saw her surprised look and replied not with shame or embarrassment, but with a smirk. Karina felt hurt, betrayed. More than that, and beyond the feeling of not wanting to share something, she felt as if a part of her had been taken and was being used. A feeling almost as if someone had used her toothbrush or underwear, but this was much stronger.

Karina's first thought was to take back the shoes by force. Zoe would fall from her pride. Those thoughts formed an image in Karina's mind. As the image got clearer, her anger disappeared, replaced by worry. In her mental image, there was blood surrounding Zoe's head, as if Karina's desire had escaped her control and had become an independent monster. The awful image looked real, felt so real it was disturbing.

Zoe was about to descend the stairs. They were just stairs—surrounded by a steel handrail. But the impression remained. Karina ran as fast as she could towards her friend. The image in her head had almost become true; Zoe slipped. Had it not been for Karina holding her mid-fall, the girl would have landed face down from the top of the stairs. Not only had she slipped, the steel handrail had cracked.

2

VISITS

The day was so dark that Karina took longer than normal to wake up. But no. Her oversleeping had nothing to do with the grey clouds covering the horizon. It was exhaustion from the previous night. Zoe walking in the gym was the last clear image in Karina's mind. After that, all memories were a jumbled blur. Lights being turned on, an ambulance coming in, hoards of people surrounding them, the shoes flying off Zoe's feet, the shoes folded inside Karina's purse. The shoes—and what they seemed capable of doing—sent shivers down her spine.

In the kitchen, her mother blamed the poor maintenance of the school but was thankful that everything ended up well and added, "It was nice of you to go with Zoe to the hospital."

Karina recalled that part then. Just a broken leg. It could have been worse. Everyone said it, but she was the only one who understood the full extent of how worse it could have been. She felt guilty, certain that the shoes had played a part in Zoe's fall, although she had no idea how.

She ate quickly, helped her dad with the dishes, and ran back to her room. The shoes were still in her purse, rolled into a small size. Unbelievable that amidst all the confusion there had been time to hide the shoes and nobody— not even Tori— had noticed them. For everyone, it seemed that Zoe had come to the dance barefoot, because she'd never answered anything when asked about her shoes, claiming she didn't remember them, as if a near-death experience could make Zoe forget what kind of footwear she had on.

Enough from the previous night. The cracked handrail gave Karina chills. The shoes were evil, pure evil; succeeded in breaking a leg and nearly breaking up a friendship. Perhaps they should be returned or thrown away. But no, they were too precious for that. Karina would keep them, hide them, and never wear them or let anyone see them again. She placed the purse on a high shelf in her closet.

DESPITE THE WET and gray weather, Karina's parents went out in the late afternoon, after inquiring a thousand times if she was okay, which was dumb since she wasn't the one who'd fallen. As a result, she found herself alone with her thoughts and decided to take a walk for the sake of sanity. A walk. She knew where she had to go.

Karina came to the same street where she'd found the sign. Of course there'd be no yard sale in this weather, but she could at least find the old house. But it wasn't in the street she thought it was—or in any street around it. Wasn't she able to recognize the house without the junk in front of it? Or maybe someone had renovated or demolished it. But there were neither demolished nor recently renovated houses anywhere. Maybe she was mistaken about the street. Maybe her memory was just bad. Maybe—she had no other explanation. The grey clouds were now coming down in minuscule droplets of rain, almost like a thick fog. She felt as if the dampness reached her bones, despite knowing well that it was a scientific impossibility. And she had definitely forgotten where the house was. Bad memory was not any type of impossibility.

THERE WAS something odd about opening the door and getting home by herself. How strange that not so long before, her parents needed someone to look after her, as if she would set the house on fire, run away, or starve to death. Now, a couple of years later, everything was different. That night, however, she felt lonely and slightly scared. Her mom had left dinner in the fridge, ready to be heated, but Karina decided to make toast instead. While cutting some moldy pieces from the old bread, she noticed that the lights in her room were on. And they changed as if something had moved near them. Karina told her stomach to chill. It could be Zoe. With a broken leg? Karina took a deep breath. What was the point in wondering, if she could walk there and find out? She felt stupid for that, but she actually had to gather her courage, get up, and go to her bedroom.

Indeed someone sat on her armchair: a beautiful woman wearing a long white dress that contrasted with her long, very shiny black hair. Her eyes were black too, deep, like old eyes that had seen many things, which was odd because the woman didn't look older than 35, 40 at most. Karina no longer felt scared or surprised. She had almost been expecting someone like that, not that she thought her parents had changed their minds and hired a cool-looking babysitter, but more that she had a feeling someone would come looking for the silver shoes, and the woman's looks fit the part. Karina's first thought was to run to her closet and check, but that didn't make sense because if the woman had been a thief, she wouldn't be hanging around. Karina wanted to say something but had no idea what.

The woman broke the silence. "You know why I'm here."

Karina thought she did, but thinking and saying are different things, and plus she didn't want to mention the shoes. "Uh, not really…"

The woman stared at Karina for a few long seconds, then said, "The silver shoes you have, I need them."

Karina closed her eyes, heaviness in her chest.

"Don't worry," the woman said. "I won't take them from you. In fact, that's something you should know already. The shoes cannot be stolen."

Or even borrowed. That explained what happened to Zoe.

The woman continued without moving her stare, "Those shoes were created by me, and they are magical, as I believe you noticed. Now you see, you might think magical shoes are a good thing to have, but that's not true unless you know how to use them. I am the only person who can take full advantage of the power of the silver shoes. Sure, other people have worn them and thought a tiny fraction of their power was good enough. But the problem lies in all the power they don't know how to control."

Karina didn't like where the conversation was going. She didn't plan on wearing the shoes again or letting anyone see them, but she still wanted to keep them, just to know that she had something rare and special. "So you're saying I should give you the shoes?"

The woman shook her head. "By no means. I want you to sell me the shoes. In exchange for them, I'll grant you a wish."

Karina almost scoffed but held herself back. The woman looked otherworldly and all, but she didn't look like a genie or anything. "And how can you do that?"

"Well, if I don't grant your wish, I'll be stealing the shoes. As I explained before, and as you witnessed yourself, the shoes cannot be stolen."

"But they're yours. Doesn't that have, like, a different rule?"

"They belong to you now. Now tell me: what is it that you want?"

Did she think Karina was that stupid? But on the other hand, the woman had said it with such conviction and power that it was almost contagious. It was hard not to trust the woman's voice and calm eyes. The idea was fair enough, even if a little crazy. No harm in trying. "World peace."

The woman looked confused and stared down for the first time. She was barefoot. "No, no, no, you have to wish something for yourself."

"Why? That's a good wish."

"It is. But you see, you cannot mess with other people's free will."

Oh well, that meant there would be no new era on Earth thanks to her. Still, she had to protest. "But you said I could wish anything."

"I said you could make a wish, and I forgot you people on this world don't know how to make wishes. Now wish something for you."

That meant ending poverty and pollution were out of the question. Karina had an idea. She almost hated herself for the stupid, silly thing she was about to ask, but it was the only thing she could think that would not affect other people, and her conscience was clear that she had tried to wish for something more important. "I... I would like to be popular. Not necessarily in school but be recognized, I guess."

The woman sighed. "You see, that's still about other people, because you want to change their perception of you."

Karina didn't agree. "No, people will perceive me as popular if I'm different, so the change is in me."

Again the woman thought for a moment before answering. "Yes and no. Right now what you want is only to change their perception of you. Think of something else, quickly, because my time's running out."

Karina waved her hands. "What can I wish? Everything I come up with you say doesn't work."

"I can't tell you what to wish, or I'd be wishing for you. It shouldn't be that complicated."

"It is. Everything I say is wrong…"

"It's not wrong. You just have to learn. Listen, I don't have any more time here. Let's do this: I'll come back tomorrow evening. I'll think of another way to buy the shoes from you. Ah, the shoes —try not to wear them. Keep them safe. There are other creatures in many worlds who want them, and not all of them are good. They can't steal the shoes from you or take them by force. But that doesn't mean they won't try."

Karina gulped at the thought of evil creatures looking for her and the shoes.

The woman continued, "I'll be back tomorrow. I have to go now."

Instead of disappearing in a cloud of smoke or flying out of the window, the woman simply walked to the front door and left. Perhaps she was just a great actress playing a trick, but then Karina noticed there was some sparkly dust floating on the place the woman had been seated. The woman—she had forgotten to ask her name.

3

GETTING REAL

Slowly, the sense of reality came back to Karina. Sparkly dust. Yeah, that was from blinking or whatever. Grant a wish. Was Karina still at the age of believing in fairy tales? She was a normal, logical person. Most fairy tales she knew were from a time when she had no word on the kind of entertainment assigned to her.

I want to be popular. Really? No. Really? That was the cherry on top of her stupidity. How could she have fallen for such crap? Thankfully she didn't sell the shoes for an empty promise. Wait. Did the woman have the nerve to steal the shoes right under her nose? Karina hurried to the closet and picked up her purse. The shoes were still there. What had this visit been all about then? Maybe Karina was just tired and seeing things, but what troubled her most was not having visions, but believing what they said. She went back to the kitchen, finished her toast, then returned to the bedroom, put on her pajamas, turned off all the lights, and lay on her bed. If she was going to believe in fairy tales, she'd better sleep before nine.

While midway on her journey between being awake and asleep, Karina heard what seemed to be something heavy falling in her bedroom. The sound would have startled her, had she not had enough of weird stuff and decided just to convince herself she was dreaming. Then she heard girls' voices.

"Ouch."

"It's all dark in here. I didn't think it'd be like that."

"Ayanna, you weren't even supposed to come. We need lights."

"We can try to find them."

"No, I'll take care of that."

"Cayla, you're not supposed to!"

"Shhh. Nobody will know about it."

"That's so cool."

At this point, Karina had the notion that she was awake and the voices were in fact in her bedroom. Her eyes were still closed in the hopes the voices would fade away on their own, but instead, they only got clearer and more real, to a point she could no longer hold her curiosity and had to look. She opened her eyes just enough to see without being noticed. A strange, orange glow illuminated the room. Two teenage girls stood near the window, reminding her of the woman she had previously seen, but dressed in simple green and orange summer dresses. Karina's study lamp lay broken on the floor.

This was getting to be too much. Arguing in her room was one thing, but starting to break things? No. Karina sat up. "Hey, what are you doing here?"

The girls looked surprised and scared. The oldest composed herself quickly, then walked to Karina and bowed.

"Our apologies for disturbing your sleep and breaking your, um, *thing*."

The younger girl hesitated at first, then also bowed. Their formality was artificial and almost comical. Still, Karina was so puzzled at having more strange visitors that she just kept listening.

The oldest girl continued, "My name is Cayla. I'm a Whyland Princess. This is my little sister Ayanna."

Ayanna rolled her eyes. "Little sister?" She then turned to Karina and said, "Whyland princess as well. And your name is?"

Cayla pushed her sister back. "I ask." She turned to Karina. "Who are you?"

Karina just stared in amazement. After the phony genie, now it was time for two princesses. Special shoes can really make one feel important. In the dim glow, all she could see was their shapes, their dresses, and their dark hair. The situation was too strange to be real but too real to be a dream. She didn't know what to make of this visit and had no idea where that light was coming from.

Karina looked around puzzled. "What's with the orange glow?"

The room fell dark.

"What orange glow?" a voice asked in the darkness.

Some nerve these girls had. The light from the window would have been enough to make shapes distinguishable in the dark, but not right after a light had been turned off. Still, Karina knew her room well enough to walk up to the switch on the wall.

Now clearly visible for the first time, the girls were simply two normal looking teenagers. They both had dark hair but looked different. The older girl, Cayla, seemed about fifteen or sixteen, wore a beige dress and had sharp facial features. In a plain blue dress, not green, Ayanna had a pleasant round face with bright eyes. She seemed around twelve.

"What are you doing here?" Karina asked.

Ayanna jumped ahead and talked fast. "We're really sorry. We didn't mean to disturb you. It's important. We need your help. It's the sh—" She noticed her sister's stare and looked down.

"Continue," Karina said.

"Right." Ayanna looked at her sister, who nodded, then took a deep breath and started, "Sometime ago, a day or two, Lylah, the witch, came here." She almost stumbled over her own words as she went without pausing to catch air. "We think she came here, to this room, and talked to you. We think she wanted her shoes. We think you still have them. And if she gets them, it is bad, like, really bad—the end of the world." Then she breathed again.

End of the world? A day before? That wasn't making much sense. The girl's fear and urgency were probably contagious, because Karina felt a chill in her stomach as she sat on her bed.

Cayla crouched in front of Karina, looking right in her eyes. "Do you still have the shoes?"

"Yes." It was no occasion for lies. "But, no. I mean, the only visit I received was tonight, and she didn't seem to be a witch. I mean, I don't know. But still, it was a little less than an hour ago, not yesterday."

Cayla's eyes widened. "The time difference. It's greater... So you're saying she came tonight?"

"Yes. But, I'm not sure she's this witch you are talking about. She seemed nice."

Ayanna rolled her eyes. "She had to seem nice! She's cunning."

"We followed her path to get here, so we know it was her," Cayla said. "Was she really convincing?"

Spot on. Karina nodded. She remembered with embarrassment her delight at the opportunity of making a wish. But one thing bewildered her. "If she's evil, why didn't she take the shoes?"

Cayla snorted. "Whatever protection she placed on them is backfiring."

That made sense. "She said she's coming back tomorrow evening."

"She'll have a plan by then," Ayanna said, sounding scared.

Cayla paced back and forth as she ran her hands through her long dark hair. "Yes, but that will give us plenty of time to act. If she's coming one day from now, and if one hour here is a day and a half back home, that should give us—"

"Over a month, in whatever you are thinking." Karina had no idea of which time difference they were talking about, but she was sure that if one hour equaled one and a half days, one day minus one hour equaled 34 and a half days.

"Right," Cayla said, apparently not pleased at the interruption.

"It can't be that much," her sister said.

Cayla scratched her chin and looked down, addressing no one. "It seems right, I think. We'll have to ask when we get back, but if we have at least one month, we'll be able to beat Lylah."

Things were getting clearer now. Karina got up and asked the dreaded question, "Is it the shoes you want?"

Ayanna shook her hands in front of her. "We don't want the shoes! They're evil."

Well, yeah. Karina knew that, but then she was confused as to the reason the girls were there. "What is it that you want, then?"

Cayla took a deep breath. "I'm gonna try to explain this from the beginning. That's why we came here." She tucked a strand of hair behind her ear. "Lylah is very powerful—"

"I get it," Karina interrupted. "She wants the shoes. You're saying she can't have them, so I won't give them to her. Does that solve your problem?"

Ayanna shook her head. "She'll find a way to get them. You'll be in danger, and us too."

"She can find you," Cayla added. "Then she'll steal them from you, or worse, make you give them to her. Next time she might not be nice about it."

Karina sat on her armchair and rested her head on her hand, with a slightly sick feeling in her stomach. Something didn't sound right in this story. The girls seemed fine, maybe a little annoying, but certainly not any of the so-called evil creatures that would come looking for the shoes—if it was true that evil creatures would come looking for the shoes. Unknowingly Karina still believed in what the woman had told her, and she was getting confused.

"Listen," Cayla said. "You don't want to keep those shoes; they'll only bring disaster into your life." She knelt and took one of Karina's hands in hers. "Lylah wants to take control of my father's kingdom. She is already gathering followers, but without the shoes, her plans can't go very far. My father has a strong army and can defend our people. But with the shoes, she'll be invincible. And there's more; with the shoes, she'll be able to cross over to different worlds easily, and that'll allow her to expand her dominion all over the universe. That means even the very world you live in might fall under her dark reign."

That sounded scary, but perhaps over-the-top, exaggerated scary. And something didn't make sense. "She just came. I mean, she just crossed over, didn't she?"

"Uh, yes," Cayla squinted. "But I think it would be different then. She would have power."

Fair enough. "And what do you want me to do?"

"Help us destroy the shoes," Cayla answered.

As Karina feared.

"You need to come to our father's castle," Cayla continued. "From there we'll set off. I'll help you, don't worry."

"Me too," Ayanna said.

Cayla scowled.

Did Karina hear right? "So, you mean, I have to go to your, uh, kingdom, place or whatever?"

Cayla blinked slowly and nodded. "Yes, you need to go to our kingdom. It's in a different vibrational frequency, so you can call it another world or dimension, for lack of a better definition."

Karina had a big smile. The idea of different parallel worlds was not that impossible in scientific terms, and if she could see it, she could perhaps try to understand the logic behind it. Why hadn't the girls mentioned this earlier?

Cayla returned her smile. "So, do you agree to come and help us?"

Karina shrugged. "Yeah, I think I could make, you know, the effort."

The right thing to say would have been "of course!" but Karina didn't want to sound too eager. The girls looked at each other, seeming hopeful and relaxed for the first time. Karina was also happy and excited, but suddenly, the thought of leaving her room in the middle of the night bothered her. "Wait... do you mean, now?"

"We can't waste time," Cayla replied.

"How long is it going to take?"

The girls looked at each other, and Cayla answered, "In our world, about a week or two, we think."

"Are the shoes that complicated to destroy?"

Ayanna opened her mouth to speak, but closed it when she noticed her sister's look.

Cayla answered, "Yes, a little complicated, but nothing we can't manage. But if she came yesterday, it means that a few days in our world will be just a few hours here."

That was true. What if not? Maybe the whole time difference talk was a way to convince Karina to go. Still, curiosity itched to the point of being unbearable.

Cayla insisted, "You'll be back in a few hours. We need to hurry."

"How will we get there?"

"Through the portal."

Karina was puzzled, and Cayla added, "It's hard to explain, you have to experience it."

Curiosity won in Karina's heart. A few hours could never hurt her. It would be like dreaming. Some cushions under the blankets would hopefully fool her parents in case they opened the door. All she had to do was get dressed and pack. From her wardrobe, she pulled her backpack, threw the books and notebooks on the floor, then realized it could be almost a week. "Can I bring a suitcase?"

"What for?"

"Clothes."

"We'll lend you some. Bring only what's absolutely necessary."

Karina packed socks and underwear and the small purse with the shoes. She ran to the bathroom for her toothbrush, face wash, moisturizer. Should she take shampoo, conditioner?

"Hurry, we can't take long." Cayla's voice came from the bedroom.

Fine, no shampoo then. Back in the bedroom, Karina changed into jeans, a t-shirt, and tennis shoes. A good thing Karina was not Zoe, because for her, the strictly necessary would never fit into one small backpack. It was better this way; she felt light and free. Very light indeed—she felt as if she had no abdomen and if the floor below her was about to collapse. Was she being brave or insane? Well, she could always justify her decision with a perfectly logical desire for scientific inquiry. No one could argue against that.

Karina took a deep breath. "I'm ready."

She realized she had no idea how they would "travel" and wondered if a door would open in her room, if her mirror or window would become a portal, or if a spaceship would appear outside.

Cayla smiled, looked at Karina and asked, "What about the shoes?"

"They're here, do you want to see them?"

"No!" Both girls said at the same time, as if the shoes were made of some kind of infectious material.

"Fine." Karina felt a little offended and thought they were exaggerating, but at the same time regretted having ever touched them.

Cayla walked to the window and put one of her hands on it,

holding her sister's hand with the other. Ayanna extended her free hand to Karina, who turned off the light then walked carefully to where the girls were and took the younger girl's hand.

"Close your eyes and hold tight," Cayla told her.

Both girls had their eyes closed, but Karina kept them slightly open, just enough to try to see what was happening in spite of the darkness. But nothing was happening yet. Again she wondered if it was a big scam, but what would be the goal of it if they didn't even want the shoes?

"Now close your eyes and relax," Cayla said.

Karina closed her eyes a little more so that even her short eyelashes clouded the small horizontal slit from which she tried to see something incredible.

"Can you close your eyes please?" Cayla insisted, this time sounding annoyed.

Karina looked at Cayla, figuring she would be staring at her, but no, her head was down. Since the girl insisted and nothing was happening anyways, Karina shut her eyes.

Immediately she lost balance and almost fell. She would have let go of Ayanna's hand if it weren't for the girl's firm grip. Through her eyelids, she felt strong flashes of light and didn't dare open her eyes. Her body felt no movement other than her first loss of balance. Maybe the older girl was pulling the light trick again, but a lot stronger, like daylight at noon, except that it flashed. After a few seconds, the flashes stopped, and just the feeling of being under direct sunlight remained.

4

WHERE?

Karina heard footsteps and, for the first time, started to believe she had actually traveled. Ayanna let go of Karina's hand and she assumed it was safe to look. In spite of the daylight, they were indoors, in a very tall but not very large, circular empty room with dark blue walls. Blue, not like painted blue, more like marble or rather some opaque blue stone she didn't know the name. The walls were smooth, with no apparent division between blocks. Sunlight came through a whitish, semi-translucent ceiling.

A blonde woman came running in from what seemed to be a hallway. "My girls!" She hugged Ayanna and Cayla, each with one arm. "What took you so long?"

"We were there for just a few minutes," Cayla answered. "The time gap is bigger than we thought."

"I see. I was so worried."

The woman didn't seem very happy to see Karina. She wore a loose dress that was not loose enough to hide her big baby bump. She looked too young to be the girls' mother, but then, perhaps people in this world aged differently with all the time difference and stuff.

A tall, thin, bald man with a long gray braided beard, wearing a long robe, came in the room. He had wrinkles, so people aged, and yet, there was something youthful about him. Odd.

He turned to Karina and the girls. "Follow me."

They walked through a hallway with green walls and that same whitish translucent ceiling. The floor seemed to be made of wood, but it was greenish instead of the usual brown tone Karina was used to. Ugly abstract paintings with colored lines and circles decorated one wall. Karina's poor understanding of art seemed to be universal. When they got to a big, green wooden door, the bald man led them into a room.

When the girl's mother was about to enter, the man blocked her—"Not you."—and closed the door.

"Nia's pregnant," Cayla whispered, as if it wasn't obvious and as if it explained why she was left outside.

Karina shrugged.

Cayla continued, "She can't have strong emotions."

Karina nodded, not sure if she understood. She looked around to make sure she was really in a room, not a roller coaster. Fine, it was a room in another dimension, which was super awesome. For her, not for the pregnant woman left out.

They all sat at the table. The bald man asked them, "Do you have the shoes?"

Karina took a second to realize that the question was for her, and then she nodded while a shiver ran down her spine.

"Can I see them?" he asked.

Karina took a deep breath. She hadn't really given much thought to the fact that destroying the shoes was the price for her otherworldly visit. She opened her backpack, took out the small purse, and opened it.

As she was about to take out the shoes, the bald man interrupted. "That's fine. They are real." He looked at the girls. "Well done."

Awesome. Karina was the one giving up unique shoes and the

opportunity to make a weird wish, and the girls were the ones getting the credit.

The bald man with the long braid coming out of his chin then turned to her. "What's your name?"

Some attention at least. "Karina."

"I am Odell. I teach Ayanna and Cayla. You are a very brave girl to come all the way from your world to help us. We appreciate this very much."

That was getting better. She smiled. "Thank you."

"No need to thank us. Now, you'll need to rest. You'll set on your journey tomorrow."

Did Karina hear right? "Journey?"

"To destroy the shoes."

That sounded exaggerated, but she didn't want to protest because going on a journey sounded cool.

Odell looked at all girls attentively. "You'll travel at night, and you'll go on foot, it'll draw less attention."

Cayla squinted. "That'll take days."

As much as Karina didn't want to ask, she had to, because she wasn't following the conversation. "Where exactly are we going?"

Odell looked at Cayla. "You didn't explain to her?"

"You told me to bring her as fast as possible. That's what I did."

"You took hours," he said.

"It's the time difference. We were there for about fifteen minutes only."

Odell raised his eyebrows. "Really?"

His surprise seemed somewhat fake, to the point Karina again started to think that they were all actors fooling her. But if that was the case, at least the production was first class.

"That's even better then," Odell continued. "I'll redo my calculations."

They seemed to have forgotten Karina's question, so she had to repeat it, "And... Where are we going?"

"Of course. You haven't been told." Odell turned to Karina. "Those shoes were made by Lylah, and only her magic can destroy them. You'll have to go to her dwelling."

"So we'll need to bring the shoes to the scary witch who seems nice—the one who can't have the shoes?"

"Yes," Odell replied, a weird smile on his face. "But all you'll have to do is throw the shoes in her fire, and that can be done very quickly."

Karina thought she had heard something like that somewhere. "Fire? You mean like the crater of an active volcano in her land?"

Odell stared at her as if she was crazy. "That would be very hot—and dangerous. But no, it's nothing like that; it's her fireplace. That's where her magic is."

Karina almost face-palmed herself. Of course a volcano crater would be incredibly hot. Now, where was she getting those ideas? The real plan made a lot more sense.

"We can't waste time," Odell continued. "You'll leave tomorrow afternoon. I'll provide you with supplies."

"Who's coming with us?" asked Cayla.

"We cannot compromise this mission. Nobody can know about it," Odell replied.

Cayla asked, "So I'm going alone with Karina?"

"I'm going to go too," Ayanna said.

Odell nodded. "Yes, you three are going."

Cayla exhaled. "I'll have to take care of her?"

Ayanna frowned. "I'm not a baby."

Odell got up. "We'll meet again tomorrow. For now, rest."

Karina followed the older girl to the end of the hallway and stairs. On the upper floor, she had the impression she was above the hallway where she had just walked. But how could that be, if downstairs sunlight came from the ceiling? In this floor too, the ceilings looked the same translucent white from which light came through. She figured she was tired and mixing directions.

Well, of course. She needed to sleep—too much weird stuff for a single evening, even though it was no longer evening. Cayla led her to a room with a normal double bed, complete with pillows and covers, which was a relief, because one could never guess how people slept in other dimensions.

Cayla stood at the entrance. "I'm right next door. Call me if you need anything." She closed the door and left.

Karina was left in that room with no idea how to call the girl or anyone else if she needed, as there was no phone by her bed, which made sense since she was not in a hotel, and they probably didn't have phones anyway. And how was she supposed to sleep when she was in a whole new dimension? She looked around. There was a narrow door in the room. She opened it, and it led to a bathroom. A pleasant surprise, even though the toilet bowl was a hole in the floor, and didn't seem to have any flushing mechanism. A small egg-shaped bathtub stood in one corner. She would ask about the bath later. Karina opened her backpack and realized she hadn't brought any pajamas. She remembered Cayla telling her to bring only what was strictly necessary. Right. Her mental grumbling stopped when she noticed a shelf with some nightgowns made of silk or something like it. They smelled clean and Karina slipped one on.

Once under the covers, she closed her eyes. The sheets or whatever were soft, but she had no idea what they were made of. Well, to be fair, she had no idea what her normal covers were made of, except maybe for cotton or fleece. Here she had many thin layers that were like a mix of those two kinds of fabric. Cozy. That ceiling was very bright, though. She wondered if she would be able to have a decent sleep. But despite the light, her eyes closed, and she started to doze off, until a sudden fear woke her. She had to check the shoes. As she got out of bed, the room was much darker than before. Had she slept that much? She opened her backpack and took the purse. The shoes were still there. She lay down again, this time with the purse by her side and the straps around her wrists.

~

KARINA WOKE when it was still dark. She turned sideways to look at the clock, but there was none. On the other side, no light came from the window, in fact, no window, only a faint glimmer coming from the ceiling. Of course, she was not in her room. There was a shadow on one of the chairs. Karina grabbed her purse tight and almost screamed, thinking Lylah was visiting her again, but then she saw a glimmer on long blonde hair.

"Did I scare you?" It was the blond woman from before.

Obviously. Was sitting in people's bedroom a local thing? "No. I mean, not you. I... I thought it was Lylah."

It was probably dawn because the room was getting lighter. The woman narrowed her eyes. "I'm Nia. Didn't you see her?"

Meaning that confusing the two of them was really stupid. Fine. But it was dark. "Yes, I saw her. Wasn't that the reason you sent the girls?"

Nia's expression darkened. "I didn't send them anywhere."

Of course. Anyway, Karina hadn't meant "you" as *you,* but still.

The woman sighed and continued, "I think they are too young to be risking their lives." She looked at Karina from head to toes. "And so are you."

Karina gulped at first, but then realized that the woman was probably just scared because she didn't know how simple the plan was. "I'm not risking my life," Karina explained. "They have it all planned; we just need to throw the shoes in her—"

Nia's horrified expression meant she had said too much. Way too much.

The woman got up. "Throw the shoes? Where? In Lylah's fire, I suppose." She put her hand in her heart and took short deep breaths. "Do you by any chance have the slightest idea of the danger of going into her dwelling?"

"No," Karina mumbled.

"And yet, you think it's a good idea to give it a try. You think it's a good idea to put my girls in such danger."

"I... I don't know anything, I just came to... I'm just trying to help your daughters."

Nia stepped back. "They're not my daughters. But that doesn't mean I would ever agree to send them on a suicide mission."

"Suicide?"

Nia raised her eyebrows. "Well, do you think you can just sneak into her fortress?"

"No. I mean... Fortress?"

Nia put her hands on her waist. "Where do you think she lives? A little house in the woods, without any protection?"

As silly as it sounded, that was exactly what Karina had imagined. "I..."

Nia got closer to Karina and stared at her. "It's a fortress, better protected than any castle on Earth."

"We're still on Earth?"

"Don't change the subject."

Karina waved her hands. "It's not my fault. I didn't plan anything. I was sleeping, the girls woke me up, they asked for help, and I came. That's it."

Nia pointed her index finger towards Karina. "That's exactly it. They are only going because you are going."

"And what do you want me to do?"

"Go home."

"How?"

"The same way you came: through the flowing tower. I'll take you there, and you'll go. That's the best thing to do."

That was a little unfair because Karina still hadn't had the chance to see anything outside the castle. She was also afraid of going back home and being visited by some kind of evil creature, but at that moment what Karina was most scared of was the evil or perhaps not evil creature standing in front of her. Broad daylight came from the ceiling. Karina closed her eyes. "Fine. I'll come with you."

She took her backpack, put her clothes inside it and didn't bother changing because she figured a nightgown was a fair exchange for bothered sleep and a frustrated visit to an alternate world. The saddest part was saying goodbye to any hope of brave Karina saving the world. But if brave Karina could not even confront a pregnant woman, what chance did she have against a powerful witch? As they walked to the door, it opened, or rather, Cayla opened it. She was yawning, rubbing her eyes and squinting.

"Did you call me? I thought I heard something." She noticed Nia. "What are you doing here? Why are you two awake?"

"We were talking," Nia answered, sounding a lot less furious than a couple seconds before.

Karina bit her lip, torn between asking Cayla to help her get away from that crazy woman or acting like a good abductee and staying quiet.

Cayla looked at Karina and squinted as if to check if she was seeing well. "Why are you holding your backpack?"

Karina opened her mouth, but no sound came.

Nia answered instead, "I was going to take her for a walk."

"Oh. You don't need to carry all your stuff," Cayla said.

Karina again wondered if she should tell the girl what was going on, but Nia settled the matter. "To the flowing tower. Back where she came from."

"But you can't!" Cayla protested. "That's our only chance."

"According to whom?" asked Nia.

"My father and Odell."

Nia shook her head. "I don't like Odell, and I don't trust him."

"I do. And this is my chance to prove what I can do."

"You shouldn't have to prove yourself!"

Cayla was very serious. "If I am going to rule Whyland, I need to prove I'm capable."

Nia snorted. "Stop wasting your time. You're not going to rule anything."

"Who's going to rule then?"

Nia pointed to her belly.

Cayla stepped back. "You want to keep me from doing my duty in order to make way for your son instead?"

"You are accusing the wrong person. I'm only thinking about your safety. You don't need to go on a dangerous mission just to prove yourself. Let Karina go back home and take the shoes with her."

"But then Lylah's going to get them!"

"What's the difference? Do you prefer to deliver them in person?"

"At least then we'll have a chance."

Nia crossed her arms. "Oh, you want a chance to get killed?"

Karina wondered when they would ask for her opinion, not that she had any yet, but being ignored on a matter that concerned her was not very pleasant.

Cayla looked down, as if thinking, then stepped closer to Nia and took her hand. "Nia, please. Don't try to stop us. You know you can't. I'll tell my father. I'll tell Odell. You'll only get in trouble, and we'll go anyways."

Nia pulled her hand and resumed her menacing stance, this time directed at Cayla. "You think I can't stop you?"

The girl seemed more concerned than intimidated. "Even if you can, please, let me go. Let me destroy these shoes. I know we can do this, and that it's for the best."

Nia turned to Karina. "You. What do you think? Do you think it's worth risking your life for a crazy plan that doesn't even concern you? That you know nothing about?"

Karina wished she had made up her mind earlier, because she wasn't sure what to say. Brave and craven Karina battled in her head. In the end, neither won. There was another, stronger contender: curious Karina. "I think we can at least try."

Nia looked shocked as if she had never expected Karina to decide to stay. Ha! Got that wrong.

"You want to get killed? Get killed then," Nia said.

Karina wondered how to answer, but Cayla beat her to it. "No, we're trying to do the right thing. Nia, if you are doing this because of us, because of our safety, please stop. Let us do it. It's my life, I have the right to do what I want with it."

"You're both too young to decide. This is wrong. Odell is a liar. You'll only see it when it's too late."

Cayla hugged her. "Thank you for letting us go."

That was the opposite of what Karina had understood, but whatever.

Nia didn't respond to the hug, but she let the girl finish, then said, "As for Ayanna, by no means will I let her go."

Cayla shrugged. "I don't want her to go either. It's Odell that insists."

Nia took a deep breath then said, "I'll deal with that." She then narrowed her eyes and looked at both girls. "I might not see you before you go. And probably not after. Just remember I warned you." She walked away while her words hovered in the air.

Cayla didn't seem bothered by her confrontation. Or was it a conversation? She asked, "You didn't take her seriously, did you?"

Well, in a way, yes. Karina had no idea who she was supposed to listen to anymore. But the girl was so cool about it, Karina thought she could be just as nonchalant. She shrugged. "Nah."

"I knew you'd never believe such nonsense."

Karina cleared her throat. "Of course not."

Cayla yawned. "I'm glad you woke me up. We need to get used to staying up at night."

Night? But sunlight came from the ceiling. Perhaps it was summer and nights were quite short. "Isn't it morning already?"

"I guess it depends if you count four o'clock as morning."

Before Karina pointed the ceiling, she realized this light had gone off and on too quickly to be the sun, so it had to be something else; something she didn't quite understand, and she felt really dumb for her assumption. At least she could still hide her dumbness. "I... just... I think I'm getting the hours mixed up."

Cayla laughed. "No wonder. Do you want to eat something?"

Food? Since the sleep had been interrupted anyway, that was a great idea. "Sure."

"Let's go to the kitchen then."

Cayla walked toward the door and Karina followed, but then she remembered the reason she was there to begin with and quietly returned to pick up her purse with the shoes. Again she looked inside to check if no one had stolen them, because who knew what kind of evil creature could be lurking in her bedroom. Oh no, that was a terrible thought—she wouldn't be able to sleep there anymore. Then she remembered it was Lylah who told her about the evil creatures, so she was probably lying. But then, if Lylah was the evil creature, Karina had proof that they could indeed sneak into her bedroom. Terrible thought again. The woman's words about the danger of the shoes echoed in her head, now mixed with Nia's words telling Karina she would get killed.

"So? Are you coming or not?" Cayla asked, snapping Karina out of her dreadful train of thought.

Or maybe not. Karina had already embarked on the fear ride. Her eyes met Cayla's, who'd become serious and asked, "What's wrong? Did Nia's talk scare you?"

"Uh..." Karina closed her eyes, realizing with despair that she was not very good at being brave or even pretending it. "It's just, I mean, what if something happens? What if Nia is right? She said Lylah lives in a fortress, how can we expect to enter it?"

Cayla nodded. "Well, first, as to Lylah's dwelling, it's not really a fortress, it's just a castle with walls." Before Karina had time to figure out what the difference was, the girl continued, "And there's an easy way to enter it, Odell knows it. Before we go, tomorrow, he's going to give us all the details."

"And what if he's wrong, like Nia said?"

"Not him, no way. He's like, uh, I've known him since I was a baby, and he never makes mistakes. He knows things... He's our teacher and he's... very learned. Now, I think you took Nia too seriously. I should have warned you, but I didn't think... Anyways, she's been paranoid lately. It's awful, she used to be like a mother to me, but now, she's been accusing Odell, saying he's in league with Lylah, imagine that!" The girl bit her lip and her eyes were misty. "She's... she's been saying things against my father. Something isn't right with her, and now for some reason, she doesn't want us to destroy the shoes. I don't want to think anything bad about her, but... never mind." Cayla shook her head as if shaking away a thought.

Karina wasn't totally convinced. "Fine. Maybe Nia is worrying too much. But still, what if the plan goes wrong? What if, by any chance, your teacher is wrong? What then?"

"It won't go wrong. Do you think my father would want me and my sister to risk our lives? My little sister! And this is our chance to do something great. Don't you want it?"

Something great. Perhaps that was what Karina had been wanting. "I guess you're right."

"Trust me, everything is going to be fine. Shall we eat now?"

Maybe Karina's problem was not fear but hunger. She smiled.

AFTER MANY DIMLY LIT CORRIDORS, a large hall with high ceilings and a smaller corridor, they came to a very bright room, so bright that Karina's eyes took a while to adjust. It was a huge room with some small round tables in a corner, and a couple of counters and large cupboards in the other. Everything was made of some kind of stone Karina would describe as marble, but although it was white it was not really marble, because it was shinier, kind of sparkly. All that whiteness gave the place a dream-like quality, which contrasted with the relative normality in the rest of the castle. Was that a castle? Did it have walls around it? Would it be considered a fortress? Some silliness.

The dining room had real windows, tall and large, but because it was night, all Karina could see was blackness and a few stars in the sky. An old woman who seemed to be a cook or servant attended them, offering food options that Karina had never heard of and didn't even catch the names, so she relied on the princess to choose something for her. The woman set to work on one of the counters. The "food" was a green gooey thing. Karina almost didn't eat it, but then she remembered that it was a good idea to try things first before deciding she didn't like them. That logic had some big flaws, as there were things some people should never try, but she did take a spoon. It tasted kind of like broccoli soup, but with different spices. It was actually quite good, and perhaps that logic was generally applicable to food. Cayla had told Karina not to talk about their journey in common areas, so the questions that popped in her head remained unanswered, moved over to a 'later' file in her brain that soon got too crowded.

She finally decided to ask Cayla a question that had been bugging her and was not forbidden: "Your lights, they are different from the ones I know, how do they work?"

"Lights?" Cayla seemed surprised at the question, then pointed to the ceiling. "You mean that?"

"Yes."

Cayla shrugged. "Well, it's sunlight."

"But it's night now."

"It's saved sunlight."

Saved sunlight. Wouldn't that be wonderful? To put sunlight in a little can, then open it later, quite useful in an electricity outage. "Of course not."

Cayla squinted. "Well, what is this light then?"

"That's my question."

The girl just shrugged. Karina looked down, thinking. At least her assumption that she saw sunlight was not so dumb after all. But it didn't make any sense. She tried to rephrase her question. "I see. So you use solar energy to produce light. Is that it?"

Cayla seemed to be making an effort to understand the question. "Uh... well, yes, light is energy."

No kidding. "But how does it work?"

The girl looked up as if thinking. "There might be something on the roof. I'm not really sure."

It was funny how the girl just took it for granted. Would Karina be able to explain her own lights? In general terms yes: electricity, wires, and stuff. But now she was in a completely different place. Then a thought hit her, and Karina almost laughed at her silliness. "Is it magic?"

"What?" The girl looked surprised, offended, or a mix of both. "No. That's really evil."

"Oh, sorry." Karina looked away. The girl's distaste of magic seemed strange and didn't match with the idea Karina had about her. Had she simply assumed she was in a magical place? Well, maybe being in a castle in a parallel dimension or whatever explained her impression. But there was something else. Karina remembered. "What about the light you cast in my room? Was that m—"

Cayla didn't let her finish. "No, no." Alarm and fear showed on her face, as she gesticulated frantically. "There was no light. It was dark. It was dark."

One would think the girl had been caught stealing or something. "Yeah, yeah, it was dark. I'm tired, confused, and imagining things." *Yeah, right.*

"You are," Cayla said as if to put an end to the subject.

The girl had cast a light in her room and they both knew it, but Karina didn't want to press it any further, so she just nodded and returned to her soup. But then, if magic was something forbidden like it seemed, how come they traveled through dimensions? Or was there a scientific explanation? Now, that would be a really interesting thing to learn. Maybe she should ask Odell if he was the know-it-all. A pity he didn't seem to be the teach-it-all.

When Karina returned to her room, there was still some night or early morning left, and apparently almost everyone was still sleeping. The light on the ceiling dimmed; the opposite of what was probably happening outside. Karina tried to forget the whole idea about evil creatures in her bedroom, but trying to forget the thought just kept it present in her mind.

5

HOW?

Darian looked at the panel in front of him. The lights represented the army's lifts. He had a good idea about who was in each one and knew how many people were on their side for sure. Some of them were maybes. Those were the most dangerous and could be their downfall. Still, their numbers were enough. He counted again, in disbelief, and then again, as if it counting could change the numbers. They were enough. Enough. Darian swallowed. He should have been thrilled. He should have been glad. He should have been relieved that his dreams were about to become true, but he didn't feel any of that. His own reaction surprised him. And now it was time to tell the council, so they'd plan the next move. That was his duty. He knew it. After a long, deep breath, he put on a cloak and walked to the river waterfront, feeling the drumming of his heart. A war drum?

Perhaps he didn't have to tell anything. Having played both sides for so long, lying had become as easy as breathing. He tried to understand what he'd been thinking. His thoughts turned to the castle and to who lived in it. A knot formed in his chest. He'd been wrong. Lying was much easier than breathing.

~

KARINA FELT a soft touch on her shoulder.

"Wake up. You have to come with us."

Ayanna was in her room, smiling with her pleasant round face. Karina was thankful that for once an intruder didn't just sit waiting for her. She reached for her purse with the shoes, and almost didn't need to look inside, as she could feel them with her touch, but she still looked just to confirm her impression. "Are we leaving now?"

"Leaving?" Ayanna laughed. "No, it's just lunch. They said maybe you'd like to eat before we pack."

Ayanna had excitement and anticipation on her face, meaning she still thought she would go with them. Karina was about to change clothes when she noticed the girl was wearing a nightgown—or was it a dress? — similar to hers, so she followed her without changing first. Perhaps they were informal, and that was a brunch.

They went to a dining room with a high ceiling supported by arcs, and a central round table in green wood and glass. Cayla was sitting there already, together with Nia and Odell. There were also two men Karina didn't know. One seemed to be around 40 and had a pleasant face. He wore a tunic in a light fabric. The other man was a little older and had a graying beard. He wore a silver overcoat and looked definitely overdressed for the occasion. He was probably the king. Nobody made any introduction, and Karina remained silent. Nia had eyes lost in the distance, a fraction of the impressive woman who had visited her bedroom that night. Karina felt a little guilty for making the woman so sad.

They had what appeared to be chicken, or some other kind of bird, with vegetables. Karina was not sure if she knew the vegetables, but in truth, she was terrible at naming or recognizing vegetables anyways, so she would never know whether or not they were different.

After lunch, Cayla led Karina back to her room, asking her to pack and get ready. Karina learned about the bathtub and washed quickly. Back into her jeans and t-shirt, she picked up her backpack. When Karina came out, the girl stared. "Are you going to wear that?"

Maybe her clothes were beyond unfashionable in that place. "Why? Should I try to, uh, blend a little?"

Cayla shrugged. "No. It's just, you might get hot. But if you're comfortable..."

The girl was wearing a nightgown dress, which by now Karina realized was a real dress, not that a nightgown would not be real, but meaning a dress that wasn't for sleeping. "Fine. Just a moment."

Karina went back in the room, changed into one of the dresses, and put a couple more in her backpack. She kept her sneakers, though. Not that they had offered any shoes, and not that she would wear... well. When she came out, Cayla smiled and nodded. Karina followed her through sunlit, saved sunlight, or whatever illuminated corridors. Strange that even though it was day, and it had to be day, if they had just had lunch, there was nobody walking in them.

Cayla descended a flight of narrow steps. Midway through the stairs, she opened a door that had no handle. In fact, it was a door Karina hadn't noticed. They entered a round room in which ceilings and walls were in one uniform piece, like a bowl turned upside down. Light came from what looked like a hole on top, but it was probably the same thing as the lights in other parts of the castle. This room was darker than the others, which gave it a mysterious, shady quality. Odell and Ayanna were sitting at a small table. Cayla saw her sister and squinted.

Odell waited for them to sit, then he got up. "You are here for the most important part of your task: planning. Stick to the plan, and you'll have nothing to fear."

He opened a map on the table, with mountains, a river, and

some strange drawings. Or were those names? They seemed to be in another language.

He continued, "I don't want you to carry anything identifying you or where you are going, so make sure you memorize this."

That only reminded Karina of her bad grades in geography, and how often they involved bad memory and maps.

Odell pointed at the mountains near the river. "You'll walk through these woods, on the base of the mountain. There is a path. It's ancient, and it's safe. It also means you are not too close to the river villages, and yet not deep in the woods. People won't see you, and you won't risk running into jaguars."

Karina's knees trembled. "Jaguars? Like, uh, big cats?"

"More aggressive than cats." Odell pointed some blue spots deep in the mountains. "But they live near the lakes, here. They don't usually cross these hills." He looked at Karina, who was still unsure, and spoke slowly as if to make sure she understood each of his words: "And even when they do, they never come near the path."

"Isn't this the cursed path?" Ayanna asked in a weak voice.

Cayla rolled her eyes.

Odell laughed. "Ayanna, how often did I tell you not to believe in silly superstitions?"

The girl looked down, her voice almost a whisper. "Sorry, uh, I don't mean it's cursed, I just wanted to know if that's... the one I've heard about."

Odell nodded and pointed at the map. "Animals don't come near this area, and so, well, people speculate. So, yes, you might have heard something about this path. Again, all it means is that it's safe."

On the map, Karina saw lines, which she assumed meant roads, in other parts, but not where he pointed, so it was not a regular road or path. Ayanna seemed upset, probably offended that Odell laughed at her question. Cayla stared at her sister with worry. When her eyes met Karina's, she glanced at Ayanna, as if asking what she was doing there. Karina shrugged. How was she supposed to know?

Odell pointed then to the border of the mountain range, near a place where two rivers met. "You'll walk all the way to the crossing banks, then you'll cross the Black River, and go to Lylah's castle from the other side, here. Walk down those woods carefully, in the beginning of the night, then you'll dive to her island. There's an underwater tunnel which leads straight to her castle. Once there, you can destroy the shoes. It's that simple."

Simple? Hiking, diving, this journey was looking a lot more extreme than Karina had expected. They didn't even bother asking her if she was an outdoor adventurer. Meanwhile, Cayla just nodded as if everything was indeed quite simple. Ayanna, on the other hand, seemed terrified. She was pale, and Karina hoped she would be the one to ask a question or at least raise an objection.

But it was Cayla who spoke. "When are we leaving?"

"In one hour."

Cayla squinted. "Already? But, do you think Karina will have time to learn everything?"

Odell raised an eyebrow. "There's plenty of time to go over the details and make sure the three of you are more than prepared. We can't postpone this any longer. Come, I'll show you your supplies."

He walked to another table in a darker part of the room. Karina and Cayla followed. The table had a few objects Karina didn't recognize at a first look, maybe some kind of climbing or diving equipment.

"Ayanna?" Odell called the girl who was still in her chair.

She got up, trembling. "I, I..."

Ayanna turned around and vomited. Colorful pieces of what had been their lunch splattered across the floor. Karina stepped away and avoided looking at it any more. Cayla seemed relieved instead of worried, but Odell, who didn't notice Cayla, lost his calm composure and ran to the girl. "What did you eat?"

Ayanna grunted. "Just... lunch, with you."

She closed her eyes then rested her head on the table. Odell shook his hands. "Cayla, go get a doctor. Now." He sounded furious.

The older girl's eyes widened, then she ran outside. The man took Ayanna's pulse and lifted her head. "Stay awake, can you hear me? Don't sleep."

Ayanna's eyes closed, her head resting on one of the man's arms. Fear and worry were visible on his face, which probably meant the girl had something serious. He breathed heavily and looked around as if trying to find an answer or solution somewhere in the room. When he saw Karina, he narrowed his eyes. "You were with her. Did she drink anything, eat anything?"

Karina was startled. She hoped he was not accusing her. "We came straight to lunch. I didn't see her after that."

Odell shook his head and seemed to force himself to speak more calmly. "I'm just trying to understand what happened to her."

Nia popped up on her head.

Odell stared at Karina. "Do you want to say something?"

"No. Uh, yes." If Ayanna was in danger, it was best to say everything she knew. "Nia. She didn't want Ayanna to come with us. In fact, she didn't want any of us to destroy the shoes; she said it was dangerous."

Odell looked astonished. "When did she speak with you?"

Karina almost regretted mentioning Nia, after all, she was only worried, but now Karina had to explain. "At night."

"Night?" He shook his head. "Strange. But no, not Nia. I'm sure she has nothing to do with this."

Funny how he trusted Nia when the woman had said straight out that he was a liar. Odell looked sideways, thinking. The door then opened to reveal Cayla panting, with the bearded man with the silver coat. Odell rolled back the map in less than a second and glared at Cayla, who looked down.

The man looked around. "So this is one of Odell's secret rooms. Funny I've never been told about it."

Odell clenched his fists. "I asked for a doctor."

Karina started to think that the man was not the King.

"We have first aid training in the army," the man said.

Odell snorted. "I have way more than that." He lifted Ayanna, her upper body resting on his shoulder. "Let's go. I'll take her to the examination room." He then turned to Karina and Cayla. "Wait here."

Odell left in front of the man, who followed in slow steps. Karina and Cayla stood far from the table and the dirty floor surrounding it.

"Who's that?" Karina asked.

"General Keen. He leads my father's army." She shrugged defensively. "He was the first person I saw."

"I thought he was the King."

"The king's my father. You saw him at lunch."

The one with the pleasant face, then. Karina nodded. The girls remained silent for some time.

Eventually, Cayla broke the silence, "It stinks here."

Of course it did, but that was the last thing Karina imagined would be in Cayla's mind. "Aren't you worried?"

"About what?"

"Your sister?"

"No."

Was Cayla that cold blooded?

The girl seemed to notice Karina's disapproval and added, "I'm sure she's fine."

Karina hoped that was true, even though the sudden fainting was impressive. "Do you think it was Nia?"

Cayla squinted then nodded.

"She could have done that to us as well," Karina said.

"No, she couldn't."

Her answer didn't make any sense. "Why not? She didn't want us to—"

"She needed help. Now, please don't mention this anymore. Ayanna got sick and that's all. I know she's fine. And we'll be much faster without her."

What a sister. But Karina knew when to quit a subject, so she left it at that. Still, she had already told Odell half the truth and she could not *untell* him.

"Uh, I can't stand this smell," Cayla said. "Let's go to my bedroom. We can leave our stuff here."

"But he told us to wait."

"He wasn't even thinking, all worried about precious Ayanna."

Because the girl was already stepping outside, Karina had no choice but to follow her, otherwise she would have to stay alone in that weird, bad smelling room.

The girl's room was somewhat like the room Karina had slept in, but bigger, with bookshelves and paintings on the walls. It had a bed but also a small table and chairs, where the girls sat. A good thing Karina was past the age of considering princesses glamorous, or she would have been disappointed at the regular teenager sitting in front of her. Cayla was silent, pensive. Was she feeling guilty about Ayanna? Worried about their trip? Karina for her part felt as if she had agreed on skydiving, was standing on the door of the plane, then someone told her to wait, and keep waiting while staring into the abyss below. But there was no abyss, just a room that was not much different from her friends' room in her own world, or dimension, or whatever. Fine, maybe this room was a little bigger, and maybe if Karina knew someone who lived in a mansion they would have a similar room. Hopefully her imaginary mansion-living friend wouldn't dare poison their own sister, though.

The door opened, breaking their silent inertia. If Odell had hair, it would have been disheveled to match his expression.

"There you are. I think she's fine. But we might have to postpone your departure. Wait here. I'll be back."

Cayla got up. "But you said we couldn't waste time."

"That was before. Wait here. She's being examined."

He stepped out and Cayla sat, now looking worried. She turned to Karina. "He said she's fine. See? I knew it." Cayla spoke with certainty, but she had a look of relief that might have meant otherwise. "Why can't we go then?"

Karina didn't understand the hurry if the so-called time difference meant they had a week or something. And something else bothered her. "Is he going to have time to explain everything to us?"

"I understood everything."

Nice for her, because by that time his short explanation had become a mushy mess in Karina's head. "But I…"

"Oh, don't worry; I'll be there to help you."

Karina felt the girl was patronizing her. "Well, maybe, but I barely saw the map."

Cayla got up and started moving towards one of her bookshelves. "If you want to take a look at a map, I think I have one here. But I know all the maps by heart."

Karina got up and stood by the girl, who fumbled through her books. Perhaps she knew the maps by heart, but not their location in her room. How encouraging. The door opened. Odell entered, looking glum. "Come with me. Bring everything you need."

"Our things are in the globe," Cayla replied.

"I'll bring them to you. Go to the study room. I'll meet you there."

He left in swift, large steps. Cayla led Karina downstairs and they entered the room where they had their first meeting the previous night.

A couple minutes later, Odell walked in, arms full of bags and other objects. "You'll have to go without Ayanna; she has to rest for a few days."

"What's wrong with her?" Karina asked.

"Food poisoning, but not serious. She'll be fine." He shook his head. "It's really unfortunate. To happen now." He then took a map and opened on the table. "But we have to move on."

His explanation was a top speed recap. Odell showed the supplies; some kind of dried food, water skins in some kind of gray leather or rubber, some weird gloves and socks, extendable tubes, hooded cloaks, and a bag. The robes were for them to leave the castle unrecognized. The bag was a tent. Karina tried to be cheerful. Camping trip! Exciting, exciting, in the good and bad way. Odell handed Cayla a large black key. She took it as one receives a prize.

He then explained, "This key opens the underwater tunnel."

Karina tried to remember that part. Something in the river, the Black River, to get to the island. Well, she would eventually figure it out.

Odell continued, "Once you go up, you should see her fire." He looked at Karina. "Throw the shoes there."

"I will," Karina answered in a certainty that matched his tone, having muffled her little internal voice who protested against destroying her pretty shoes, first because that was not a good time for inner arguments, second because she was excited to do something important.

Odell looked at both girls seriously. "Do not deviate from the plan. Don't tell anyone what you're doing, and I absolutely mean anyone, even if it's someone you trust. Don't go to any towns or villages. You have enough supplies for your journey. Stick to the plan and you'll be fine. Is that clear?"

The girls nodded and Odell smiled.

Karina was excited, but some of what Nia had told her echoed in her head. She had to ask, "And what if... what if we are caught and can't throw the shoes? What if something bad happens?"

Cayla grimaced.

"You'll be rescued," Odell answered. His tone was certain and assuring. He paused for a moment. "Then, again, there's no reason to assume that scenario."

"Of course not, we'll do everything right," Cayla added.

Odell nodded in agreement.

Karina didn't appreciate having her question dismissed. "Great. So everything goes well. Then what happens to Lylah? And how do we come back?"

Odell had a half smile that lasted less than a second. Or did Karina imagine it?

"Things will be different," he replied, now serious. "You'll be brought back." He looked at Karina. "And you'll be taken home." He looked at both girls. "That's the second part of the plan, and I'm responsible for it. All I need you to do is your part."

As vague as his answer was, somehow Karina felt assured, as if her task was just a cog in a wheel. Not that her task was not great: it was, but at the same time it was comforting to know there were more people involved than just her and a sixteen-year-old girl.

Cayla and Karina put the supplies in their backpacks, the hooded robes over their dresses and walked to the corridor, while Odell stayed in the room. Karina wanted to laugh at how ridiculous Cayla looked in that ugly brown cloak, but then she remembered she was wearing the same thing and it was no longer funny. They would leave the castle through a small door by the kitchen. Before stepping out, Karina asked to go to the washroom, and almost asked again when she saw the door, but she knew it was just jitters. How long could she delay her departure by peeing? On the door, Cayla turned a sort of combination lock, which opened it. They stepped out. Karina was about to discover a whole new world, but in spite of all her goosebumps, it only felt like stepping outside a door. There were no drums or trumpets. Nobody wished them good luck or farewell.

6

COMMUNICATION

The afternoon smelled fresh, the smell of woods and water. They were at the foot of a mountain range, on a plateau high enough to allow a vast view. There was a river not far below, and even though Karina had seen it on the map, seeing it as a real river, much wider than she had thought at first, felt different. The sun was lowering on their left side, hiding beneath mountains, reflected on the river and painting the sky orange. Karina looked back to see the place where she'd been. The castle looked rather small. A large part of it must have been embedded in the mountain, which explained the lack of windows. The walls seemed to be made of a dark brown stone, or else the late afternoon light gave that impression. In front of the building stood a platform, with some silver round things, like giant umbrellas or air bags.

Cayla asked,. "Also wishing we'd take one of those?"

Karina was startled. "Uh?"

"We'd go much faster."

"Do you travel in those things?"

Cayla shrugged. "Well, I haven't traveled much, but people do."

Karina still couldn't make out what they were. "Are they pulled by horses?"

Cayla was puzzled. "Horses?"

"I mean, how do they move?"

"They fly."

"Oh."

How silly, where did she get the idea of horses? The things did look a little like zeppelins, except they were less oval and rounder, and didn't seem to have a basket beneath them. Karina would describe them as roundish things (it was a little dark) with airbags on top.

"Do you ride horses?" Cayla asked.

"What? Me? No, I—"

"Why did you ask about horses?"

Because it was a castle, there was a witch and yada, yada, yada. But that was not a good explanation. "I thought I saw a horse."

Cayla looked back and squinted.

"I think I'm a little confused." The confusion was indeed true.

Cayla sighed. "I know. Walking all the way just seems so…" She put her hand over her chest, as if thinking, then shook her head. "Well, that's what Odell told us, so he might have his reasons. Let's go. We have to find the path before it gets dark." She pointed up. "It's in that plateau."

That "plateau" looked like the base of the mountain, but perhaps that was what it was. The girls walked upwards while moving away from the castle, in a diagonal direction. The trees were close together and had broad leaves. The trunks were brown, and Karina was somewhat surprised, because with all the green wood furniture she'd thought the tree trunks would be that color. Of course, that idea was really silly. In fact, the forest looked rather normal, with tall trees with broad trunks and moss on the ground. Her scientific mind would classify it as a tropical or semi tropical forest. Nature wasn't much different from the nature she knew, which made sense, if they were on Earth, wherever they were, whenever they were or whatever.

The sun was setting, but instead of cooler, the day was getting warmer, unless the walking made her warm. And the ugly robe. But it was true that the dress underneath seemed to cool her. The girls kept walking up while the sky turned pink then purple then dark and darker blue. A quarter moon brightened the forest. There were sounds in the distance, like some insects or birds. Karina had a strange feeling she was being followed or watched, and even though she thought the feeling was pointless, it still bothered her. For the first time, she realized she was walking at night, in the middle of nowhere, with only another girl as a companion.

Karina froze with fear and stopped. "Isn't this dangerous?"

Cayla turned around. "What?"

"Us two, alone in the woods."

"We're getting near the path," Cayla said. "It's safe there."

The girl was so calm, Karina felt calmer as well, but then another thought bothered her. "But how are we going to know we're in the right place?"

"I think we'll notice. Come."

Karina walked, and she felt hot from walking and the temperature. But her head was not cool, she heard strange sounds, and heard their steps as being extremely loud and bound to attract something or someone, but she had no idea what or who. After some time, the girls came to an area that was flatter, and they stopped going up, which was a relief. The wind stopped, and the air felt stuffy. All Karina could hear were their own footsteps; the forest had grown quiet. There were fewer trees in this area, and Karina could see the black sky full of stars. *Stars.* They could tell her where she was. Or not. She didn't know those stars. Maybe this was Earth, but in the Southern Hemisphere. Maybe it was something else. She decided to focus on where she was walking, not where she was geographically. What difference would it make? The ground was bare, without grass or moss, only covered here and there with fallen trunks. So much stillness and silence, and, strangely, that silence bothered Karina more than the noises she had heard earlier. Had she not seen trees around her, she would have believed she was in a desert. That place felt gloomy even though the moonlight illuminated their path. Oh, that was what it was.

Karina asked in her softest whisper, "Is this the path?"

"I think so," Cayla replied, also with a whisper.

The girl removed her cloak, and Karina did the same. She felt cooler, but not more comfortable. That place was weird. She told herself no animals or people would get near, so, in spite of the awful stillness, at least the path was safe. But then, if even animals avoided that place, there was a reason. She gulped and debated whether or not to ask what the reason was, but the girl probably didn't know it, and perhaps it was better not to know.

"THE PRINCESS DID WHAT?" Sian had heard it right, but he wanted to double check that the boy in front of him hadn't gotten his words mixed up.

"She left the castle."

"You mean like that? Puff? And nobody noticed it?"

The boy lowered his eyes. "My sister saw her coming out of the kitchen door."

Sian looked around to the alley where they were. Nobody paid attention to them, and yet, he knew people could be listening. He gestured for the boy to follow him in silence. Sian ran his hands through his long brown hair and tried to think. Had the princess run away or been captured, the king would have raised an alarm. Word would have gone out—unless the King wanted to keep it quiet. But then he would probably trust his closest general and advisor. That was Sian's father, and Sian would hear something about it. Perhaps they were just taking long to realize she left, or, more likely, the King knew about it. But for what purpose? Another option was that the boy was mistaken. Still, there had to be some truth in this information. They walked to one of his meeting points, a room in the basement of a market. Sian sat down.

"Who was with her?"

"Another girl. Not her sister."

Surprised, he rose. "That's it?"

The boy cowered. "Yes, yes, that's what my sister saw."

Sian was stunned to realize that the boy was afraid of him. At around twelve or thirteen, the boy was no more than five years younger than Sian himself. But then, standing up, Sian towered him. He sat down and smiled, trying to speak more softly.

"I'm happy you came and told me that. I'm really glad. Thank you." He winked. "Maybe you could be a good candidate for the military academy."

The boy looked down. "Maybe."

That meant no. Anyway, all Sian wanted was the information. "And who's this other girl?"

"Nobody knows. My sister didn't see her, but she heard that an unknown girl spent the night in the castle."

Sian nodded, as if it was the most natural piece of news ever. He thanked and paid the boy. Years of training had taught Sian how to tell when people lied, and the boy had been telling the truth—or at least believing he was.

What Cayla did or didn't do was the least of Sian's concerns, except if meant that something was out of order. Cayla walking out alone or almost alone didn't make sense. For him. Because he was probably missing a vital piece of information. There was something happening, and he had no idea what it was. Not knowing something, that was dangerous and could spoil all his plans.

He commed Jason, one of his trusted officers. "News on my brother?"

"Yes, sir, and there's something quite interesting. He disappears from the radar from time to time."

More unexpected news. "And you couldn't have told me this before?"

"I found that out yesterday and I was waiting for you to contact me. Sir. I fear maybe he could be helping with the insurgence."

Sian didn't trust Jason that much. "Keep your fears for yourself then, before my father hears any of that."

"I didn't mean—"

"It's fine. But report when he shows up again. And don't get any ideas. My brother knows what he's doing."

He closed the channel. Of course Darian knew what he was doing. Nothing good. But it was too early for anyone to know that. To rush and expose him now would be foolish. Everything in its time.

AFTER SOME THREE hours of walking, Karina's feet hurt, but she didn't want to complain. Eventually they stopped to set camp even though in theory they should be walking at night. Cayla set up the tent in a matter of seconds. Inside it, the girl had a little light, from a clear crystal looking thing. This time Karina didn't want to sound like a primitive person and assume it was a magic crystal. Of course not. It was just science that she didn't understand. And probably neither did the girl, though she took it for granted. They ate some of the food they carried, which was like cake and dried fruit. Karina worried about crumbs on the bed, but maybe it was better than going outside. Sitting and relaxing, Cayla looked like a regular girl, someone that could even be her friend.

Karina tried to start a conversation. "Are you excited? For doing this?"

The girl smiled. "Yes."

They fell silent again. Karina still had a question concerning Nia. "And you are sure, uh, the queen won't try to stop us?"

Cayla looked thoughtful for a moment, then replied, "As long as she doesn't know what we are doing, we're safe."

That made sense. No, wait, it didn't. "But she knows what we are doing."

Cayla seemed troubled. "What? But how could she know? How come you didn't tell us?"

"I thought... it was obvious, since she wanted to stop me from coming, no?"

"Of course not. Seriously, we could be in danger."

Karina stared at the girl, wondering if she had been hit in the head. "Fine. Now you are telling me Nia is dangerous."

"What? No. I was talking about Lylah."

That clarified things, a little. But then the girl had clearly misunderstood her. "I was talking about the queen."

"That's who I was talking about."

"Isn't Nia the queen?"

"Of course not."

Karina was more and more confused. "Who's the queen then?"

"Lylah. She calls herself the queen. Some of her followers call her that as well. When you said queen, that's what came to mind."

"I see. So Nia is—"

"Nia. My stepmother."

Karina nodded, almost laughing at the misunderstanding. But there was something she wanted to know. "You mention she's dangerous, Lylah. What has she done?"

"Lots of bad things."

"Like?"

Cayla lowered her head. "She tried to overthrow my father, and she'll try again if given the chance." The girl took a deep breath, exhaling slowly. "People died. Like... my mother."

Karina felt bad for asking. "I'm sorry, I had no idea."

"You couldn't know." She looked at Karina. "Do you understand now, how important this is for me?"

Karina nodded.

Cayla then added, "And yes, perhaps I don't know much, but Odell does. He says this is what needs to be done and I trust him."

They remained in silence for a while, until Cayla broke it. "What do you think of all this walking?"

Karina was so surprised at the change of subject that she blurted out the truth. "It's a little tiring."

"And we didn't even walk that much tonight."

"How many days are we going to go like this?"

Cayla shrugged. "Six, eight. I don't know. It depends on how far we get each day."

"But I thought," Karina was unsure, "I thought you didn't mind walking for days."

Cayla squinted. "It's not about minding or not. Do you think it makes sense?"

Karina shrugged. "Is there another way?"

Cayla had half a smile and a glimmer in her eye that could be seen even in the dim glow. "See, we're not in enemy's territory until after we go to the other side of the river. I understand why we must be careful there, I really do. But, you know, our mission is not to walk, what we need to do is get those shoes to her castle, and get rid of them. That's what we need to do."

Karina wondered where the girl wanted to lead this conversation. "Sure. But I don't know what the alternative is."

"I'm just explaining why I'm considering this... uh, option, so you don't think I want to disobey Odell for no reason, or, uh..."

"Well," Karina almost rolled her eyes but refrained in time, "he's not my teacher. I don't care."

Cayla seemed relieved and surprised. "You don't care?" She looked around and smiled. "So, you don't mind if we go to the end of the path, like, in a different way?"

Karina stared at the girl and almost answered, "Of course I do. I really, really want to get tired and spend an entire week in a silent, gloomy and eerie forest, doing nothing interesting", but then she decided against it. She didn't know the girl that well.

Cayla noticed Karina's hesitation and became serious. "Do you mind?"

Karina laughed. "Of course I don't. I just don't understand what you're planning, that's all."

Cayla smiled, then quickly became serious again. "First thing, I can only consider this option if you promise never to tell anyone about this. I mean, not even Nia, Ayanna, or Odell. Nobody can know about it."

It wasn't as if she was best buddies with any of them. "I won't tell anyone."

Cayla stared at Karina. "Can you promise?"

"I promise."

The girl sighed. "I have a friend. He's just a friend. He pilots a lift. I think he could take us to the end of the path, if he can of course. I've thought about it. We don't need to tell him anything. We say we're going camping, walking... He doesn't need to know, and nobody needs to know, and we won't necessarily be disobeying Odell, you see? And it's not that I can't walk or that I need his help, or that I want to see him. It's just that it makes sense. Right?"

Karina assumed a lift was one of those flying things. She would love to know how they worked. "Why didn't you mention this earlier?"

Cayla looked at Karina. "I... I don't know. I thought you wouldn't agree."

Karina laughed at how funny it was that the girl seemed almost afraid of her, as if she was going to judge her or something.

Cayla got serious. "Why are you laughing?"

Karina kept laughing. "I'm also afraid to say what I think to you, because I don't know you well. But, you know, we're in this together, we should trust each other."

"Yes," Cayla answered, seeming thoughtful. Then she laughed. "You're right."

They laughed together. Maybe Karina could start considering Cayla her friend.

"I'll contact him tonight then," Cayla said. "You understand why I'm doing this, right?"

"Sure."

Actually, not really. If it was just getting a ride and going faster she wouldn't need to make all these explanations. Anyways, Karina didn't really care. She just hoped she would have the chance to get on one of those flying things. Another question was how exactly her new friend would contact anyone, considering they were in the middle of nowhere and didn't have a phone, but she was ready to be surprised, so she just waited to see what the girl would do.

Cayla looked down and hesitated. "You're sure you're not going to tell anyone in the castle about any of this?"

That was getting annoying, but then, maybe there was a good reason Cayla was so afraid. Karina tried to reassure her. "Don't worry."

Cayla looked down and smiled, her face soft. She pulled a necklace from under her dress. It had a silver chain and an orange clear stone. Karina realized both dresses her companion wore had the same high collar, and that it was perhaps on purpose. It also explained why she brought her hand to her chest. It wasn't her heart, but the necklace she was touching. Cayla glanced at Karina and a flicker of embarrassment crossed her face. The stone turned a little brighter, as if it had a light of its own. Karina had seen enough weird stuff to accept that it was a communication device. Lovely idea in fact. After some seconds, the girl pulled the pendant close to her mouth and spoke to it. Of course, the thing was indeed a communication device.

"Darian," Cayla said softly, as if waking someone who is asleep. "Darian?"

No answer came from the stone, assuming, of course, the thing was supposed to answer. She sighed and tried again, this time a little louder.

"Darian? Are you there?"

Cayla kept staring attentively at her stone and repeated the question a few more times, sounding more and more impatient at each time. She looked worried and disappointed. Finally, Cayla took off the necklace and tossed it. "It's useless."

So that was the answer on how they would contact anyone in the middle of nowhere: they wouldn't. But Karina tried to be cheerful. "We can still walk. That was the plan anyways."

Cayla waved her arms. "I don't mind walking! That's not the point. I mean, why wouldn't he..." She took a deep breath and looked down.

Karina shrugged, having no idea who he was or how that stone was supposed to work. She felt a little disappointed as well, because since Cayla had mentioned the possibility of flying, Karina was eager to try one of those flying things, curious about how they worked, and also eager to speed up their journey. But again she tried to cheer up her friend. "Maybe he'll still reply. Just wait."

Cayla looked down. "I hope," she mumbled.

Karina didn't know what to say. She wondered whether Cayla's friend had a stone identical to hers and if, by any chance, it had caller ID. It obviously didn't have voicemail.

Karina had been so interested in the communication stone that she had momentarily forgotten about the shoes. *The shoes!*

The very reason she was there. They were still in her purse. She had to stop thinking they would just walk away by themselves, or perhaps forget the idea that evil creatures would come and catch them. Oh, no, why did she have to think about evil creatures again, right when she was in the middle of a forest in a "cursed" path? She took the water skin for another sip, but, unlike her purse, the skin was empty. And she was thirsty. There was a stream close by, but she dreaded going out alone.

"Can you come with me?" Karina asked. "For some water?"

Cayla at first looked as if she hadn't understood the question, but then answered automatically, "Sure." The girl then picked up her stone necklace and put it around her neck.

Karina was about to pick up her little purse, but then she had an idea. "Do you have any string? Or anything to attach something?"

"What for?" Cayla asked.

"I want to tie the shoes on me."

Cayla squinted. "What?"

"They're flexible. I think I can tie them around my waist. I don't want to keep checking them."

"Are you sure? Isn't it dangerous?"

"It's better than taking chances, no?"

Cayla shrugged. "Maybe."

She opened her bag and took out something that looked like a narrow silver ribbon, which she cut with a little knife she carried. Karina lifted her dress and tied the shoes around her waist. The ribbon was somewhat sticky, which was quite helpful in keeping the shoes in place. She was about to ask her friend to help with the final knot, when she realized Cayla was turned backward, probably not to see the shoes. Now that was excessive superstition. One day Karina would tell her that her friend had worn them, and... oops, her friend had broken a leg and a handrail. Maybe it was best this way. Still, Karina felt a lot more assured with the shoes close to her body, hidden under her dress.

She wouldn't need to check them again; she could feel them. Cayla still had her back turned, so Karina called out, "I'm ready. Let's go."

The stream was some twenty meters from their tent. The water reflected the stars and Karina smiled, thinking she would drink starry water. This could be a lovely place if it weren't for that dreadful silence. She had never realized how a forest is supposed to be alive with sounds before this strange place. Even the stream could not be heard but very closely. It was as if there was something blocking sound. Karina filled then closed her water skin. When she got up, she saw Cayla with her necklace, no longer hidden under the dress. But of course!

"Cayla," she pointed at the orange stone, "have you ever used this in this path, or any similar place?"

"I've never been here before. Why?"

"Could it be that this path blocks it? Prevents it from working? Like it does with sound?"

Cayla looked at her stone. "I don't see why." She looked at Karina. "You think?"

"It makes sense, no?"

"I... don't know."

"What if we walk... uh, closer to the edge of the path?" Karina suggested. "Then you try again?"

Cayla nodded. "Maybe. Come."

They walked in the direction opposite to the mountains, just a few steps, until the ground was no longer flat, but started descending. Karina thought going down a slope in the dark was slightly dangerous, and almost protested that she had suggested going close to the edge of the path, not away from it, but soon Cayla stopped. Karina was not sure if it was her impression, but she heard soft forest sounds coming from below the slope. Cayla's orange stone had a faint glimmer, and the girl lifted it close to her face. Even before she spoke, the stone started speaking, or transmitting a boy's voice.

"Cay, where are you? What's happening? Are you all right?"

"I'm fine, I just—"

"Wait. I see where you are. I can't really talk now."

The voice disappeared, and the stone's glimmer slowly faded. Karina's deduction about unknown technology had been correct. "See? I told you it would work here."

Somehow, Cayla was not as happy. "I guess. Let's go back to the tent."

"What's wrong?"

She mumbled, "Nothing."

Back in the tent, they sat in silence. Cayla then lay down and turned to the other side. Karina decided to do the same, even though it was still early. All she managed was to feel uncomfortable; the discomfort one has when going to bed and not wanting to sleep. Karina stared at the top of the tent, trying to cheer herself with the thought that she was in an adventure, even though that moment didn't feel like one. Perhaps that was what real adventures were like: they felt ordinary and mundane when one was in the middle of them. Only later, when looking back, people would realize what it had been, which was sad because it meant nobody ever truly lived an adventure, only remembered it as one.

7

ONE MORE

Cayla tried to close her eyes and in an attempt to stop herself from thinking. After more than one year away from Darian, should it be any surprise that he would be too busy to talk to her? She'd been holding on to a faint hope against the fear that time had changed everything. That he'd forget her. But it shouldn't matter. What should matter was getting to Lylah and defeating her. By destroying shoes. There was something silly in the idea, but Odell had to be right. His hope had worked so far, as it had brought a friend willing to help her without asking for anything in return. It felt good to remember that there were still people in the world who would go far to do what was right.

Cayla had to stop thinking about Darian. She shouldn't even have contacted him. Maybe it was for the best. She looked at her bright necklace stone, casting a glow around it. Beneath it, her heart was dark with fear.

⁓

CAYLA WAS SNAPPED out of her sleep by a soft sound of someone —or something—scratching the tent. Karina also shot up in surprise. The sound had come from outside. No point wondering what it was. She pulled the knife from her bag, lit her crystal, and stepped out, ready to fight whatever it was.

"Who's there?"

Before she had time to illuminate the person's face, she heard the voice.

"It's me."

Knife and crystal fell on the floor. The light from the moon and stars allowed her to see the brown-eyed young man in front of her. She would have gasped for air anyways, because he was so good looking, but her surprise was double, because this was Darian, not as she remembered him, but older, different.

"What's happening?" he sounded worried.

"How did you find me?"

"Find you? I've been trying to find you for over an hour. Do you realize where you are?"

His angry tone surprised her, but there was something even more puzzling. "I never told you where I was."

He took a deep breath. "It's the necklace. I think... I didn't know it did that, but I can feel where you are." He then sounded angry. "What are you doing here?"

He was snapping. She could snap as well. "I'm confused. Could you or couldn't you find me?"

"Well it's not a tracker on a map. What are you doing here?"

He sounded as if she owed him an explanation, and she didn't. She shrugged. "I'm camping."

He frowned.

Cayla pointed. "Here's the tent."

"And you decided to camp on your own. In the hidden path."

"I'm with a friend."

He crossed his arms. "Friend?"

As much as his shoulders and arms were not as she remembered, what bothered her most was his bad attitude. He'd never been like that before.

At this point, Karina got out of the tent and waved. "Hey."

Darian frowned and stared at Karina, as if looking for something wrong.

Karina was probably super uncomfortable, because she added, "Cayla was showing me the forest. I... I study plants."

He raised an eyebrow and turned to Cayla. "Is that right? How come they let you out?"

As if Cayla were a prisoner or something. "Why wouldn't they?"

Darian snorted. "Well..." He changed his tone, and again sounded concerned. "Are you sure everything is all right?"

Cayla rolled her eyes. "Yes. We're fine."

"I see." He turned to Karina. "Hello, I'm Darian. Sorry, I should have introduced myself. It's just, such a strange place and all." He shook his head. "Sorry."

"No problem." Karina shrugged.

He turned back to Cayla. "I was worried about you."

"Really? Why didn't you talk then?"

"It's, it's complicated. I can't even start to... But you shouldn't be out by yourselves, this is dangerous."

Dangerous bla bla bla. As if Cayla were some helpless child. "We're fine. We've come all this way, and nobody's seen us."

"Well, look where you are!" he said. "I couldn't even find you."

"You just did, didn't you?"

He sounded nervous. "We should go. This place is not safe."

Karina asked, "Why?"

"This path isn't for anything alive," he said.

"Well, why did you come then?" Cayla asked.

He looked down for a while before saying, "My lift is near. Come."

Come? Yeah, it was Darian and all, but he wasn't going to order her around. "Who said I wanted to go anywhere?"

Darian looked down again and bit his lip. "I'll take you back, or wherever you want to go. Please don't stay here, not by yourselves."

"At least now you're saying please."

He stepped back. "What? I have to beg now?"

Perhaps it wasn't only his arms that had gotten thick. "Not beg. Ask."

"Well, I'm asking."

"And it makes a difference." Cayla smiled and turned to Karina. "Let's pack."

She shoved the covers in her bag in a matter of seconds, and even helped Karina with her stuff. Cayla then pulled a few strings to fold the tent, the structure spiraling and twisting the fabric in a cylinder the size of a thick bottle. Darian only looked, waiting.

Cayla looked up. "Where's your lift?"

"I told you, nothing comes here."

"Even in the air?"

He nodded. Cayla picked up her light and followed him as they went to the edge of the path. Karina was right behind her. As they descended a slope, he turned around and extended his hand. That was sweet, but Cayla was perfectly capable of descending without any help, and he wouldn't be able to walk backwards anyways.

She shook her head. "I'm fine."

He puffed, as if annoyed or offended, and then turned around. What had she done?

~

KARINA FOLLOWED as they went to the edge of the path and this time they really descended a slope in the dark. She wished she had a light, but then, that would mean one less hand to hold onto bushes and trunks. Thankfully there were lots of trees. Or perhaps not, because that also meant there were lots of roots one could trip over and fall. Cayla walked close to Darian. He looked back to check on her, and offered his hand a couple times, but she refused. Oh, she could at least turn around and offer her hand, if she was so sure of herself. But Karina didn't say anything. Slowly the forest came alive again with sounds. How glad she felt. It was as if her ears had been blocked and now they started working again.

She wondered where his lift would be parked, considering there were no clearings. Or would they walk outside the forest? Soon the moonlight illuminated what looked like a thin white pole. Actually, it seemed to be moving. As it turned, it revealed another pole, and beams between them. It was a ladder, a rope ladder, but made from what looked like silver or white ribbon. Karina looked up and saw the oval bottom of lift above them. Had she not known better, she would have thought that was a flying saucer, but of course it wasn't, it was a floating flying machine in a different dimension, something a lot more logical.

"You two can go first, I'll go last," Darian said.

Cayla gestured for Karina to go first. She felt nervous, because once she set foot on the ladder it became a lot more dangling than she had predicted. She then heard or imagined a voice saying, "Don't. Don't go!" It sounded like Cayla but when she glanced back the girl was silent, so it was only Karina's own fear. Still, she went up a few steps, but all the shaking made her even more nervous. The lift was high above, twice the height of the tallest tree, and she couldn't picture herself going all the way up on that dangling thing, especially with that dreadful voice echoing on her head. Well, but wasn't adventure and great things that she'd wanted? She was about to achieve new heights. She ignored the voice in her head and her own fear, and went step by step on that shaking, dangling thing, ignoring how high she was going.

CAYLA WATCHED as Karina went up and grabbed the ladder. She felt a hand over hers and her entire body trembled. Perhaps she'd avoided holding his hand because she wasn't sure how she'd react. It had been smart to avoid it on a dark slope. She turned and looked up at Darian. Looking up to see him was new and weird.

"What's happening?" he whispered.

That tone again. Demanding, ordering, so unlike the boy she remembered. She pulled her hand and went up the ladder.

WHEN KARINA ENTERED THE LIFT, she noticed it was much bigger than she'd imagined, with green windowless smooth walls, made of some kind of metal. There was a large empty area in the middle, a large bench on each side and a little table near the back. The place was illuminated the same way as the rooms in the castle. A small wall with a door separated what would be the cockpit or the equivalent of it, since there were no controls where they sat. Cayla came up, and then Darian. Karina took a better look at him. He was a regular looking teenager, the same age or maybe a little older than Cayla and a little taller, with brown eyes and brown straight hair down to his chin. He wore dark blue long-sleeved shirt and pants in some kind of synthetic material.

Cayla sat down. "Well, we're here now."

"And... were you even planning on going anywhere?" he asked as he closed the hatch from where they had come and rolled the ladder into a small compartment

"Yes," Cayla replied. "We were going to continue on the path, down until, uh, the mouth of the Black River, and I thought you—"

"Are you out of your mind?"

"Put me down if you have a problem with it," Cayla said.

Darian rested his forehead on his hand, as if thinking. "Just... tell me what's happening. Does your father even know you're out?"

"Well of course," Cayla replied. "Or else I suppose everyone would be looking for me, wouldn't they?"

Darian nodded. "I guess. But why do you want to go so far? Why the mouth of the Black River?"

"That's where we're going. But I can still walk. We were going to walk there anyways."

He laughed. "Really? You mean to tell me you were planning on walking for at least five days?"

Cayla shrugged. "Why not?"

He took a deep breath. "Maybe. But I'll tell you what, we could go somewhere else, I could take you somewhere safe, and, if you're running away, maybe—"

"I'm not running away!"

"What's happening then?"

"I told you. I'm camping."

He snorted. "You're not going to tell me?"

Cayla just stared.

Darian crossed his arms. "Maybe I'll take you back to the castle."

Cayla also crossed her arms. "My father will love to see you bringing me."

Darian looked down and sideways. Was that guy the trustworthy friend who would give them a ride? He and Cayla stood silent.

Karina thought it was her turn to say something. "It's the

plants. Rare plants. Only near the, uh, Black River, and we need them."

He raised an eyebrow. "Which plants?"

"*Falucata stonensis*," Karina said, hoping the made-up Latin sounding name would be convincing enough. Now wait, were their plants named in Latin? Did they even know Latin? Why did they even speak English? But perhaps this was not the right time for those questions. Darian and even Cayla had puzzled expressions, so Karina tried to explain some more. "That's, uh, the scientific name. It doesn't have a real name, because people just call it... grass, because... that's what it looks like."

Karina actually enjoyed pretending she was a scientist, even if not a very precise one.

Darian looked at Karina as if seeing her for the first time. "Who are you? Where are you from?"

Yikes. She hadn't considered how to answer those questions.

Cayla replied, "She's Odell's newest apprentice. His niece. She came to live with us a couple months ago."

"How come you never mentioned her?"

Cayla looked down. "We... haven't talked much lately, have we?"

"I know." He sighed. "I'm so sorry, it's just, and so many things, and you disappeared."

Cayla stepped closer to him. "I'm sorry. I... couldn't contact you, or else I would. You should know it."

He sighed. "I know. I just... missed you."

Cayla looked down and away. "I missed you too."

"This is Odell's doing then?" Darian asked, his voice much calmer and softer than before. "Why would he send you out to study plants in the brink of an uprising?"

Cayla squinted. "Uprising?"

"I mean, it's just, the military thing, the generals think there's always the possibility of some kind of conflict, or uprising, and you'd be in great danger. Also, don't forget who supposedly dwells on the upper Black River."

"I know," Cayla said.

Darian raised his eyebrows. "And you still want to go there?"

"I'm not asking you to take me to the upper Black River, just the mouth."

Darian passed his hands through his hair and looked at Cayla. "I'm telling you this is dangerous and you should trust me."

"I trust you, but I'll walk there if I have to."

"Fine," said Darian. "I'll take you there. Tomorrow, during daylight. And I'll come down with you to pick the plants."

"No, no. We need to be alone, and it takes at least a day, uh, to spot the plants."

Darian was about to answer when the door to the other part of the lift opened, revealing a teenage girl. She wore pants and a shirt similar to Darian's. She had a pleasant, pretty face. "Can we move now?" she asked.

"Sure," answered Darian, "I'm coming in a moment."

The door closed. Cayla stared at it as if she had just seen a three-headed monster. "Who is she?"

"Oh, Zayra. She's my partner."

Cayla looked livid.

Darian continued, "In the ship. She flies with me. We are supposed to fly two by two. I'm sure you know it."

Cayla stepped back and crossed her arms, squinting as in an effort to make sense of a blurred image. "Is that why you wouldn't talk to me?"

He frowned. "What? No."

There was fury in her eyes. "Why would you come with someone else?"

"I had no choice," he said. "We were on a patrolling assignment. But she's my friend, I trust her. You don't suppose I could leave the ship floating by itself, do you?"

Cayla shook her head in disbelief. "Nobody was supposed to know about us being here." She lowered her voice. "And she's heard everything we said".

"She didn't hear it; the door was closed. And she won't tell anyone about you. Besides," he lowered his voice, "she doesn't even know who you are."

"How can she not know?"

"I told her you work in the castle, and, uh, she thinks you're my girlfriend."

Cayla made a disgusted face. "What?"

Darian stepped back. He looked even more bothered than when he was on the path. "I had to explain why I wanted to help you." He put his hands in front of him, as if to distance himself from Cayla. "No pretension here."

He then turned around, entered the other part of the ship and shut the door behind him. Cayla sat quietly, looking sour and shaking her head. She covered her eyes with her hands. "We're doomed."

Karina thought that was an exaggeration and that her friend was jealous, but she didn't say anything. After a while the door opened. Darian's flying partner came in their compartment, or room. She seemed friendly, and was indeed very pretty, with large blue eyes and perfect brown curls.

The girl stepped in front of them and smiled, turning to the princess. "Hello, I'm Zayra. I'm really happy to meet you, Cayla." She sounded as if she really meant it. She then turned to Karina. "And what's your name again?"

"Karina."

"Kayna?"

"No. Karina."

"Oh, right." She sounded as if she still had not understood, then turned to both girls. "I just wanted to tell you we're going to spend the night in a small island in the lower Silver River. It's empty and we can all sleep in the lift. Tomorrow we'll take you to the crossing banks."

"Thank you," Karina replied.

Zayra seemed pleased and had an even bigger smile. "Oh, it's my pleasure." The girl then turned to Cayla. "You have the same name as the princess. How's that?"

Cayla, who had been staring straight in front of her, barely moved her eyes and shrugged. "How am I supposed to know? I never had another name."

Zayra laughed. "You're right. Do you know her?"

"Who?"

"The princess."

Cayla grimaced. "I live in the castle."

Zayra smiled. "Yes, of course. But, doesn't it cause confusion?"

For the first time Cayla looked at the girl. She stared as if examining her before answering. "People in the castle are not like you."

Zayra seemed confused. "What do you mean?"

Cayla had a half smile. "They are not dumb."

The girl stared at Cayla, as if trying to understand. After a few seconds, she laughed. "Oh. Right. Well, I have to get back." She opened the door and disappeared in the compartment.

Cayla looked sour. "Did you see?" She mimicked the other girl. "It's my pleasure. As if she's the one who's doing us a favor."

Did she change her mind about people hearing them? Cayla had been a little rude for no reason. Still, Karina tried to calm her down. "Don't worry, everything will be fine". She winked. "We'll collect all the plants we need."

Cayla sighed. "I really hope so."

LATER THAT NIGHT, the lift landed on what was supposed to be an island in a river. Only Darian went outside to bring drinking water. The lift had a small bathroom, like a bus bathroom, inside the other compartment, which Karina had mentally named the cockpit, so she had to go there to use it. The most exciting part was of course being alone in the cockpit or control room, even if for a short period. Further inspection, however, revealed that it was not very impressive; it had three chairs, a window in the front (a windshield actually) and a black panel without any button, joystick or steering wheel. Karina wondered if that black panel worked like a smartphone screen, or if the pilot just conjured some magic, but then she reminded herself to stop being primitive and assume people used magic. She would need to catch them piloting or controlling the thing to learn how it worked. Or perhaps ask. She looked out the windshield. Since it was evening, she saw only a night sky and what seemed to be some water in front of her.

Karina went back to the main compartment. The table that had seemed somewhat small at first was actually bigger than she'd first thought and could easily sit eight or ten people. But only three people sat by the table. Four when Karina joined them. They didn't have a proper dinner, but rather snacked on bars and dried fruit, which seemed to be their staple travel food. Darian and Cayla were quiet and gloom. Zayra tried to make some conversation, but didn't insist much. One time Karina caught Zayra looking at Cayla like a scientist examining a rare specimen, but other times Darian's flying partner looked relaxed and almost happy, oblivious to the heavy mood around her.

DARIAN GLANCED at Cayla then looked down. For so long he had dreamed of seeing her again. Never would he have imagined it would be like this. And she was different. Cayla had always been fierce and stubborn, but now it was almost as if she was stubborn against him. He had almost died of worry wondering what was happening with her, and she didn't even care about him. He glanced again at her. She was prettier than he remembered, as if that could be possible. With princes coming from other kingdoms just to see her, Darian wondered for the first time if she thought he wasn't good enough for her. The thought stung.

CAYLA GLANCED AT DARIAN. He had changed. His bright eyes had turned deeper and more thoughtful, serious, with an intensity that she hadn't seen before. In a way it was scary, but it was also... She had to get used to the idea he was no longer the cute boy she liked to spend time with. He was still cute all right, but not a boy anymore. But he shouldn't have brought them to Zayra, he shouldn't. Cayla wasn't sure what bothered her most: the fact that an unknown girl knew at least part of a plan that should be secret, the fact that Darian could be killed if that girl told anyone they were anything more than friends, even if Cayla wasn't sure anymore what they were, or the fact that she had just learned that Darian spent his time with a girl that was at least five times prettier than herself.

No. What really bothered her was that the girl could endanger her plan to go to Lylah. There was something odd about her and she didn't trust her. Maybe contacting Darian had been a mistake, but then, how could she know he would be with someone she couldn't trust? Fair enough, Darian didn't know that this was an important and secret journey nobody could know about. Well, of course she couldn't tell him. Still, he could have asked her if it bothered her that someone else would see them. He could have asked. He could... so many things. Among them, stop talking to her as if he had the right to tell her what to do.

TWO LARGE BEDS were pulled from beneath the side seats. Each of them was as big as a king sized mattress. The three girls lay on one bed, and Darian on the other. Karina had to sleep between Cayla and Zayra, because she assumed the princess would not want to spend the night near the other girl. Thankfully each had their own cover, but the middle position was not the most comfortable, as Karina couldn't move much to either side or she would bump onto one of the girls. Still, this was nicer than the silent tent in the middle of nowhere, and if she remembered that she was skipping a lot of walking, she could ignore the bad mood that still hung around the place.

Karina's eyes were open even after the lights had faded and everyone's breath had become smooth and steady. Cayla was now deep asleep and spreading her arms, squeezing Karina against Zayra. Was it that even asleep she felt entitled to a princess space? Not really because in truth Darian was the one with the biggest space, just because he was the only guy there. Karina sat up and looked at him. How old would he be? Sixteen, seventeen, not much more. Zayra also seemed to be the same age. Karina felt a sick feeling in her stomach when she realized she'd been flying in the hands of teenagers. Well, maybe people there aged differently, maybe lifts were really easy to fly or maybe she should just stop being paranoid and remember the tougher challenges ahead of her. Actually, perhaps it was better not think about future challenges and just try to sleep and enjoy the comfortable bed. Cayla had gotten what she wanted; they would fly a big chunk of their way, but somehow, she was really upset about being there. If she was jealous, why wasn't she simply nicer to the guy who had brought her here? Oh, mysteries of the Universe.

KARINA WOKE UP ALARMED, fearing someone was stealing her shoes. She sat up but then realized she could still feel them around her waist. She then turned around, because she heard someone. Zayra was near their bags, and for a second seemed to be looking into them. But the girl smiled when she saw Karina, without any sign of alarm, surprise, or fear.

"It's good you woke up, we're almost there," Zayra said, as she folded a blanket.

Karina felt confused. She was still debating whether she saw or not the girl looking into their things.

"You'd better get ready," Zayra added, then looked at Cayla's direction. "Both of you."

The girl put the blanket in a compartment near the side seat then walked back to the controlling room. Karina decided she had confused the girl's blanket with their bags. Regardless, they didn't have anything important in their bags, not even a map or anything that could identify them, so it was no big deal. Karina got up and tried to see where they were, but quickly realized that was pointless, first, because there were no windows, and second, because she would not know where she was anyways, although it would be nice to admire such a different view. Cayla was still asleep. Karina knelt and shook her friend's shoulder. The girl jumped up scared, until she looked around, probably realizing they were not in the middle of any emergency, and sat down.

After a couple minutes, Darian walked in, addressing Cayla. "Are you sure you want to do this? There are dangers... you are not aware of."

Cayla shook her head. "I'm well aware of the dangers."

Darian looked down and bit his lip. "I could come down with you, stay close, just as a precaution."

"Don't you need to be patrolling?"

"I could leave Zayra by herself."

"Oh, now you can leave her. How interesting."

Darian looked at Cayla attentively, as if trying to understand something, before asking, "Why does she bother you?"

"Because nobody was supposed to know about us."

"I see. You're ashamed."

Cayla squinted. "No. It's just, it had to be secret."

"Well, you don't want me come with you I won't. I'll pick you up in the afternoon."

Cayla shook her head. "No, no, it's fine. We're going to take a boat home. From the Last Town."

Darian raised his eyebrows. "It's dangerous."

"Everything for you is dangerous, I suppose you consider breathing dangerous."

He nodded. "In these days, out there on your own, yes."

"You want me to suffocate then."

"No. I could protect you."

"Ah, you want to suffocate me personally. No, thanks."

He stared at her for a long while, then to the floor, then to her again. Cayla had a defiant look.

He stepped back, fists clenched, arms trembling. His voice came out soft and smooth, "That's it then? Don't you worry, Princess Cayla," he spoke slowly, emphasizing every word, "you will never run the slightest risk of me suffocating you."

He then turned around and got into the other compartment. The lift shook as he slammed the door. Cayla stared at the door with a confused expression, and then sat and looked down. Karina didn't know whether she should say something or not, and either way she didn't even know what to say.

Because the lift had no windows, she had no idea whether it was moving or not, until it slowed down and descended. Zayra came out and opened a back door. Had the door not been opened, Karina would never have realized it was there. She felt relieved that this time they were on the ground, in a clearing, so she would not have to jump, or worse, descend a loose dangling rope ladder. Better than jumping, actually.

Zayra stood by the door. "Bye, good luck."

"Thanks," Karina replied softly, because someone had to say something.

Cayla didn't look back or say anything. Karina watched as the flying machine went up and then far away.

Only then did Cayla look, and shook her head. "This could ruin our mission."

"We just skipped a five-day walk."

Cayla sighed. "I'm not sure it was worth it."

Karina was about to point out that it had been Cayla's idea, but then decided to stay quiet and just be glad they didn't have to walk all the way.

THE IMAGINARY PURSUERS

The mountains were low at this part, lowering to what was probably the place where the two rivers met. That much Karina remembered from the map. Cayla looked at that direction, then to the other side, as if trying to decide something. Karina didn't understand what the girl was thinking, because even she knew to which direction they were supposed to go.

Karina pointed. "Isn't the mouth of the river that way?"

"That's what worries me," Cayla replied.

"Why?"

"That girl knows where we are going."

Oh, no, Karina was hoping any annoyance against Zayra would have stopped once they stepped out of the lift. "So?" she asked, refraining from rolling her eyes.

Cayla frowned. "I don't like it."

That much Karina was aware, but she still tried to calm her friend. "Well, she doesn't really know where we are going and what we are planning to do. And if she's your friend's friend, maybe you should trust her."

"I'm not even sure I trust him." She said this as if acknowledging a painful truth.

Perhaps... it was too late to think that? But Karina asked something else, "Is there anything we can do about it?"

"Well, they think we're going to the mouth of the river, there, or perhaps that we'll stay in the woods near or between the two rivers. What we can do instead is walk to the other direction, and cross to the Black river through the mountains."

That mention reminded Karina of the bit of Odell's explanation she liked the least. "Don't jaguars live there?"

"Not there, they live further up, protected by real mountains. This part here," she pointed to the low mountains beside them, "they are not even mountains, just hills. Very little difference from walking close to the river. It just takes a little longer, but we're ahead anyways."

Karina looked up. Indeed the hills didn't have rocks that seemed difficult to climb, just trees wide apart. It would not be much harder than when they went up the plateau to the path. But that was not her problem with the plan. "What's the point in changing our itinerary?"

"If anyone follows us, they won't find us."

As much as Karina hated to argue, she had to point out something. "Right, but they have fast flying uh, things—lifts. If anyone wanted to find us, I don't think we'd be able to walk far enough from the last spot they saw us."

Cayla looked seriously at Karina. "You're right. But the mountains will be the last place they'll look. Let's hurry then." She turned around and walked fast towards the mountain

Karina regretted having said anything. She calculated that they would walk at most five kilometers in an hour, probably even less, considering they were going up. That meant that even if they walked eight hours straight they would only make forty kilometers. Karina had no idea how fast those things went, but she was sure that whoever was inside would have enough time to look for them in a forty kilometer range, regardless of the direction they went. She debated whether or not to mention those numbers to Cayla, but then decided against it, afraid that the girl would come up with an even crazier idea. Indeed, her pace started to get hard to follow. Karina then considered that at least the hills had some trees, meaning they would not be easily spotted by air, but then she told herself to stop calculating the odds that they would be found, because nobody was following them.

THE PACE WAS SO tough that soon Karina stopped wondering about the reason they were going up and concentrated on her walking, breathing fast. The walk was rather smooth; few spots were steep or had rocks. After some two or three hours, when Karina's legs had already started to hurt, Cayla stopped. "Maybe we should rest now."

For a split second Karina almost reminded her friend that if they wanted to run from imaginary pursuers they should keep going, but then realized that if the pursuers were imaginary there was no need to hurry. What a brilliant conclusion. In fact, she should be glad that they would get a well-deserved break. For the first time since they'd started going up the hill, Karina had time to turn around and really look down where she'd come from. Through the trees she caught a glimpse of the valley below, the river, and low hills on the other side. There were many constructions here and there, especially near the river, in bright colors: green, yellow, red, blue, purple and others. She wondered what material they were made of, whether they were houses and if the colors meant anything.

When Karina turned around, she noticed the tent had been set up. That was fast—and silent. She was surprised, because she had assumed "resting" meant only stopping and perhaps sitting a little.

Cayla seemed to notice her surprised look. "We sleep during the day, walk at night, remember?"

Karina nodded. Of course she remembered the instructions, but what was the point in keeping to the rules if they were off course anyways? Still, a tent meant they could relax much better than sitting on rocks or branches. Cayla sat on the entrance of the tent, and started drinking water. Karina did the same and also ate one of her bars. Even though they could not see the buildings from where they were, Karina tried to start a conversation. "What are those buildings down there?"

"That's the Last Town."

Karina had heard this name mentioned as the city from where they would supposedly return by boat. That made sense and explained why Cayla thought they would not look for them in the mountains, or hills. "Last because it's the last by the river?"

"Ah, no, not really. The rivers continues. With a different name. 'Last' has to do with a war or revolt, it was the last city standing or something."

"I see."

Before getting frustrated that her friend knew so little, Karina reminded herself that she too was awful in history, so at least they had something in common. Unfortunately, common lack of knowledge didn't make a good conversation topic. Cayla sat down. Her black hair shone so much in the sun that it almost looked silver, in a way that was shampoo-commercial unnatural. But her eyes were sad, lost in the distance, as she touched the orange stone in her necklace that was no longer hidden under her dress. Karina debated whether to respect her friend's silence, or ask a question she was itching to ask. To favor the decision of asking, she weighted that since they were in such a difficult journey they should trust each other. "What's with you and Darian?"

Cayla let go of the stone quickly and widened her eyes. "What do you mean?"

Oh, did that need explaining? Karina tried to rephrase it. "How long have you known each other?"

"Ah, a couple years. He's, uh, almost like a brother." Cayla lowered her head. "Or was. I really trusted him."

Brother? Karina felt her lunch spinning in her stomach. Still, she thought Cayla shouldn't be so gloomy.

"But he came, he brought us here, exactly like you wanted."

Cayla shook her head. "No. I didn't want a random girl knowing about us. Who knows what she'll do with that information? This is just... wrong."

"But she's far away now, she doesn't know where we are, and has no idea what we're doing."

Cayla nodded slowly. "That's what I'm hoping. But still, she knows about me and Darian."

That wasn't making much sense. "But... aren't you, uh, like siblings? Surely everyone knows you are friends."

"They know we were friends, not that we still are."

"Why so much secret?"

Cayla sighed, bit her lip and looked down. "Well, he used to live in the castle, until my father, uh, he thought...Well, my father has forbidden me to ever see Darian again. But, it's not that I am really disobeying my father, because he imagined something that was not true. I thought my father would come around when he understood that me and Darian, we're just friends. That's what I thought, but I'm not sure about anything anymore."

Karina could well understand why her father would "imagine" something more than friendship. People are really creative. Then she remembered her friend was a princess and understood the problem. "I suppose you'll have to marry a prince or something."

Cayla squinted. "What?"

"I mean in the future." Karina was not sure if she was talking nonsense but she remembered something she had heard somewhere. "For an alliance with another kingdom or something."

Cayla shook her head. "No. I don't think he wants me to marry anyone. And I'm too young to even think about that."

"That's true. Is that the problem? That you're too young?"

Cayla agitated her hands. "I don't know. I don't know why my father won't let me... And this is not about Darian. I'm just answering the question you asked. You brought it up." She went inside the tent. "I'll try to lie down a little and rest. Close the tent if you come inside."

Cayla was a textbook example on how love made people illogical. Anyways, she didn't want to sit by herself. "I'll lie down as well."

With that, they entered and Cayla closed the tent. Karina was surprised that the tent felt cool inside, and was darker than she had imagined. It was a good place to rest during the day, even when it was hot outside, perhaps especially then. She lay down and put her legs up, over her backpack, so as to rest them. Cayla had her eyes closed even though she didn't sound like she was asleep. Karina's waist hurt a little from the sweat caused by the shoes, so she removed them quietly and put them beneath her legs, so that she could still feel them. But instead of relaxed, she felt worried. She heard a voice somewhat like Cayla's saying, "Karina, get up and run. Run, quickly." She looked at the girl, thinking that the princess' earlier paranoia had gotten contagious.

Cayla opened her eyes. "What?"

The question surprised Karina. "Oh, nothing."

Cayla closed her eyes again. Now, if she was calm, why was Karina feeling so edgy, as if they were on the brink of some disaster? Was it that they had deviated from the plan? Maybe Odell's words had impressed her more than she admitted. Maybe it was just that she needed to rest the mind more than the body, but that was nonsense, because it had gotten plenty of rest during that tough walk. Karina tried to think about something different, but fear and worry started to bother her so much that she made up her mind to convince Cayla to get up and keep moving. But before Karina said anything, Cayla opened her eyes and sat up. "Did you hear that?"

"What?"

Cayla gestured for silence. Suddenly, she opened her eyes wide. "Someone's coming. We need to hide."

She got up and got out of the tent. Karina still hadn't heard anything, but she thought perhaps her companion was suffering from the same anxiety that had gotten her. Karina started to put the shoes around her waist, but before she finished, Cayla came back and pulled her hand. "Come."

One of the shoes fell as they walked outside the tent. "My shoe!"

Cayla was strong and had already pulled Karina away from the spot. "We'll get it back later. Come." She headed to a tree and started climbing it.

Karina followed with a lot of difficulty, while the princess looked down in desperation, trying to hurry her. When Karina was a few branches below her travel companion, the girl gestured for her to stop and be silent. Cayla lay on top of her thick branch, so that she was partially hidden from whoever was below, and Karina tried to do the same. She looked down, trying to find the fallen shoe, but she couldn't see it. She felt the remaining shoe on her waist, and wondered whether she could lift the other one using magic, but perhaps she needed to wear the shoes for them to have an effect, or have someone else wear them. Or something. Or perhaps this was some big nonsense. She wished the shoes had come with an instruction manual.

Karina couldn't hear anything other than leaves, the wind, and small insects. Perhaps their fear had been just paranoia. Grabbing a branch was uncomfortable, not only the physical discomfort, but also that uncomfortable feeling of expecting something not to happen. How long does one wait for nothing? Not long, as she saw a group of five or six people, walking silently and yet fast towards their tent. No wonder she hadn't heard them. Someone walked to the tent and looked inside.

"Empty," a young woman said softly but loud enough to be heard from the tree. "They can't be far. You two stay here. The rest, come, we'll find them."

At that moment Karina's heart started to race, because the woman's words meant they were looking for someone. She rested her face against the branch, hoping it would hide her. Below them, people were moving around. After a few minutes, everyone seemed to have gone somewhere else. Karina wanted to look down to see what was happening, but her body refused to move. That proved a good thing, because seconds afterward she heard a woman's voice.

"I don't know. I still think this is a trap."

A man replied, "You think our commander's sister would set us up?"

"Not her. The boy she hangs out with."

"Wow, now, some respect," the man replied. "He's done more for us than anyone."

"I know, but I won't forget that he's General Keen's son. And has that brother. How do you suppose she knows the sisters are here?"

"He's certainly well connected," the man replied.

"Too well connected, that's what I think," the woman said. "Now tell, me, what would two princesses be doing down here, all by themselves? Isn't it, just... too easy?"

There was some silence before the man replied, "Well, it is odd. Still, if they are here, it's our great chance."

"And yet, if it's a trap, it might be our end."

"Why did you come then?"

"I'm not a coward."

The man didn't reply and the woman didn't say anything

anymore. The mention of two princesses meant that they were really looking for them, perhaps thinking Karina was Ayanna. But nobody knew they would go to these hills. On the other hand, two people knew they had been dropped off near the foot of those mountains. A guy and a girl, just like "the traitor" and "the sister" in the conversation. And who were those people anyways?

After a while, the man said, "They're still searching, no sign of them."

"Hum," the woman replied, "whoever walked up the hills and set this tent must still be close, or else they would've left tracks. They can't have disappeared by magic."

"Well, technically, what if..."

"What, magic?"

"Why not?"

The woman laughed. "Some hypocrisy from our adorable king. But I still doubt it. Trust me, they're close. I'm going to climb the trees and look."

At that moment Karina didn't know if her heart stopped or sped or jumped. She certainly stopped breathing for a few seconds.

The man asked, "Didn't you think this was a trap?"

"The sooner we find the bait, the sooner we find out. Whistle if you see anyone, even if they're friends. I'll whistle as well."

The woman's voice sounded farther away from before, as if she had already made her way to another tree, thankfully not theirs. Still, she would eventually find Karina and Cayla, unless she missed their tree, gave up, or someone called her somewhere else. Poor odds there. The feeling of patiently waiting to be caught was anything but pleasant, and yet, it felt unreal, as if Karina had to disconnect herself from the reality awaiting her.

But before she disconnected too much, Cayla brought her back. "Two against one. It's our chance. Let's go."

Go? Seriously?

Cayla had already climbed down from her branch and she pulled Karina. "Down, quickly. We can run."

Karina started climbing down, unsure if that was really a good idea. Cayla was already further down. Karina then heard the sound of a loud bird. Or was that the man whistling?

"Jump and run!" Cayla yelled before doing what she had suggested.

A jump from that height could result in a broken leg, but Karina didn't want to wait by herself on the tree, so she jumped, falling on soft ground, without any broken leg or sprained ankle, realizing the jump hadn't been as high as she'd thought. She saw the back of a man running after something: Cayla. Before Karina weighed her options, someone pushed her to the ground and sat on her, then pulled her arms with one hand and pushed her face down with the other. The coarse ground scraped her cheek. Then the person above her—the woman—grunted and got up.

Cayla yelled, "Get up, fight!"

This time it was really Cayla, not some weird voice. Karina got up and saw Cayla against the woman, who was younger and smaller than she had imagined, and wore clothes similar to Darian's and Zayra's. Then another girl came, and she went for Cayla. The princess kept both of them away mainly by moving fast, turning and kicking. Karina looked around, searching for something to throw at them, but soon realized that they were moving too fast and she would miss, or worse, she might hit Cayla. She decided then to kick the girl and see if, together with Cayla, they could defeat both her and the woman. But out of the corner of her eye something glimmered in the sunlight: her shoe. It was far from the tent, farther than their equipment, which had been spread on the floor, and far from the fight. Karina ran to the shoe, grabbed it and started running, but she soon tripped and fell. The shoe flew far ahead of her. She felt some rope around her feet, meaning that she had not fallen from sheer incompetence.

"Get up and come with me," the man told her.

Karina obeyed, but with a lot of difficulty because her feet were tied, and jumping with feet together in an uneven slope was not the easiest thing to do. The man pushed her forward, back to where, from the grunts and yells, the fight was still going on. The woman now had a little knife in her hand, but Cayla kicked it then picked it up. The other girl mainly circled Cayla, and backed up, afraid.

Strangely, the man clapped. It didn't sound mocking or sarcastic, but a regular clap. "Great effort girl, now that's enough."

Cayla either didn't hear or pretended not to, as she kept advancing towards the woman.

"Enough, girl!" the man repeated.

The princess still ignored him. The man ran towards Cayla, and as the girl and the woman distracted her, he pushed the princess. As she fell to the ground, the woman quickly sat on her and immobilized her, the same way she had done to Karina. The man tied the princess's hand and feet. Being ignored, Karina accomplished a couple jumps, distancing herself from them, but she soon realized she would go nowhere tied like that. She sat and tried to untie herself, but found it difficult because she had strips of a jagged cloth tangled and adhered to each other everywhere, not a rope with a simple knot or opening. She fumbled through the strips, then heard people near her. Cayla was sweaty and red, and had hands and feet tied. The man and woman tied Karina's hands and tied both girls to a tree. The girl went somewhere else. Cayla whispered to Karina, "Did you see the advantage of two against one? Thank you for your help."

In a way, Karina understood that she hadn't helped, but, on the other hand, it had not been her fault. "I don't know how to fight."

"Seriously? All I needed was a little help."

"I tried. It was fast, confusing, and that thing that got my feet."

"Your feet got caught? I jumped. See? You have to think."

Karina didn't like the accusation, and plus, she was not even sure fighting or resisting would have helped. "They have people all around the hill. How far would we have gone?"

"Farther than we did, that's for sure."

9

FINGERS

The woman approached them and looked attentively at Karina. "What's your name, girl?"

"Don't answer anything," Cayla whispered.

The woman didn't insist on an answer and instead turned to the man. "That's not Ayanna."

"How do you know?" he asked.

"She's too old to be the younger princess."

Cayla then said, "You know I'm not a princess either, right? Why would I be here without guards? This is a trap, and you should let me go and save yourselves while you still have time."

"You fight too well, girl," the woman replied. "Lots of free time. You're the real thing."

Cayla squinted and stared at the woman, then, after a while, said, "Maybe I was sent here because I can fight, so that I can take all of you at the right moment."

The woman laughed. "Well, for one, if you were an impostor, you wouldn't say so. And two, if you were here to fight, why would you have a partner who can't defeat a flower?"

Ouch, that hurt Karina's feelings.

Cayla laughed. "Sure, trust that. You'll see. You're all alone and soon you'll be caught."

The woman looked at Cayla. "Is that supposed to be funny or scary?"

"Funny," Cayla replied. "For me. I'm going to be laughing soon."

The woman nodded. "Oh, I see." She turned to the man. "Lionel, I don't think she's the princess. I think she's the fool."

They both laughed. Cayla spit on the woman's face. Karina was impressed with the precision, speed, and distance, wondering if spit contest was a royal sport in those parts.

The man became serious but the woman only cleaned her face with the back of her hand and kept laughing. "Great aim. You really have some misused talent, girl." Then she became serious. "Little advice: don't do this to Rose."

"I don't need advice," Cayla replied.

The woman turned to Lionel. "See? Any doubt who's the princess here?"

"Nope."

Cayla yelled, "I might not be a fool but I can fool you."

The woman raised her eyebrow. "Of course. You're an expert impostor and I'm sure a swarm of lifts is coming to catch us."

"I'm glad you're aware." Cayla smiled.

The man and woman stepped away and talked quietly to each other. Even with effort, Karina couldn't hear what was being said. Cayla wiggled and struggled trying to untie herself. Karina didn't see the point in it but she moved a little, pretending she was also trying to free herself, just so that her friend didn't get mad. Karina was anxious to get this situation solved soon, wondering if they would be taken to Lylah's castle and if throwing only one shoe would do the trick, even though she had no idea what the trick was. Or maybe everything was going wrong, but then she remembered Odell telling them that they would be rescued, that everything would be all right. Those thoughts put her at ease, she only wished Cayla would also remember what she was told. But perhaps Karina had to remind her.

She whispered as close as Cayla's ear as she could, "Remember what he told us? Before we came?"

Cayla looked as if she had not understood, until she finally seemed to remember. "No, no. This is different..."

The woman approached them. "Different from what?"

That was Karina's question as well.

Cayla replied, "From the way *you* are going to be captured."

The woman sighed. "I know. Unfortunately, not everyone is as nice as we are."

Cayla looked away. At least she didn't try to come up with a smart reply, because it would have been awkward at that moment. Karina heard steps approaching the clearing, and soon three people joined the man and woman who had been watching them, but two of them soon went away. The person who remained was a young woman with short hair, and, unlike the others, wearing a dress. Karina made an effort to hear their conversation even though they were not very close.

The short-haired woman who had just come said, "Sonja, Lionel, good job. Did you confirm their identity?"

The woman, Sonja, replied, "The oldest girl is princess Cayla. I have no idea who the other one is."

"We haven't questioned them," Lionel added. "We identified the princess because of her behavior. I suppose one princess is enough."

The short-haired woman approached the girls. Karina noticed she had thick black lines painted on her cheeks, like some war painting, or perhaps meaning that she was their leader. Strangely, the paint looked good on her, in a menacing way, but still good.

The woman crouched, pulled a short knife then addressed Cayla and Karina. "I'm going to do this once. Who are you and what are you doing here?"

Karina trembled with a dreadful sense of danger, noticing that the woman's eyes were pure hatred. And to think Karina had been afraid of Nia. The woman held the knife as if she meant to use it, and if this had been a game, it would have stopped being any fun. But since Karina could not quit, she started blurting the truth. "My name's Karina, I'm not from here—"

"We're not saying anything! We're not saying anything!" Cayla continued to shout until Karina stopped trying to tell where she was from and what she was doing.

"Just take us to Lylah," Karina pleaded.

At this point, all Karina wanted was to find the woman, witch or not, give her the freaking shoes, and go home.

The woman laughed. "Sure, Lylah, our savior, the one we wait and wait and wait. Or else, Lylah, the enemy, the faceless threat hanging upon us." She faced Karina. "I'm not taking you to where Lylah is, and do you know why? One, it would be bloody. Two, I don't want to lose a hostage. Lylah is dead, girl, dead."

Karina swallowed. Somehow, the news distressed her a lot, especially now that she was starting to consider the so-called evil witch a very nice woman. It also made their journey useless. Why were they out facing dangers to defeat a dead woman? Also, if Lylah was dead, who were those people, and why were they after them?

A teenage boy came panting and spoke to the shorthaired woman, "Nothing. They're alone."

He turned around, as if to walk away again, when something caught his eye. He knelt in front of Cayla, pointing to her necklace. "What is that?"

Cayla looked elsewhere and remained silent.

The boy got up and addressed the woman with the face paint. "Rose, that's Darian's twin, I'm pretty sure. I told your sister his necklace must have had a twin, she never believed me." He glanced at Cayla. "They must be... you know. Does he know she's here?"

Rose rolled her eyes. "Of course he knows. How do you think we found her? Now, I need a big favor from you, very important. I need you to check the Black River bank, see if anyone's coming from that side."

"You want me to go alone?"

"I'm sure you can handle it. Go."

The boy nodded and departed. Rose, Lionel and Sonja exchanged glances. Rose crouched in front of Cayla and looked at her necklace, then got up and whispered to the others, but this time Karina could still hear them. "He's right, it is a twin necklace, and it's just like Darian's."

Sonja turned to Lionel. "I told you he was too well connected."

Lionel was serious. "Speaking of which, does Darian know about this?"

Rose stared at him. "You too? Take your guess."

The man looked down.

Sonja put her hand on his shoulder. "Sometimes we got to do what we got to do."

Rose glanced again at Cayla then turned to the others. "We'll figure Darian later. I just want to deal with the girl." She crouched in front of Cayla, and touched her necklace. "So you are the mysterious girl."

The woman grabbed the orange stone on her hand and pulled the necklace, but it didn't come out.

"Don't," Cayla pleaded.

Rose kept trying until she succeeded in pulling the necklace. She threw it on the floor and stepped on it, making a crashing sound. Tears ran down Cayla's eyes. The princess then spat on Rose's face. The woman wiped it, and some of the paint on her cheek came out, revealing a thick red scar.

She knelt in front of Cayla and put her knife on the girl's face. "Do you want one like this?" she asked, touching her own scar.

Cayla remained silent, staring at her.

"Do you?" the woman repeated, and her knife was pierced the girl's face, revealing a little blood. Sonja and Lionel stepped closer, watching Rose.

"No," Cayla answered, the voice just loud enough to be barely heard from such a close distance.

The woman pulled back her knife, but not before cutting Cayla's face some more, but just a superficial cut, with a little blood, hopefully nothing that would scar the girl forever.

Rose turned to her companions. "I say we cut a hand from each and send to the king. That way he knows we have the girls and mean to harm them. If he doesn't back of his army in one day, we send him the other hands."

This time Karina really got scared. All she wanted was to disappear, teleport, or for an earthquake or some other natural disaster to save her. This adventure had definitely stopped being fun. Lionel and Sonja stared at Rose as if in shock.

"I thought we would only keep them as hostages," the man said.

Rose shook her head. "Then we won't pressure the king. We can't fight brutality with mercy."

Sonja and Lionel still stared at her, both wide-eyed.

"Oh, please!" Rose added. "We can make this fast and painless. I'm not evil, I know they're just girls." She turned to Lionel. "If you were in the army you'd have to obey."

He shook his head. "I deserted. I can desert again."

Rose shrugged. "Nobody's tying you."

"Wait," Sonja intervened. "You can't do that without consulting the rest of the group. I for one agree with Lionel. I'm here to fight violence, not support it."

Rose sighed. "What about cutting the girls' nails? Would we need to consult the rest then?"

Lionel scratched his head. "I'm not sure the king would be able to identify the nails. I mean, perhaps, but..."

"I was joking," Rose said. "Now, really, I know what we stand for, but I also know what we're up against, and who we're up against. We have a unique opportunity. We can't show weakness."

"Fingers then," Sonja said. "Starting with the little ones."

Lionel stared at her.

Sonja raised her shoulders. "I don't like it either, but Rose does have a point."

"Little fingers then it is," Rose said. She turned to Lionel. "Do you still want to desert?"

He looked away. "Not yet."

Sonja took a deep breath. "I'll prepare the equipment."

Now where was the promised rescue mission if it all went wrong? Karina felt betrayed. Her mouth was dry, and she felt a knot closing down her throat. She looked sideways, and her eyes met Cayla's. The girl had been strangely quiet, and her eyes showed fear as well.

Karina then remembered Zoe. Zoe, falling from the stairs. Now, why was that image coming into her mind then? Of course! The shoes. If the shoes could break a handrail, they could certainly cut some rope, even weird, sticky, tangled rope. But had it really been the shoes? Still, even if it had been, Karina didn't have both shoes now. But the shoes were not with her when Zoe had fallen either. She closed her eyes, trying to concentrate, trying to think, trying to make something happen, even though she had no idea what. She opened her eyes and saw another young woman coming to their direction. She had something in her hand, and walked towards Rose, who was standing far from the girls.

"What is this?" the young woman asked. She had the missing shoe in her hand. "Is this some kind of magical—"

The girl didn't finish. She tripped on something on the floor, and the shoe flew away from her. Karina got up and grabbed it, without noticing she had ripped the ropes that tied her as if they had been made of paper. Rose and Lionel saw Karina and ran towards her. Rose had the knife on her hand and the menacing look of someone who decided not to mind losing a hostage. Karina froze for a split second, before realizing she'd better run. After that, she could not understand what happened and in which order. There was black smoke around her, but no smell of anything burned. The floor trembled. Rose fell. Karina found herself beside Cayla, but away from the tree, not sure how they had gotten there with all that smoke and earthquake. Was it an earthquake? She held Cayla's hand, also not knowing how the girl got untied. More black smoke, nothingness, a feeling of falling, then a thud on hard floor. Somehow, the strongest image in Karina's mind was Rose falling. Who said she couldn't defeat a flower?

Karina coughed. She had difficulty breathing, and no idea where she was. People approached her and she feared that she would be captured again, until she realized she was in the place where she had arrived at the castle: the circular tall blue room. She had teleported, or been teleported. She was safe. Tears of joy and relief came out of her eyes. This time she would just find Nia and go back home. She didn't want to go on any more journeys, and she couldn't care less who took the shoes and controlled the world.

Some four or five people encircled her. Because of her tears, she had trouble recognizing them. Why were they surrounding her? They seemed to carry something in their hands, pointing at Karina, but that could not be. She wiped her tears and took a better look. Indeed, they seemed to be some kind of guards and had something pointy, like spears. Perhaps it was just precaution until they checked her identity. Now, where was Cayla? The men had menacing looks. Why were they doing that?

"Take her. Before she escapes," a man said.

Two men grabbed Karina by the arms while someone put a hood on her. She was gagged before her scream came out.

10

THE MEANING OF YELLOW

Darian stared at the panel and the position of the lifts in the surrounding areas. There was no army and no rebels around the meeting of the rivers. And yet he felt uneasy. He touched his necklace. Should he contact Cayla? Or *suffocate her*. Right. Let her breathe. But at what price? No price. There was nobody in the area, no danger, and nobody knew she was there. He'd repeated these words some twenty times by now. And yet... he was the one suffocating with worry. Worry. For a girl who wouldn't even take his hand. Over one year waiting, and she treated him like an acquaintance. Maybe the fault had been his. Perhaps he'd been mistaken about whatever they had. It was not her fault. The alternative would be to be angry. Next thing he'd be smirking and saying stupid things like "love is poison" and become like his brother. His brother. Wonderful reverse role model. He was probably in Siphoria, partying and enjoying his sense of importance, oblivious to what was going on in the kingdom.

Zayra walked in. "We should be going, shouldn't we?"

He wasn't in a mood to talk. "No."

She looked down. "I mean... there're lots of things we need to do. You especially. You can't remain here all day."

"Can't I?"

"You can. Sure. When we're so close, you're going to ignore everything we fought for so long. You're going to forget all the people who need us, who support us, who support you, and stay here moping for a girl who's not worth it."

He leaned back. "Opinion taken."

Zayra slammed her hand on one of the seats. "That's it? You don't have anything to say for yourself?"

"I outrank you, Zayra. I don't need to explain anything." He hated the stupid army ranking system, but it could be convenient sometimes.

"Fine. Why don't you go and run after her? Maybe if you beg she'll look at you. Meanwhile, ignore everyone who loves you and cares about the cause you were supposed to fight for. Ignore everything."

She slammed the door and left him alone. Her accusations were pointless and her anger was puzzling, but he didn't want to bother trying to understand his pilot. He didn't feel guilty. A few hours wouldn't make a difference for anyone. And he felt responsible for Cayla. His necklace still shone. He'd always thought that the light was proof that she loved him. He'd likely misunderstood the type of love.

A light blinked in his personal communicator. Odd channel. He picked it up.

"Is this Darian?"

"Yes."

"This is Zee, I'm in Rose's group."

The name was familiar, but not much. Some new recruit, not from the army. He kept his eyes on the panel, hoping whatever Zee had to say was short.

Zee continued. "I didn't mean to disturb you, I just wanted to make sure that you ordered the princess to be captured."

He felt as if the seat below him had disappeared. "What?"

~

KARINA WOKE on a strange bed with a splitting headache. Daylight, or whatever, came from a ceiling far above her. The room was circular, with yellow walls made of some kind of stone, but without any division between the blocks. Besides the bed, the room had two chairs, a small table, and a curtain. She got up and saw what the curtain had been hiding; a hole in the ground, a sink, and a small tub. Karina looked at the walls around her and saw no door. She felt something on her waist and noticed she still had one shoe tied around her. The other one was on the ground, near her bed, as if it were one of her slippers. The room looked a lot like the blue room from where she had come, but without doors.

Was she a prisoner? Indeed, the last time she recalled being conscious someone seemed to have captured her. But still, she had the clear impression she had arrived at the castle, the very place she had come to help. Could it be that she had gone to an identical castle? Perhaps Lylah's? Maybe. Could it be that the castle had been taken while she was away? Maybe. She realized with despair that she didn't understand anything about that place. Who were those crazy finger cutting people who had tied them? They were not with Lylah and not with the king, and that just mushed everything, because Karina had signed up to help on a battle of good against evil, and for that to work two parts were needed: good and evil.

She was feeling lonely and anxious, not knowing what was happening, and why she was being held on that place. She decided to yell to see if anyone would come. "Hello! Someone! Help! Helloooo! Helloooo!"

Even though the room was empty, with smooth walls and a high ceiling, there was no echo, which was odd. Karina sat at the table. Nice touch to give her a table, but it was missing the most important thing: food. Oh, how she wanted some real food. Actually, at that point, even fake food or weird bars would be welcome. She felt thirsty as well, and at least the sink was a real sink, with water, so she drank with her hands. Then she decided to yell some more: "Helooo! Food! I'm hungry! Hungry!"

Was there anyone near her room? She tried to touch the walls, seeing if she could find a door, a handle, something. Perhaps she was not a prisoner and was just being silly. But all she felt was a smooth, circular wall. She lay down again, trying to prevent herself from wondering whether she had been left there to die. Oops, too late.

She sat on the bed, then saw the shoe on the floor and picked it up, meaning to tie it around her waist with the other, but then decided to hold them both and look at them. She could hardly believe those were the same shoes she'd found at that yard sale. That past reality seemed so distant now. As for the shoes, they revealed to be so much more, and, at the same time, in comparison to the reality they brought her, almost ordinary. Unless... Karina tried to recall what had happened at the hill. She had meant to use the shoes to escape, and she did escape, but she wasn't sure if it had been the shoes, or if someone had captured or rescued them. Floor trembling and black smoke, all of that was quite weird for shoes to do, even magical ones. But what if they had done it? What if the shoes had saved Karina, regardless of the hostile reception where she arrived? There was one way to find out, and she almost laughed at her stupidity for not having tried them earlier. She felt like a prisoner in a cell who has a key and yet never tries it on the lock. Now, what could she try to do with the shoes? Blow up the walls? Reckless, and dangerous. Try to teleport, find Cayla? Now, wait, teleport: that was the magic word. If she had teleported away from the hill, perhaps she could teleport to the place she most wanted to be: her room, away from all those people and all this mess she didn't understand. And if any creature came looking for the shoes, this time, she would gladly give them away.

But... how was she supposed to teleport? Hold the shoes and close her eyes? Say a magic word? When they had come none of the girls had said anything, so she probably didn't need any magic word. But there had been a portal, whatever that was. Perhaps it would be easier just to forgo any logic, because magical shoes were not logical anyways, and give it a try. Karina put on the shoes, closed her eyes and imagined walking into her bedroom. Nothing happened, but she took a few steps, as if walking could make a difference. Or should she touch a wall? Before she tried anything different, she felt as if she were falling.

When the feeling subsided, she opened her eyes. She caught her breath. *Home.* She was in her room, and felt a little scared and even skeptical that it was really her room, shocked at how easy it had been. Even though it was dark, she could see well, as if her eyes had adjusted in the seconds they had been closed. The lump under the covers was there, and so were the books on the floor, which she had removed from her backpack. Her pajamas were also on the floor. Now that was really stupid if she wanted to fool anyone that she was sleeping. On the clock by the bed she saw 12:16. She had no idea at what time she had left, but it couldn't have been much more than three hours earlier than that. The time difference was indeed real. She could get in bed, and nobody would even notice she had been gone. Even better, she could go to the kitchen and make herself a sandwich and a hot chocolate.

But something didn't feel right, and perhaps it was just that "too good to be true" feeling. Or not? Was she guilty that she had left? No, it could not be, because she had been given no choice. Karina decided she needed to forget what had happened in the last hours of her life, just be glad that she was back home and appreciate it. She crouched to pick up her pajamas, but, again, something was not right. She could not see her knees or feet or shoes. She could not see her hands or arms either, or any part of her body for that matter. A few hours before, she would have loved being invisible, and finally accomplishing one of her childhood dreams. But no, this was something else. That explained why coming there had felt too easy, maybe too light. She had not really come; it was if she had been dreaming. She then felt something pulling her as if she had been tied to the tip of an elastic ribbon whose force was now pulling her back. She saw blackness around her and felt as if she was floating mid-air. What could have been awesome in different circumstances was terrifying at that moment.

"Close your eyes and let go. Let go," a man with a familiar voice said.

She closed her eyes, even though it made no difference, as everything was black, but she had no idea what she had to let go, because she was not holding anything. Unless it was her thought. The thought of home, her room, escape, safety. But how could she give up those things?

"Let go. Come back."

The voice, she recognized now, was Odell's. His voice meant she was about to be rescued, and that thought encouraged her to return to the reality of the yellow room with no doors. Karina opened her eyes and realized she was lying on the floor. She looked up and saw Odell standing beside her. Never before had she been so glad to see an acquaintance she had known for two days. But something was wrong. His face was grave and stern. Was he a prisoner as well? Karina sat and looked around. She saw an open window some two meters above the ground. In fact, that was not a window, but a door, and probably the reason Karina had only found smooth walls when looking for an opening near the floor. Cayla stood at the high door, and Karina felt relieved to know that she was alive and well. But then again, no. Something was wrong; she looked distressed. Was she a prisoner as well? Karina felt disappointed that they were not there to help her, but still a little relieved that at least she would have company in her adversity.

"What's going on?" Karina asked.

"It's useless," Odell answered, sounding cold and menacing.

"What?"

He seemed angry. "Trying to escape. Your shoes don't work here. The most you'll accomplish is to hang between two worlds, never settling anywhere. Never living, never dying."

She rubbed her eyes. Fine, perhaps trying to teleport home had been dangerous, but what was she supposed to do? "I was hungry, I... I yelled, nobody came, I, I was trying to go home."

He laughed, not a nice laugh, but, for some weird reason, a mocking laugh, then stared at her. "Home? Nice try. We know what you want."

Why was he being so weird? Could he have figured something even Karina could not? "Really? You need to tell me cause I'm curious. Unless you mean food."

Odell pointed to the table. "Come, you can eat now."

Karina saw that the table was no longer empty, and didn't hesitate to accept the invitation, ignoring his weirdness. She glanced at Cayla, who still stood at the door, looking distressed. Or was she hungry as well? She should come down if that was the case. Karina filled a plate with weird rice and vegetables. At least she was finally getting real food and for that she could forget and forgive the strange behavior around her.

After she took a couple bites, Odell said, "So, you were planning to keep the shoes all along."

Karina almost choked. She forgot her good manners and answered before swallowing, "I cou 'ave tay 'ome."

Not very intelligible. Odell only stared.

She swallowed quickly and tried again, "I could have stayed home. I didn't need to come here and I wouldn't have come if I wanted to keep the shoes. I had them." She noticed her feet with some surprise. "In fact, I still have them. I'm wearing them."

He nodded. "Exactly. You just proved that you knew how to use the shoes and meant to use them."

"What?"

Karina took off the shoes and kicked them away, then she took another bite of her food, because she was really hungry. She was starting to think that he didn't look or act like a prisoner, so she hoped he would come up with a long explanation that would clear up everything—and give her time to chew and swallow.

"You came here to seize the power," he said. "Or worse, to help Lylah seize the power."

Perhaps this was one of those awful nightmares in which everything goes wrong and nothing makes sense. But it couldn't be a nightmare because food still tasted like food. The problem was that she didn't even know how to start arguing against absurdity. "I... no. Uh... If I wanted to help Lylah I could have given her the shoes when she visited me."

He raised an eyebrow. "Except you couldn't."

"Uh, no, but..."

"And you admit you met her before coming. And that you thought she was nice."

Where was he going with that? "Well, yes. In truth, she was nice. Very different from you."

He nodded. "And that's why you betrayed us."

"No. I mean now, now you're being mean. You seemed nice before." She looked at the door—where Cayla was—and hoped to get some support. "Cayla, help me, tell him what happened. That we were close to the meeting of the rivers, then we went to the hill, then we were captured, and they wanted to cut off our hands, then our fingers."

Cayla remained silent.

"Help me," Karina pleaded to the princess. "I saved your life, or at least your fingers. C'mon, we were in this together."

Her plea caused no reaction from the girl at the door, who kept staring at some random point on the wall.

Odell looked at the princess then addressed Karina, "That means you did use the shoes to get here."

What was that now? "No. I mean, I don't know."

"How, then," Odell asked, "can you claim you saved her life?"

Karina shrugged. "I don't know what happened. Fine, maybe I used the shoes to save her life. But maybe not. Regardless, she should speak up for me." She turned to the girl. "Cayla!"

Again the girl answered only with her silence. Karina felt betrayed, and she didn't understand why she was being accused like a criminal.

Odell continued his interrogation, "You're saying you were close to the meeting of the rivers. How could you have gotten so far?"

Cayla's silence got to her nerves.

"Why don't you ask her?" Karina pointed to the princess standing at the high door. "Ask her why she had to get a ride from her boyfriend, ex-boyfriend, almost boyfriend, almost brother, whatever."

Cayla looked pale but still stoic, except for a slight movement in her head, as to say no.

"We can see through your lies," Odell said. "The only reason you need to slander the princess is because you're desperate."

If there was one thing Karina didn't like was being called a liar. She got really angry with those people who were turning against her, especially the girl she had considered her friend. "It's true. Every word."

Odell looked seriously at her. "Your lies won't help you. Or anyone for that matter."

"I'm telling the truth. Cayla even has his twin necklace, the one with the orange stone, and she talks to him using it."

Odell laughed. "What nonsense. She never had a twin necklace, and even if she had, twin necklaces can't do that. Do you know why magic doesn't work in this room?"

Karina shook her head.

"It's yellow," he said. "Yellow blocks magic. No magical artifact would be yellow—or even yellowish."

"I'm saying what I saw."

He shook his head. "You're making up lies."

As he said this, she noticed he had a ring with a yellow stone similar to the one in Cayla's necklace.

He noticed it caught her eye and waved it. "This, for example, is to protect a person from magic, which must be the case with her necklace. If she had one. Your lies won't help you."

Karina was about to ask what would help her, when she heard yells coming from behind the door where Cayla stood. Cayla turned towards the noise. Odell looked at the door and seemed worried.

"Just a moment," he told Karina before moving towards the door.

He sounded strangely normal when saying this, as if he had paused his evil-mode button. Karina heard some voices amidst the confusion.

"Go away, you're forbidden here," a man said.

"Odell's the one who should be imprisoned, he's a traitor!" a woman yelled. It sounded like Nia.

Meanwhile, Odell reached the door, pulled a ladder, climbed it quickly, then closed the door behind him, blocking all sound. Karina was again left alone in a yellow room with smooth walls, hearing nothing of what happened behind them. At least now she would be able to eat. She tried to think. Perhaps Nia was right: Odell was a traitor who had turned against Karina, but the problem was that he was not acting alone. Since Karina had no idea about what happened behind closed walls, she had to try to make assumptions based on what she saw. Odell, and whoever was backing him up, seemed to fear Karina would use the shoes and take the power. What nonsense. She would certainly not be able to handle a kingdom of crazy people. And she didn't even want it. But the weirdest thing was that if they were so afraid of the shoes, how come they left them with her? It made no sense. But then, if they were so afraid they didn't even want to look at the shoes, maybe they didn't want to touch them or something.

The idea that Odell was the traitor made sense, especially given how concerned he seemed when he heard Nia accusing him. But why was Cayla silent? Unless... what if someone was standing behind her? Actually, Karina had heard voices; someone had in fact been standing behind her. Perhaps she shouldn't have said anything about Darian. But then, he did seem involved with the finger cutting crazy people. Another weird thing was that Odell seemed to defend Cayla or perhaps Darian, even using chromo magic science to back up his arguments. Oh, Karina should stop trying to understand anything or she would go crazy. But maybe that was the explanation: everyone was crazy. Crazy, crazy. The worst part was that she would have to deal with them and try to find a way to save herself, but she had no idea who to trust anymore or even what to do. If only she had returned home when she had the opportunity. Or better, stayed home. She made a mental note never to accept invitations for other dimensions from strangers again. Hey, why hadn't anyone ever told her that? But it was too late now. And what was the point in learning with an experience that would never be repeated? Anyways, this is where Karina was, and from where she would need to find a solution and a way out.

SIAN RUSHED through the narrow passageways leading to the yellow tower, the highest security cell in the entire kingdom, built at a time when superstition and outdated beliefs overcame reason. Six guards stood by a translucent door. Behind it was the one loose piece that didn't fit anywhere. Of course, the prisoner was innocent and completely harmless. Sian would have been astonished if Odell had actually imprisoned a dangerous criminal. Now that he thought about it, he could hardly say that these times were any less guided by superstition and old beliefs. But that should change soon.

He took a closer look. The girl was sitting on a bed, muttering to herself and counting with her fingers, as if trying to figure a solution to a complex problem. He smiled. Maybe he had the answer to her problem, and she had the answer to his. Not that he would be able to discuss much of it with six guards watching them, but he could at least try to get an idea. The last he'd heard about her was that she'd been caught by his brother's criminal buddies. Then she was in the castle. The timing didn't make sense. But then, Cayla out alone with her didn't make sense either.

Sian turned to the guards. "Open the door. I'm coming in."

"I'm sorry, sir," one of the guards said, "So sorry." He looked down. "Nobody is allowed to enter."

Annoying. And surprising. Sian almost asked, "Not even me?" but they obviously knew who he was. The guard who told him he couldn't enter seemed uncomfortable having to say no. He looked at the six guards. All about seventeen or eighteen, which was young to be serving in the castle. Beginning of their careers. Eager to please. Changing their minds would be as easy as snapping his fingers. Assuring they didn't tell anyone about it would be a different thing, though. But he had to know who she was and where she fit. He heard steps behind him and turned. Odell. Sian hated the charlatan.

"What brings your illustrious visit here?" the bald man asked.

Sian snorted. "Isn't it obvious?"

Odell just raised his eyebrows.

Sian smiled. "There's a pretty girl down there."

The old man shook his head. "Aren't there enough for you in Siphoria?"

Sian shrugged. "Too many. It gets boring."

"Well, she's too young for you."

The freak either didn't know basic math or he'd forgotten Sian's age, but that was beside the point. "Too young to be executed then."

The old man grimaced, in what looked like disgust. "Nobody's getting executed."

Sian exhaled, relieved. That meant all he needed was time. He refrained from laughing as he realized he'd managed to get information from the bald man.

Odell continued, "But, again, with all due respect, I need to ask you to leave."

"The guards are here."

"Royal guards. They can remain in a Royal-only area. I do appreciate your visit and your concern, but your advice is not needed."

With Odell there and aware about Sian, talking to the girl would be impossible. Next time he wouldn't even be allowed in the corridors. But then, if she was there, perhaps whatever she knew or whatever she meant wouldn't affect the coming events. Maybe. He took one last look then turned to leave, but decided to have one last jab and turned back to Odell. "Tell her I said hi."

"She's never heard of you."

Sian frowned. "What an empty, meaningless life." He sighed and shook his head while laughing inside. The old freak had just given him another piece of information.

ALONE FOR A LONG TIME, Karina feared being forgotten, realizing that she preferred to have someone accusing and questioning her and not having time to eat than being alone without any clue about what was happening, even though the accusations didn't really shed any clue. When the high door finally opened, she was happy to see Odell. Cayla wasn't there this time. He looked so distraught Karina would have pitied him if he hadn't been acting so evil.

She decided she was tired and didn't want to argue or answer any more questions. "Listen, just take the shoes, I don't care. I just want to go home."

He raised an eyebrow. "You know it doesn't work like that."

Karina looked down, but then she remembered something. "Actually, it does. Lylah told me I could sell the shoes. I can sell them for a ticket home. How's that? Then you deal with them. I don't care."

"It doesn't work like that."

Karina waved her arms in despair. "How does it work then? What do you want?"

"First, I want you to talk about, uh, the person you said betrayed Cayla. Tell me what you know about him."

Karina felt guilty that he pressed on this point, not knowing whether Cayla was still on her side or not.

"I... I made that up."

He raised his eyebrows in surprise and seemed pleased. "I see. So now you are confessing you were lying."

Karina shrugged. "If that's helpful, yes."

"I want the truth here."

Karina sighed. "What happens if I tell the truth? Can I go? And if you don't believe me? And if I lie? Seriously, just tell me what you want."

"Just answer the questions. How did you get to the place where you claim you were captured?"

"The place I *claim* we were captured? Does it make a difference? I just want to go home. I can even take these shoes if you really don't want them. I'll hide them really well."

He shook his head. "We know that if we let you go, you'll help Lylah."

"Wasn't I going to take the power? And wasn't she dead?"

"Now you want to convince me she's dead?" Odell asked.

"Uh? No. The people there, the ones who wanted to cut our fingers, they said she was dead."

Odell laughed. "And you believe everything you hear?"

Karina scratched her head. "I really have to stop that, like when two girls came to my room and told me I needed to help them save the world and defeat an evil woman. Believing what people tell me, what nonsense."

For a second Odell had half a smile, not an evil smile, but the smile of someone really amused, then he became serious again. "Well, you're confessing then. You'll have to stay here for now. Don't try anything silly; it won't work."

He walked towards the door. She was glad he didn't insist on his questions because she would have to tell the truth, and that seemed to upset him even more. But there was something she wanted to know. "Wait!" Karina yelled. "How long are you going to keep me here?"

Odell turned around. "As long as it's necessary."

"And how long is that?"

He started going up the ladder.

She repeated the question: "How long is that? How long?"

Odell ignored her.

Karina yelled, "Hey, it's not fair, you told me I'd be taken home, you told me it was safe. I only came to help. Hey—"

The door was closed.

11

A PLEA FOR HELP

Karina sat and stared at the part of the wall where the door had been a few seconds before. Could she have gone up the ladder and tried to escape? Foolish. She picked up the shoes again. Could they blow up the walls? Even better, blow up the castle? She was so upset she thought she could do it out of spite, even though she had no idea how she would go about doing it or even if the shoes could blow up anything. She also remembered Odell saying the shoes didn't work there, but she had never heard anyone utter so much nonsense in so little time, so he could be lying—or mistaken. Or he could be telling the truth.

But perhaps blowing up walls was worth a try. She put the shoes on, closed her eyes, and tried to imagine an explosion. Was that how the shoes worked? Nothing happened. She tried again, but this time for a second she thought she was in that complete darkness, stuck in the middle of nowhere, so she stopped trying to do anything and took the shoes off. She was starting to understand why people were so afraid of them. And the idea of blowing up anything was silly anyways, why would she blow up a castle when she was inside it?

The problem with her reasoning was that she that she was relying on a lot of information given by Odell, the unwise one. Now, he did have a lot of advice on the shoes for someone who was so afraid of them. Did he have its manual hidden somewhere? Or did the information come from his league with Lylah? Why then he kept Karina locked claiming she was the one in league with Lylah? In fact, Lylah, that was the answer! Perhaps the so-called witch could help Karina go home. The trouble was how to find her. Was she sitting in her fortress or whatever, counting the days to buy back her shoes? What was she doing? Knitting? Raising an army? Planning an attack? No way to know. Still, having an object that an alleged powerful witch wanted should be worth something. Karina held the shoes, closed her eyes and tried to concentrate on Lylah, thinking about her as the nice woman who had visited her. Karina thought without saying out loud, "Lylah, Lylah, can you help me?" Nothing happened. The only thing Karina remembered was Lylah saying, "It doesn't work like that." No, wait, Odell was the one who'd said that.

Karina's new plan was to wait for someone to show up, then beg for freedom. The only problem was that nobody showed up for hours. Going to the bathroom was annoying, there was a little curtain, but she feared being seen from above, because she felt she was being watched. Nobody picked up her food tray with leftovers, which was disgusting. When she got hungry, she ate some fruit and bars that were also on the table. The light on the ceiling never changed. Still, she eventually went to bed and fell asleep, which was a comforting escape from her nightmarish reality.

KARINA WOKE UP HOURS LATER, not knowing if it was day or night. The food had been changed, and it was all non-perishable this time, perhaps meaning no one would come see her anytime soon.

This was so unfair. How would she beg then? Unless she was being watched. She could give it a try.

"Help! Let me out. I'll do anything. I don't want to use the shoes. I don't care about the shoes. I don't want any power, in fact, I don't want anything."

She kept shouting stuff like that until she got tired and her throat hurt. At least this time there was a jug of water and a glass, so she didn't need to drink with her hands. She spent the day alternating between trying to figure out what was happening, trying to tell herself that she should elaborate an escape plan, shouting pleas for help or forgiveness and even shouting threats, because hey, she still had the shoes. Nobody came and eventually she fell asleep.

Karina woke up with a hand on her mouth, and she felt terrified thinking perhaps she would be killed. The lights on the ceiling were dim. Karina looked around and saw long blond hair. Nia. Karina wanted to jump and hug her, so happy she felt, but the hand on her mouth kept her from moving.

"Try not to make any noise," the woman whispered.

Karina was even happier then, because that could only mean this was a rescue mission. How great it was to finally see a friendly face.

Nia looked around and asked, "Where are the shoes?"

Karina tried to mumble something with difficulty, then Nia lifted her hand and allowed Karina to speak.

"They're on me. On my waist. Do you want to see them?"

"No, no, it's fine. I can get you out of here, but I need you to promise me a favor."

Karina wondered if the woman wanted the shoes. "What favor?"

"I want you to get my son, then get us out of the castle."

Karina stared at the woman's belly, which was still large. "Son?"

"He was born two days ago."

"How am I supposed to get him?"

"Your shoes. You can use them to teleport."

This felt like a nicer version of Odell's accusations.

"They're not my shoes. Even if they were, I'm not sure I can—"

"They brought you and Cayla here."

"Really?"

Nia was serious. "Don't tell me you didn't know. I can't take you out of this tower if you can't get my son and me out of the castle. You know I tried to save you before without asking anything in return, but now I need your help. Do you want to come or not?"

Karina had promised herself she would follow whoever suggested taking her home, so she didn't want to refuse Nia's invitation, but she was still unsure about her ability to help anyone. Karina remembered Zoe, then she remembered Rose and the hill, and how she had done something with the shoes. She had even almost teleported home, although "almost" was a problem.

"I tried to use the shoes. To go home." Karina looked down, somewhat embarrassed. "And blow up the walls. They didn't work."

"It's this tower. It blocks magic. It'll be different outside. Now, time's running. If you want to come, then promise to help me, and come."

"I want to come. I'll help you. I promise."

Nia then gestured for Karina to follow her, and climbed a knotted rope leading to the high door, which was open. Now, the ladder would have been much nicer, but Karina didn't complain. The door was much higher than she had thought, but she put her best effort and climbed that rope, until she got close enough that Nia pulled her by the hands. At the hallway, two men were sitting, looking straight ahead. Karina gasped. For a second she feared they were dead, until she noticed they were breathing, so they were sleeping with their eyes open. Weird. The only reason she didn't ask Nia about them was that she had a stern face and gestured for silence. The woman closed the door from where they had come from, which was translucent from that side, meaning that Karina had indeed been watched.

Nia walked down the hallway and Karina followed. Further down, there were a few more men who seemed to be in that open-eyed sleeping state like the others, but Karina didn't get close to them. Instead of continuing, Nia touched one of the walls, as if looking for something. While she looked, part of the wall moved and a door opened by itself. Nia was startled and stepped back. Odell stepped out of the door and gasped in surprise. He noticed Karina, then looked at the men on both sides, as if grasping the situation. He gestured for silence. Nia took a knife and was about to stab him, but he pushed it away from her hand and took it.

"You're smarter than that," he said. "Follow me. I can help you."

Nia stepped back as much as she could. "I don't trust you. Never did."

Odell loosened the grip on Nia's arm and returned the knife to her. "Who do you trust then? The king? At least you know on whose side I'm not."

Sounds of steps were heard coming from the end of the corridor. Nia looked.

Odell continued, "You're out of options." He pleaded, "They'll arrest you. Please, come."

Nia sighed then followed him through the door, and so did Karina. Was that what she was supposed to do? The man closed the door, then walked fast through small corridors.

When they were in a long corridor, soldiers came from both sides and surrounded Odell, Nia and Karina. Leading them, a man with a silver overcoat. It was General Keen. He laughed. "Who would guess? The two traitors together."

"You should thank me I stopped them," Odell said.

Keen laughed. "Nice try Odell, but I meant you and the woman. You helped her escape."

"Preposterous!" Nia said. "I can escape by myself."

Nia shouldn't be so offended. At least the general still counted her as a person.

"Are you that much of an idiot?" Odell asked Keen.

While he spoke, Nia whispered in Karina's ear, "Hold your breath."

Karina did as she was told, but she didn't fill her lungs with air for fear of being noticed.

Odell continued, "How do you suppose I can imprison them if they don't believe I'm on their side? Now they'll escape and the king will know about this."

The general had an unpleasant smirk. "I have twelve soldiers with me. I don't think anyone will escape. But the king will know what you are doing."

Odell was calm. "Let's bring our accusations to the king, then. But if they escape, the fault is yours."

Karina started to feel out of breath.

Keen laughed. "Except they won't." He turned to the soldiers. "Seize them!"

Odell raised his arms as if surrendering. Karina did the same. She didn't know for how much longer she would be able to hold her breath, and even if it mattered. A soldier approached her and held her wrists. General Keen himself approached Odell while four soldiers walked towards Nia. Karina figured it was all over, and she almost caught some air, but she made one last effort, trusting Nia's words. She wondered whether her face was turning purple. Instead of tying her, the soldier let go of her arms. In front of her, Keen lost balance and fell. All the soldiers collapsed on the floor, and Odell and Nia ran. Karina followed, and after some seconds finally caught some air.

They ran through narrow corridors until they reached a door

that hadn't seemed to be there before. Karina wondered why she was following the man who had come up with weird accusations and kept her locked. She considered turning around and running, but she preferred not to distance herself from Nia. The secret door led to a small circular room, where he opened another secret door, leading to what looked like a cave, with rocks for walls. As the door to the cave was closed, darkness engulfed them, and Karina realized she had nowhere to escape, and how problematic that was. Odell lit what looked like a type of candle, which made things slightly better. The room, cave, cave room, whatever, had a table on a corner where Odell put the candle.

Odell turned to Nia. "Thank you for that. What did you do?"

"Thank you? I have no proof you weren't telling Keen the truth."

"Unfortunately, I can provide none. But you'll have to agree I had no choice."

"Choice? You should have fainted with them."

"I noticed you held your breath," Odell said. "Unlike General Keen. But you need to go quickly. If that was a gas bomb, as I suspect, they'll wake up in a few minutes and the castle will be on lockdown."

"I'm not leaving my son," Nia said.

"He's the best-protected person in the entire kingdom. But you have to go." Odell pleaded. "They'll be twice as careful next time. You don't suppose they had more than ten soldiers for Karina."

Nia laughed. "You're joking, right? Keen will be after you too."

"No. I'll be right there, fainted with him. And the King still trusts me. If anything, General Keen will be the one who'll have to explain your escape. If you don't leave now, I don't think I'll be able to get you out of the castle. Keen might have someone follow me. All the hallways will be watched. Either you go now or you stay and... I don't want to think about it."

"I know how to protect myself," Nia said.

"Yes. And you also know how to protect the girls. Nia, please, I know you've never trusted me, but you're an intelligent woman. You know I'm the enemy of your enemy."

Nia raised her eyebrows. "You mean to say I was always right about you?"

"Just trust that I am on your side. And the girls' side."

Nia frowned. "The girls? Why?"

"I... I've been taking care of them since they were little. Way before you, in fact."

"But you said it as if protecting them was a task assigned to you."

"It is a task..." Odell glanced at Karina then continued, "I assigned myself." He said this last part quickly, as if wanting to end the subject.

Nia still had narrowed eyebrows. "And how do you propose to help me?"

"This room leads to a way out. It's secret. I'm the only one who knows about it. Cayla and Ayanna are there already. They need to be taken away from the castle. Cayla is in trouble, she might still be safe for some time, but I can't predict how long. As for Ayanna, she's her sister, she's worried, and she's been asking questions. I can't vouch for her safety either."

Nia frowned and looked down, thinking. Karina felt a little guilty for the things she had said about Cayla, wondering if she had caused any trouble. Odell seemed to notice and turned to her. "It's not your fault. Although, why didn't you just do as I said? Why did you contact anyone outside the castle?"

Karina felt defensive. "It was Cayla, she—"

"I know," Odell interrupted. "Like I said, not your fault."

Because he no longer sounded evil, Karina had the courage to ask a question that had been bothering her. "You're not afraid I'll use the shoes?"

"Not in the way you think. But they're dangerous, and you can't control them, so don't try anything." He turned to Nia.

"Now, please, trust me. Your son will be safe. You'll be reunited."

Nia snorted. "Sure. Like Cayla's mother? Or Ayanna's?"

Odell closed his eyes as if in pain. "That's why I have to save you."

"I don't want to be saved. Now, are you going to let me pass, or do I have to get rid of you?"

This time Nia sounded scary. Even Odell looked intimidated. Or was it something else? She wondered what she would do to him, perhaps immobilize him like the guards in that corridor?

Odell took a deep breath then said, "You'll just leave the girls?"

"Why don't you go with them?"

Odell shook his head. "I can't."

Nia scowled. "Is this some kind of trap?"

"You don't know me. Or you'd never ask that question. There are other ways to protect them."

Nia's eyes were misty. "I can't try to save my son, because I have to help the King's daughters and their friend? It's not a fair choice, you know?"

"Choice is a privilege we can't always afford."

"And what do you want me to do?"

"Ayanna will tell you. You'd better leave now."

She looked down for a moment, thinking, then turned to him.

"If anything happens to Leo, I swear, I'll make sure you remain alive. You'll regret having been born."

He nodded. "I will, for sure. And if anything happens to any of the girls, I'll understand it's not your fault and you did your best."

Nia grimaced, as if annoyed.

Odell opened a trapdoor on the junction of the floor and the wall. It had a ladder leading to an underground tunnel. He turned to Karina and Nia. "You need to go down here. The girls know what to do. They are waiting for you."

A voice came from the tunnel. "We're here!" It was Ayanna.

Karina trusted the girl and felt relieved that it wasn't a trap-door leading to her doom. Okay, maybe it would lead her to her doom, but at least she'd have company. Odell looked worried and urged her to go quickly. She went down the ladder, realizing she had no equipment or supplies, and that they would be three girls and a young woman with an army after them. Still, she felt relieved when she got down and saw Cayla and Ayanna.

Nia followed, her face somber, as the trapdoor was closed above them. She stared at Karina. "You. Take me to my son."

Cayla stared at them in alarm. While Karina was thinking what to say, the woman pulled a knife and put it against her throat. "Teleport. Now."

Cayla stared at her. "What are you doing?"

The cold blade still touched Karina's throat. Nia said, "An emotional spike. She needs an emotional spike to teleport."

That made some sense, and then Karina wondered how come she had the nerve to be interested in teleporting logic.

Cayla pleaded, "You can't expect her to... she doesn't know any magic!"

"The shoes!" Nia was breathing fast. "She promised. The shoes will bind her to her word."

Cayla moved fast towards them. Karina closed her eyes, fearing something would happen to her, but as she opened them Cayla kicked the knife far.

"The shoes are dangerous!" Cayla said. "What if they tele-ported you, her, or even your son somewhere else? What if the shoes killed you all?"

Nia sighed.

Cayla stepped closer to her. "He's my brother. I also care about him."

Nia looked away, gave Karina one last scary stare, then asked the sisters, "What are you planning?"

Ayanna replied, "We need to get to a tunnel that will take us to the Apex. From there we'll get to the Black River and go to Lylah's place."

Nia shook her head as if in disbelief. "Lylah? What madness is this?"

"All this problem is because our father thinks we want to take his power," Cayla explained. "But once we destroy the shoes, he'll understand we are on his side. Everything will be brought back to normal."

Karina was astonished at the idea that they should escape only to do the bidding of the people who had imprisoned them.

Nia rolled her eyes. "Is that Odell's plan? He's trying to fool you all. And things will never go back to normal."

"Can we please discuss later?" Ayanna pleaded. "We need to hurry before they find this tunnel."

The girl started walking towards the darkness. She had a blue crystal in her hand, and, as she lifted it, it illuminated a long straight tunnel, going downwards.

Cayla looked at it. "I'd never heard about this tunnel before. How come you know it?"

"Odell taught me last night," the younger girl replied.

"Why you?" Cayla asked.

Ayanna shrugged. "He said they were watching you."

"Still... He should have told us about it before..."

"Them," Ayanna said. "There are many tunnels. He said they were secret. We have to take the third door on the right."

"There are no doors," Cayla said.

Karina agreed that she didn't see any doors, but maybe they were further down.

"We're gonna have to find them," Ayanna said as she touched the rough wall.

"I can see them," Nia said.

Karina only saw rough, rocky walls, and she made a mental note to go to an optometrist when she got home, hoping of course that she would eventually get home.

Ayanna was surprised. "You do? That's so great, because I'm still not very good at finding those doors."

Nia walked a few steps, then showed a part of the wall. "This is the third door."

"Now I can also see it," Cayla said.

"Do you want to open it?" Nia asked.

Cayla shook her head. "Odell said you would be our guide."

"I don't want to hear about him," the woman said as she touched the wall. She then pressed a spot that didn't look different from any other spot, and part of the wall moved forward. The door was not square, but roundish and irregular, accompanying the shape of the rocks, which explained a little why it was so hard to be seen.

The girls and the woman entered. Ayanna lifted her crystal. She turned to Nia, "Are you sure this is the third door?"

"If you want, we can go back and I'll show you."

Ayanna looked at the tunnel. "I believe you, but I thought it should go up."

"Didn't you learn about these tunnels?" Cayla asked.

"Yes," the girl replied, "and this one should lead us to the top of the highest mountain."

Karina looked at the straight tunnel and came to her conclusion. "But if the tunnel is secret, it has to have some distance from the castle before going up."

Ayanna nodded. "Yes, that makes sense."

"Hopefully," Cayla said.

"Yes, let's go," the younger girl said. She started walking, then stopped. "No. Wait. Can you help me carry these things?"

She dropped a large bag on the floor, then took out two bags from inside it and put some things in them. She gave one to Cayla and the other to Karina, who was relieved that someone had thought about bringing supplies. But a question bugged her, "Why only two bags?"

"I picked them up in a hurry," Ayanna replied, then started walking.

Cayla walked fast, passed her sister then took the lead. Karina took a deep breath, then followed. She was finally on the way to her freedom, something she'd been dreaming and wishing for the past two days. She should be jumping up and down with happiness, but the tunnel felt oppressive and gloomy, and she wasn't sure where this path would take her and when she'd be able to go home.

The group kept walking, and, as they moved, the tunnel became slightly sloped. So it was going up. A little at least. Cayla asked her sister a few questions about the tunnels, and Ayanna again confirmed that they would go to the top of a mountain. Now that Karina thought about it, it didn't make any sense. "If it's a tunnel, why not go straight to the other side?"

Ayanna shrugged. "I don't know."

Karina left it at that, now used to questions without answers. The group kept walking.

After a few minutes, Nia addressed Karina in a soft voice. "You're assuming whoever built this wanted to cross the mountains. Perhaps that was not the case."

Karina nodded, then felt bad that she agreed with Nia, and bad again for having failed to rescue her son, even though she wasn't sure if she would have been able to. "I'm sorry."

Nia didn't reply. She only looked at Karina as if taking in the information. The woman walked slowly, increasing her distance from the girls in front of them. Somehow, instead of taking the opportunity to distance herself from her, Karina matched her pace, perhaps curious to hear if she had anything more to say.

Nia gestured for silence and replied in a whisper. "I know. This must be hard for you. I should have understood you were afraid. But I'm afraid as well."

The idea surprised Karina, because she thought Nia was powerful and confident. Ayanna turned around to look at them, and Nia addressed the whole group. "Don't you think we should stop and sleep?"

Cayla frowned. "We're still close to the castle."

"We'll never be far enough," Nia replied. "We have to hope they won't find this tunnel. If they do, they'll catch us regardless of our distance. Either this is secret and we're safe, or it doesn't matter."

Was that Nia's lullaby? With such thoughts, Karina would sure sleep like an angel. And the worst is that Karina agreed with Nia's logic.

"Well, it's true that I'm tired," Ayanna said.

"We stop then," Nia said.

Cayla looked displeased. A good thing that Ayanna had come prepared, because she took some blankets from her bag for them to sleep on. The downside was that the floor was rough, so sleeping there would still be uncomfortable even with the blankets, but on the upside, that was better than the comfortable bed in Karina's prison. Ayanna grimaced when she realized there were only three blankets.

"I know. Two of us will have to share. I can share."

"I can share as well," Nia said.

Karina was relieved. It wasn't that she didn't want to share a blanket, even though she didn't want to share it, but she didn't want to sleep by Nia. She then wondered why only three blankets, and if one of them had not been originally supposed to be there. Nia? Herself? But this time she didn't ask.

The group sat, and they all ate some dried fruit bar things and drank very little from the only water skin they had. Cayla touched what looked like her necklace, no longer hidden under her dress. The stone was red, however, unless it was the light, or lack of light, in the tunnel. Now, was that really her twin necklace? How did she even get it back, and in one piece? Karina didn't ask anything, because when Cayla realized Karina was looking, she seemed embarrassed then quickly hid the crystal under her dress. Karina looked elsewhere, pretending she hadn't noticed it even though it was obvious she had.

Later, Karina lay down because that was what everyone else did, but she was afraid of what could happen if she slept. The bluish light from the light crystal illuminated the side of the tunnel: brown rock, slightly shiny from dampness.

SIAN WALKED through the hallways of the castle. More soldiers than usual had been deployed there, and he had on good sources that some people had escaped. All the hush hush and mystery just confirmed that the girl from the yellow tower had escaped. He couldn't fathom how anyone could escape such a high security cell, but there was certainly more to the story. He wasn't upset, though. If she was free, it meant he had a chance to learn what was happening, and adjust his course of action. And better than anything, he didn't even have to chase information. His own father had called him there.

General Keen was sitting on his usual armchair, hands steepled.

Sian walked in and kneeled. "My father."

"Get up and stop this nonsense. You're my son, not some worthless nobody. You should never kneel. Sit down."

Annoying his father was always satisfying. Sian got up and grabbed an armchair.

The General asked, "Do you know who escaped?"

"Odell's high-security prisoner."

A corner of his father's mouth lifted. "Well informed, as always. And do you know who was with her?"

Sian didn't know, and it annoyed him. His thoughts turned to Nia and Cayla, but that didn't make much sense. "I assume that information has been kept secret."

"It has, it has. The thing is: I don't think she was Odell's prisoner. Not in reality. He refused to have her executed, and I know that he helped her escape. Not only her, but our King's traitorous ex-wife, as well as his annoying daughters. I told the King, I told him that they were plotting against him, but I can't break Odell's hold on him. He wants the girls back alive."

Sian was surprised at how much, for once, he didn't know. He raised an eyebrow. "And what are they plotting?"

"Magic, Sian, magic. They'll take over the kingdom again. Those girls wield magic, and they are dangerous."

Sian refrained from scoffing, but it took some effort despite the years of experience in keeping a straight face when his father started his nonsensical rants against magic. "I assume you brought me here to deal with this matter, then?"

General Keen had a satisfied smile. "Yes, my son. I have a task for you. I'll trust nobody else. The girls and that woman must be killed."

Whatever opinion Sian had about it, he buried them. "And you want me to order this?"

"Yes, yes, my son. But nobody can know about it."

"Where are the girls?"

"They escaped. We're combing the castle and the surroundings, and nothing."

"They must be far away then. Let me just confirm: you want me to have Nia, Cayla, and the other girl killed."

"There's also the younger sister, Ayanna."

Sian nodded. But there was something Sian had to say. "As you know, my brother, Darian, fancies the older sister. It could be a good chance for our family—"

"He'll thank us for it, my son, he'll thank us. Less suffering. Think about your brother when you spill her blood. Spare his pain of a broken heart. And he doesn't need to know who did it."

Sian nodded in acknowledgement. "I will deal with this—as soon as I find them. I just have one request, my father."

Keen had mocking laugh. "A request?"

Sian didn't lose his beat. "Let me deal with this. Personally. Anyone else involved, and the chances of the information being leaked will increase."

"I trust no one else."

Sian bowed and left. Child murderer. So this was his father's opinion of him. He wondered what he'd done to rise so much in General Keen's esteem.

12

NIGHT REVELATIONS

A hand touched Karina's shoulder. She opened her eyes, surprised that she should be awoken when she shouldn't have fallen asleep in the first place. It was Nia, who covered Karina's mouth even though the girl had not meant to scream. Should she?

"Don't worry," Nia whispered. "I just want to talk." She looked at the two other blankets on the floor where Ayanna and Cayla slept. "Away from the girls."

The woman took her hand from Karina's mouth. Karina was more curious than afraid, so she got up, careful not to make any sound, and followed the woman some steps away from the blankets.

Nia sighed. "What do you think of all this?"

That was a huge question, and Karina was not sure where to start. "You mean, me being here, and—"

"I mean why do you think he wants us to go to Lylah?"

"To destroy the shoes?"

"Do you believe the story the girls told us?"

Karina was not sure where the woman wanted to take this conversation. "You think they are lying?"

"Not them. Odell. I think he wants to help Lylah, not defeat her."

The idea made sense, and yet it didn't. "Why would he want the shoes destroyed then?"

Nia rolled her eyes. "That's what he says. Now, think with me. Those tunnels are attached to the castle. Why does Odell know them and the king doesn't?"

Karina remembered what Cayla had said. "He's all wise and learned, isn't he?"

"I disagree, but it doesn't matter. You don't need learning or wisdom to know secret passages, or else Ayanna couldn't have led us here. You need only to know people who know the passages. Do you know who lived here before the king?"

Karina shrugged, surprised that anyone would expect her to know any history let alone history about an alternate world.

"Lylah," Nia answered.

"The Queen," Karina muttered. "What happened then?"

"Well, she was the queen, before the king. But then, they said she turned evil and was defeated. That's the story they tell. But what matters for us is that Odell might know these tunnels because he knows the previous owner of the castle."

"You think he's evil?" Karina asked.

"I'm not even sure Lylah is evil. You saw her. What do you think?"

Karina tried to remember the dark-haired woman who had visited her in her now distant room. "She seemed nice. But I don't know. Cayla says she killed her mother or was involved in it. And everyone seemed nice in the beginning."

"I know," the woman had a sad smile. "But regardless, I think Odell wants us to take the shoes to Lylah. Well, that's I thought before, but now I am more certain."

"So you think we shouldn't go there?" Karina asked.

"What? No. Let her have her shoes. But... I need to protect the girls. And my son. I think... I think they're being sent as hostages."

Karina remembered being tied by people who wanted to cut her fingers, and imagined how Lylah could do something similar. "We should tell them."

"No. We all have to go. You know who's after us, and Lylah might be the only person who can defeat him. We'll have to side with her, but make sure she doesn't harm the girls. And Odell or the king don't harm my son."

That was a bold change for Nia. Karina took in the information, thinking. She then said, "And you're not going to tell Ayanna or Cayla about this?"

Nia shook her head. "They're stubborn. Especially Cayla. She wouldn't believe it. Or worse, she could want to protect her father and do something stupid. It's best to let them think they will erase all evil from the world by destroying a pair of shoes."

Karina almost laughed at the stupidity of that idea, until she remembered she had kind of believed in it not long before. She cringed. But something didn't make sense. "But how can the girls be hostages if Odell said they were in danger? That the king was after then?"

"You have your answer in your question."

Karina didn't understand. "What?"

"Who said it?" Nia asked.

Odell. Of course. "Oh."

"But," Nia added, "there's another possibility. Maybe the king does know about these tunnels, maybe Odell is not betraying him, and they are waiting to ambush us and prove that we are traitors."

"Why send the girls then?"

"Maybe the King is after them."

"But," how weird that this thought only now occurred to Karina. "They are his own daughters."

Nia shrugged and shook her head. "I don't doubt anything anymore."

Karina still didn't understand. "But why? And why are *you* running away?"

"A somewhat similar reason you were put in that tower. He thinks I'm plotting against him, that I want to take his power. I was being watched, and things got worse after Leo was born."

Karina nodded, partly understanding, but she still had a question. "And where does Odell fit in all this?"

Nia shrugged. "Maybe he's protecting us. Maybe he's pretending."

Karina didn't like that second option. "What then?"

"If we get ambushed, we'll have to fight."

She liked that even less.

Nia then said, "Go, sleep, you'll need your rest. Don't mention this to the girls."

"I won't."

Karina started to walk back to her place and figured that at least she learned that Nia didn't plan to slit her throat. Karina lay down feeling calmer than before, because she had one less person to fear. That floor was really uncomfortable, and yet, she dozed off.

"KARINA, KARINA," someone called her. This time it was Ayanna.

Karina mumbled, "You too? Does it have to be now?"

"It's time to move," Ayanna said.

Karina covered her head. Getting up and continuing the walk was even worse than a secret conversation. And plus, it was still dark. "Let me sleep, just a little more."

"We're running away, remember?" This time it was Cayla who spoke.

Karina uncovered her head and sat, realizing it was obviously still dark because they were underground. And that was another reason not to get up.

"But this is a secret tunnel. It doesn't make any difference."

"We let you sleep for a while," Cayla said, "but we have to go. We're out of water." She turned down an empty water skin.

Even Nia was standing, as if waiting. Karina rubbed her eyes and stretched. "You drank it all?"

"There were just a couple sips anyways," Ayanna said. "Water's supposed to run on the walls of the tunnels, but I think it's further up."

"What if it doesn't?" Karina asked.

"Then we'll have to find a stream outside," Cayla said.

"That's a thirsty walk up."

"It'll only get thirstier the longer we wait," Cayla replied.

Karina got up, put her things in her bag, and was ready to walk with the group. They kept walking in that dark place, lit only by the dim crystal Cayla now carried. After a lot of walking, Karina felt insanely thirsty. She hoped to reach the running water soon, hoped it was clean, and also hoped they would not be ambushed somewhere. At least she was still full of hope.

Suddenly, Cayla stopped. "This is wrong."

"What?" Her sister asked.

"We're going down." She stretched her hand forward to make the crystal illuminate ahead, but not a lot could be seen.

Karina looked around, thinking that the tunnel was flat rather than sloped down, although, yes, flat was still a problem. Ayanna turned to Nia, "Are you really sure this was the third door?"

"Yes," Nia said. "Perhaps your teacher was mistaken?"

Ayanna thought for a moment, then answered, "He sounded sure."

Nia rolled her eyes. "We all know that he's good at sounding sure."

Ayanna asked, "Do you want to go back?"

Karina only imagined walking some three or four hours

without water, and didn't like it. She said, "Maybe we should keep going and see where it takes us."

"Yes," Cayla replied, "but there's no way this tunnel will lead us to the top of the mountain."

Top of a mountain. That reminded Karina of something, something unpleasant. "Wait. Aren't there jaguars in the mountains?"

"Not on the top. Around the lakes, in the valley." Cayla replied.

"Lakes and a valley explain going down," Karina blurted out.

"And water dripping," Nia added. "Perhaps we are in the right tunnel, but even if we aren't, I don't see any option other than going forward."

After an hour or so they found water dripping running along the walls. Karina finally drank. The tunnel didn't slope up, but apparently, everyone was satisfied in getting to its end to find out where it would lead them. So much walking was tiring and the continuous darkness was oppressive.

They walked the whole day. Karina felt exhausted, but somehow her curiosity to find out where they were kept her feet moving and her body standing. A couple times she considered asking for the others to stop, but she didn't want to show that she was more tired than everyone. Finally, Ayanna asked to stop.

Nia refused. "Look," she pointed to the ceiling and walls, "the tunnel is getting wider and higher. I think we're getting somewhere."

Karina was sure they were getting somewhere: somewhere meaning further down the tunnel.

Nia continued, "We walk just a little more, to find out where we are. Then we stop for the night."

Cayla nodded and got going, and somehow her sister followed. Karina didn't protest because she noticed that the tunnel was in fact a little different. Did it mean they were near its exit? But then, wouldn't it be safer to sleep inside? On the other hand, a few more minutes walking wouldn't kill her. A few more minutes. After that she would put her blanket on the floor and lie down, regardless of what the others decided. But the tunnel got wider and wider, and the only reason they could not see much ahead was that it was curved. After a sharp curve, they reached a wide opening, more like a large cave, some five meters wide in each direction and high enough that the light from the crystal didn't reach the ceiling. Nia's idea had been good, as this would be a more pleasant place to sleep than in the narrow tunnel. Karina didn't wait for the others and spread her blanket on the floor. Ayanna did the same.

Cayla, for her part, seemed restless and illuminated all the walls, with Nia beside her. "Do you see a door?"

"Let's keep looking," Nia replied.

That conversation made Karina realize that there was something wrong with that cave: only one entrance, or exit. Her eyes met Ayanna's, who seemed to have realized the same thing at the same time. But maybe that fear was pointless. After all, Nia knew how to find secret doors. They had come through one, and this place would sure have another. Perhaps that was why Odell said the girls needed Nia to guide them. Karina watched as Cayla and Nia examined the walls. This looked like a very difficult door, as they circled the place twice, going slower the second time, and also illuminating the higher parts of the walls. This didn't look right, because the other time Nia had found a secret door she had acted as if they were quite obvious. The duo circled the place for a third time, and even walked back a little in the tunnel.

Nia was the one who decided to stop. "We need to rest. We'll look again tomorrow."

They all sat and ate. After that, Karina lay down and tried to forget everything around her, while the others started to discuss their situation. Cayla accused Nia of having lead them through the wrong door, and Ayanna of not having heard well the instructions. Nia thought perhaps this was a trap, Odell had made a mistake, or Ayanna had been mistaken. Ayanna thought Nia could have been mistaken and even started doubting her own certainty about the directions.

In the end, despite what each of them thought, they were all tired and had to sleep. Karina remembered that the time difference was not as much as she had first calculated, and it would be already two or three in the morning. If she didn't find a way back soon, her parents would notice her absence. Still, at this point, upset parents was the least of her worries. She had to stay alive first, and then make sure she found a way back.

Cayla opened her eyes. She shouldn't have fallen asleep. Her travel companions' chests moved up and down, peacefully. Sleeping. She walked away from them, back to the tunnel, and took her necklace.

"Darian?"

The previous night it hadn't worked. She didn't have much hope that it'd be different this time. The stone was still red. It had never done that, and it wasn't because that woman had stepped on it, as she'd picked it up in one piece. Darian was trying to reach her, and had been trying for the last couple days. But Nia and Ayanna couldn't know about the necklace. Now, in the middle of the night, she wasn't sure he'd reply. But before she expected, his voice came out of the stone.

"Cayla? Where are you?" he sounded sleepy and sad.

She'd still been a little mad at him, but hearing his voice made it all go away.

"Can't you find me?"

"It doesn't make sense. It's as if you're trapped somewhere, but you're in the mountains."

"I'm in a tunnel underneath the mountains," she said.

"That makes sense. You're beneath the Apex."

If he was right, there was an entire mountain above them.

He continued, "I'm so sorry. I trusted the wrong people. I was betrayed."

She'd imagined this conversation, and she thought she would yell at him, tell him he'd put her life in danger, but she didn't feel like doing any of that. The pain in his voice showed he knew what he'd done. And it hadn't been his fault. "It happens." She had a question, though. "But are you with them? With those people?"

"There's a lot that I need to tell you, but it needs to be in person. Just be assured that I serve the kingdom."

These words put her at ease. She trusted him.

He continued, "And you? What's happening? How are you?" His tone was soft and sweet like she remembered.

"Fine, I guess. Escaping the castle. I need to finish a mission for my father, or he'll still be upset at me."

"That can't be fine. I'll come and meet you. Take you somewhere safe." He sounded sad and pleading.

"You know how meeting me worked last time..."

"I'll be alone."

"I'm supposed to go to the Apex. You can go there. But I'm not sure I'll reach it. These tunnels didn't go up."

"I'll dig until I find you."

Cayla smiled.

He continued, "Also, I understand you want to be just friends—"

The words hit her like a boulder. "What?"

"It's what you told me."

That didn't make sense. "I never did."

"You never..." he paused.

Her heart was about to explode, unsure why he was saying that. Was it an excuse? Had he changed his mind?

He continued, "You mean... to say... you want to be... more than friends?"

That was a question? "What do you think?"

"I'm asking."

"Since when do you have to ask?"

"We never... I mean, usually people ask, right? I guess I should have asked, but I never had the chance. But... when I told you Zayra thought you were my girlfriend, you weren't happy about it."

"You do realize my father will kill you if he learns that, right?"

"Sure. But we weren't near your father. It was people I... trusted. I guess you have a point. Was that the reason you wouldn't take my hand?"

"What do you think?"

"I don't know. What about the suffocating and stuff?"

"You were all weird, questioning me, giving me orders," she made a thick voice, "what are you doing? I'll take you back to the castle."

There was a pause before he started speaking again. "I was worried. Maybe I was angry. I thought you didn't..."

"You were thinking it just now, and you were nice."

"I had made peace with the idea."

"Next thing you'll tell me the sky is yellow."

He spent some time silent, then said, "I'll meet you at the Apex then."

"Again, I'm not sure I'll make it."

"I told you I'll dig and find you. Or I'll move the mountain. Or something."

Cayla's cheeks got warm. The way he said these words, it reminded her why she liked him so much. And she did. She was sure of that. But there was something she had to tell him. "Darian. I'll be with Nia, Karina, and my sister. They can't know about us. I won't take your hand."

He was silent for some seconds, then asked, "But would you like to?"

Her face got hotter. "You shouldn't have to ask."

Darian spent an even longer time in silence. Cayla thought she'd have to say something, when she heard his voice again. "I guess you won't let me kiss you either. Would you like me to, though?"

The only reason her face didn't get any hotter was because it would catch fire. "What do you think?"

"I want to hear it. Make sure there's no misunderstanding."

Cayla took a deep breath. She thought the answer was obvious, but, from the way he said it, it wasn't. Why were these words so difficult? She forced herself to blurt them out. "Yes, Darian, I want you to kiss me. I've wanted it for a long time. But please don't."

"I'll get this all solved then I'll kiss you a thousand times."

She smiled. "That's not a lot."

"A billion. Trillion. Infinite."

Cayla laughed. "Now you're being reasonable." They were both silent for a few seconds. She then said, "I have to sleep."

"I have to prepare. Make sure nobody follows me. Sleep well. Cayla. I luh... look forward to seeing you at the Apex."

For a second she thought he'd say something else. But it didn't matter. She laughed. "Or in a hole somewhere."

"I'll find you. Goodnight."

Cayla walked back to her blanket feeling giddy and light. Maybe he'd been right, and nothing between then had been obvious. But now it was. She would fall asleep thinking about kissing him, knowing someday it would be true, knowing for sure that he liked her. He was her steady rock among all the things that had been shaken recently. All those things she'd rather not think about, otherwise she'd be consumed with fear that her father would not accept her back, that everything would change. No. The shoes would be destroyed and everything would be turned back to normal. This hope kept her moving forward.

$\sim$

KARINA WOKE up while the others were still sleeping. The big cave was quite different from the small tunnels. The dim light from the crystal had been multiplied in many tiny rays, lining the cave with thin light streams. She looked up and noticed that she could see part of the ceiling high above them, and its texture. But the tiny rays didn't reach the ceiling: they rather came from it. Karina recognized a fraction of something she had not seen in days: sunlight! There was something up there, like an opening of sorts. She decided to touch Cayla's shoulder softly, just to check if she was really sleeping. The girl sat up quickly and looked around. "What?"

"Sorry, I, I just wanted to know if you were awake."

Cayla looked around, squinted, then laughed. "Then I wouldn't be sleeping."

"Indeed. But I have good news." She pointed at the ceiling. "Can you see it? There's light coming from there, so there must be an opening."

Cayla looked but didn't seem convinced. "That's impossible."

"But we can see the ceiling. We couldn't last night. And it's not the crystal."

Cayla looked for a longer period. "I see what you're saying, but there can't be any opening, because we're under a huge mountain."

She was grinning, which was a bizarre reaction if she thought they had no way out. And that certainty about their location was strange. "How do you know where we are?"

Cayla looked down. "I... have ways to find out."

"Why didn't you do that before?"

She pointed her necklace. "You know... But it didn't work before. The thing is, we're at the right place, but I think Odell misread a map. He saw a line stopping at the middle of the mountain and assumed it went to the top."

Incredible. "So you think Odell made a mistake?"

"I guess." Cayla looked down, then took a deep breath. "We'll find a way to fix it, but I wanted to talk to you. Can you come with me?"

Karina nodded. The girls walked back to the narrower part of the tunnel.

Cayla spoke softly, "When you were in the tower, I couldn't help you. Neither could Odell. I'm sorry. He told me to stay quiet and that he had to play along."

"Who was he playing along with?"

The girl looked down. "I'm sorry for my father. I think... he's under a lot of stress. Maybe he's receiving bad advice, maybe... He'd never harm you, and... I'm sure it's the shoes that are messing with his head. He'll be back to normal once they're gone."

Karina stared at the girl, almost asking "Are you out of your mind?" but thankfully her thought was silent. Instead, she said, "No problem. We'll get to Lylah's and make things right—once we find a way out of here, of course."

"We will." Cayla then became serious and thoughtful. "But you shouldn't have mentioned Darian. I'm glad you didn't say his name, though. It could've cost his life."

Karina felt bad for that, but then... "What would you have done in my place?"

"I would have kept the secret. I trusted you. You are the only one who knows about it."

That was not true. "And Zayra, that angry girl Rose, and that man..."

"I mean here. Nobody else knows. Not even Odell. I had to make up a story, and it was a lot of trouble to convince my father."

Karina wasn't sure she had to apologize, but she did it anyways. "I didn't know what to do, Odell was accusing me, I... I'm sorry. But later I said I had lied, so you see, I made up for that."

Cayla waved a hand. "Don't worry. It's past. Just please don't mention this anymore."

"I won't." Karina noticed the necklace again. This time it looked orange. She pointed at it. "Is it the same one? How did you get it back?"

Cayla shrugged. "I grabbed it. But I have no idea how we got back to the castle. Do you know what happened?"

Karina was about to say that she thought she had used the shoes to teleport, but then she decided it was best not to sound confident about that. "I... no. I have no idea."

"That's what I thought. But," she looked down, "there's some-thing else I wanted to tell you."

"Yes?" Karina was even more curious.

"Darian." She sighed. "I was mad at him, but... we spoke. He apologized. It wasn't his fault. That girl, Zayra, it was her. I knew it. I told you. But Darian, he's on our side, just in case we, uh, by chance, happen to meet him or something."

Karina face palmed. "Again? That was what got us the first time."

"Because of the girl."

"Wasn't he on the side of those people who imprisoned us?"

"Not him."

Karina started to search her memory, because she thought she'd heard something different, but she decided to leave it at that. There was another problem, though.

"If by chance we meet him," Karina hoped it wouldn't come to that, "won't Nia and your sister notice?"

Cayla shrugged. "They'll think we're just friends."

Wait. Was that a confession? "Aren't you just friends?"

Cayla squinted. "Of course! But they won't know we're close friends and have been talking. Nobody can know about this."

"But they saw your necklace."

"But they don't know what it does."

So that was what Cayla was worried about? Karina made an effort to sound serious. "Don't worry. Your secrets are safe with me."

How could Cayla be worried about such trivial matters when she was running away from her own father, who had turned evil or at least weird, when they had an army looking for them and when they were in a tunnel without exit? Oh, a "close friendship" really messed with one's mind.

Cayla started walking back to their sleeping place when she turned. "What do you think of Nia?"

The question surprised Karina. "She's... nice?" She was starting to hate that word.

Cayla looked down then looked around. "Yes, it's just... It's not that I don't trust her. Odell trusts her, but he doesn't know that she tried to prevent us from destroying the shoes, and he doesn't know what she did to Ayanna."

"And that you helped," Karina added, before thinking whether it was a good idea to mention that.

Cayla opened her eyes wide. "Yes. But that was for her own good." Cayla then squinted and continued. "As I was saying, yes, he trusts her. But he says our father locked her for conspiring against him, and we know that it's not far from the truth."

Karina felt she had to defend Nia. "She was only worried."

"Yes, but... I know she has at least some magical knowledge, and Odell doesn't know that."

"I'm sure he knows," Karina corrected her friend.

"Fine then. Still. He trusts her blindly. Sometimes, sometimes I think she might have done something to him. Like, I don't know. Anyways, I like Nia, and I want to help her, but... there's something odd about her. I'm not saying I don't trust her, but just— keep an eye on her. And don't listen to what she says."

Karina just nodded. "I'll pay attention." She felt bad because she knew Nia was planning on siding with Lylah, and she didn't tell Cayla any of this. She tried to change the subject. "Should we go back and look for an exit?"

"I guess."

They walked back. Ayanna and Nia were still sleeping.

Karina still thought there was an opening and asked Cayla, "What if you're wrong about our location?"

"I'm absolutely sure."

At this point Nia asked, "Sure of what?"

Cayla looked embarrassed. "Nothing, I mean," she pointed, "look, we can see the ceiling."

The woman looked and smiled. "There's the exit we were looking for."

13

A LONG WAY TO THE TOP

Nia sounded hopeful and relieved, and made Karina feel the same way.

Cayla didn't seem to agree. "But there's no opening."

"The opening is never obvious," Nia said. "I think it's either a secret door, or perhaps there are vines of some sort, I can't see much from down here."

"Can you go up there?" Karina asked, hoping the answer would be yes.

Nia looked up. "There must be a way, but we have to find that out."

Ayanna still slept, and Nia started again to look around the walls, but this time she was looking for a place to climb, rather than an opening. Karina also looked, thinking that the room was a puzzle to be solved, and how she liked puzzles. But she didn't like them when she couldn't find the answer, so trying to find a way up soon stopped being any fun. Still, she was proud of herself for having been the first to see the opening for what it was. She was getting good at recognizing otherworldly logic.

After a while, they sat to eat, realizing they were running out of food. Ayanna woke up and was happy to hear they had found a door.

Nia then got up and looked at the walls over and over. She finally sat again. "I don't see anything." She sighed. "We would need to go straight to the ceiling. A rope with a hook or something similar would work. But I can't think of what we can use instead. I... I don't know." She shook her head and looked down.

Ayanna asked, "You want a rope with a hook?" She got up and picked up her bag. "I have one." She pulled out something white and shiny from inside it and gave it to Nia, who looked surprised.

Cayla stared at her sister. "You had a rope all the time? And didn't tell us?"

The girl stepped back and raised her shoulders. "Nobody asked!"

Cayla rolled her eyes. "We were looking for a way up."

"How was I supposed to know?" The girl replied.

"You're right. I should have asked," Nia told Ayanna, then turned to everyone. "But at least we found the door and we know we're in the right place, or else she wouldn't have brought this rope. I'll climb to the ceiling."

She said this as if the climb was quite simple, even though it looked nothing like it, at least for Karina. In fact, Nia tried to throw the rope some eight times before she started reaching the ceiling, and even then, it took a couple more tries to get the hook safely placed. The girls only looked. Nia then jumped, grabbed the rope and started climbing it without any difficulty.

When she got to the ceiling, she touched it then yelled to the others, "They're vines. I need to cut them."

She held herself with one hand and legs while fumbling through her clothes, then came back down, looking distraught. "My dagger. I lost it. Does anybody have a dagger? A knife? Ayanna?"

Ayanna looked through her backpack, searched, then shook her head.

Cayla frowned, then took something from her bag. "Is it this one?"

Nia at first seemed surprised, then upset the girl had kept her prized object. She took it without saying a word, then climbed again and started cutting the vines as if they were made out of paper. Karina realized the blade was sharper than she'd imagined, and shivered thinking that it had been near her throat. The cuts on the vines revealed more dim light and an apparent opening.

Nia said, "I can see stairs." She moved up through the opening and disappeared in that dark ceiling. Only her voice could be heard. "Come on up."

The girls looked at each other. Karina thought the sisters were also wondering how in the world they would climb that thing. But no, apparently it was just indecision. Ayanna jumped, grabbed the rope, then climbed up, even if a lot more slowly than Nia. Cayla held the light, so she gestured to Karina to go first. The rope was straight, with no knots, unlike the one she had used to climb out of her yellow prison in the castle, and even then, close to a wall, she'd had a lot of difficulty.

Karina looked at her friend then whispered, as if speaking softly diminished the truth she was about to admit, "I don't think I can do it."

Cayla sighed, impatient. "There's no other way. Do you want to go back?"

Nia put her face in the opening. "What's going on?"

Cayla replied. "She says she can't climb it."

Nia didn't seem upset. "I'm sure she can. Cayla, climb first, that way she sees you and can do the same."

The girl nodded and climbed, holding the light between two fingers. She was fast and precise, almost like a circus artist, and Karina realized that she had seen circus and gymnastics stunts many times, and that they'd never increased her chances of being capable of performing them. But soon Cayla disappeared through the hole, keeping only the light pointing down. It barely reached Karina.

"Take your time. We're waiting," Nia said, in a tone that implied the opposite.

Karina tried as best as she could. She managed to grab the rope, but she was never capable of pulling herself up only with her arms. A few more tries yielded only exhaustion and pain. Karina sat on the ground, feeling defeated. She then tried to think, seeing if she could find a logical solution to make up for her lack of physical skills. She wondered if she could teleport, but more and more she felt it was impossible, and that perhaps she had not been responsible for their escape from the finger-cutting people on the hill. A loud thud snapped her out of her thoughts.

Cayla had just jumped down, and was beside her, looking annoyed. "Is that your plan? To spend the day sitting? How's that going to bring you up?"

"I was trying to think."

"You won't go up by thinking. Let alone trying."

Karina only stared, wondering if the girl had really gone through the trouble of jumping down just to scold her. Cayla was right beneath the rope, and pointed up, then pointed to her shoulders. "Here."

Karina crossed her arms because she was well aware she had to go up and she had to use her arms. "I tried, okay, I'm trying."

Cayla laughed. "No, no. I want to help you. Climb on my shoulders." She then crouched.

Karina climbed on the girl's back, then on her shoulders. She held the rope and stood up on Cayla's shoulders carefully not fall. This time, she could touch the rope with both hands and feet, making her way up easier. With a lot of effort, she got close to the opening, and Nia pulled her up. She found herself on a metal grid, surrounded by a tube made of a sparkly white stone. There was a transparent spiral staircase, made of glass, or something similar. Dim light came from the steps above. Those were some huge stairs. A tunnel upward.

Cayla soon came up. "Well, at least we'll finally move. I was afraid we wouldn't reach the top by day."

Nia took a deep breath. "Let's just hope nobody's waiting for us outside."

Cayla shook her head. "No. I think this time everything will go well. I know it."

"Good for you," Nia said.

Karina feared they would start arguing, but they didn't. There was no point in trying to predict the rest of their journey when it stood above them. Karina then wondered how high that mountain was. From what she had seen from the castle it was an old mountain range. The highest peak couldn't be taller than some two kilometers, which meant that they could get to the top in no more than a couple hours.

After a few minutes climbing, Karina realized that she had greatly underestimated the effort and time to get to the top. After just a few turns, everyone's pace was reduced, and soon they all sat to rest. Nobody talked, because they were panting, even Nia and Cayla. They just passed the water around. Karina felt a little dizzy from all the turning and her legs hurt. They spent their next hours either climbing slowly or sitting and resting. At least the more they climbed the more light reached them, and it felt good to be moving away from darkness. The downside was that the more they climbed the taller the steps felt. They were the same size, but the strength in their legs wasn't. Karina would never again complain about going up four, ten or even twenty floors. Not after she climbed the equivalent of some six hundred. Assuming her estimate was right, of course.

As interminable as the staircase had first looked, after many hours of slow climbing and resting they reached a place where they could see a small opening and patches of blue sky above them. The stairs finished, and they reached a smaller tube, some six meters high. A metal ladder led to the top. Cayla climbed first, and Karina last. She hated being last again, but at least she knew her arms and feet could take her out of that place. Actually, it wasn't as easy as it seemed. Trembling tired legs are not very efficient climbers. When Karina finally put her head outside, among branches, she saw that the tube from where they had just come out looked like a tree from the outside. That was a neat way to hide a huge staircase from anyone who went to that mountain.

Exhausted, Karina reached the ground, which was covered with grass. There were other trees around them. Karina realized how much she had missed the sky. The few clouds above them looked orange and pink. How magnificent it was to be out in the open.

"We need to find a place to spend the night," Nia said.

Cayla looked at her sister. "What did Odell say? I mean, what are we supposed to do now?"

Ayanna seemed to think for a moment. "Other than going to Lylah's castle, I don't think he had any more advice." She looked down, thinking. "No, he didn't. But I think it should be easy from here, right? I mean, because he didn't say much about it."

Nia narrowed her eyes as if thinking. "As far as I know this is an impossible place to reach—except by air. So we just have to make sure we're not spotted from above. Other than that, perhaps we're safe—hopefully."

They walked to a place where the trees were closer together, so that no lifts could spot them from above. They spread their blankets and sat. Karina felt exhausted, but she was curious to see the path ahead. She got up. "I just want to take a look there."

"I'm coming with you," Cayla said, and also got up.

Nia narrowed her eyebrows, then said, "Careful. It's getting dark. And don't go far."

The girls nodded, then walked about one hundred meters, until the forest, and the ground, stopped suddenly. There were mountains further away, in a crooked horizon. Beneath them, an ocean of thin clouds, covering a valley and a dark river. So that explained "black" river. Somehow Karina had imagined a more eerie meaning to the name. Amidst the clouds, in the middle of the river, she could see something white and shiny, similar to the stone surrounding the long spiral staircase. Karina took a better look, and realized it was a white castle on a small island, contrasting to the waters around it. It looked like a toy in the distance, or better, an icing cake decoration, and yet, that little thing was their final destination.

Karina then realized she had been so caught up in the tunnel and stairs she had completely forgotten the purpose of her journey. Her task was so much more than getting out of a tunnel. The darkness and enclosing had made her forget the great beautiful sky outside, and that this world was just part of some great bigger something.

14

LOOKING AHEAD

"I'm glad we're out. This is beautiful, isn't it?" Karina said.

Cayla, who stood beside her, smiled. "It's amazing. And we're near her castle, so we are finally back on track."

"Back on track with everyone after us."

Cayla didn't seem worried. "We'll make it right."

Karina then thought about her change of mind about Lylah, her change of mind about the King, and how the mission seemed completely different now. She wondered if Cayla was at least open to feeling something different from the way she felt before. "And what if the reason we're here is different from what you expected?"

Cayla had a puzzled look. "Like?"

Karina shrugged. "I don't know. And you think we'll go in, throw the shoes, then puff, Lylah disappears?"

She had made an effort to sound serious, but she wasn't sure if it had been successful.

Cayla laughed. "You make it sound silly. I don't know, all I know is that Odell wouldn't tell us to do something dangerous or that didn't make sense."

Karina looked down. "It has been dangerous."

"I know, but if we didn't have any problem on our first journey, we could be down there, on the other side of the river, on this same day, waiting for nightfall, without anyone following us."

Getting to the mouth of the Black River should have taken five or six days, so Karina corrected her friend. "Actually, we would still be near the meeting of the rivers."

"See? I was right. We did speed up our journey."

Karina laughed. In reality, she thought that a long and boring camping and hiking expedition around the mountains would have been better than all the trouble and danger they'd been through the last few days. But, would it really? She would still believe that the tyrant and crazy King was representing the good guys. She would still believe she would save the world by destroying the shoes. Of course, Karina wasn't thankful that she had been imprisoned and threatened. But still... like Cayla said, they had even sped up their journey.

Cayla noticed that she was thinking, but probably imagined something else, and said, "I know. Maybe we should have done as Odell told us, we should've walked all the way, I know. But I can't change that now."

Karina nodded, accepting what she thought was the closest to an apology her friend could muster. Another thought, unrelated to their conversation, hit Karina. "It doesn't have walls around it."

"What?"

"The castle. You said it had walls."

Cayla seemed to remember. "It's true. But it doesn't look like a fortress either."

"It doesn't."

Karina was no expert in fortifications or castles, but that delicate, white, shiny thing certainly didn't look like a fortress. She then tried to imagine what it would look like from the inside but the thought gave her a knot in the stomach. Even though the castle looked like a little toy, it was there, it was reachable, it existed. So different from the theory of Odell's explanation which now seemed to have happened an eternity before.

"Let's see the way down," Cayla said.

The girl walked closer to the edge, and Karina followed. She knew the descent was steep, but when she looked, her heart almost stopped. "Steep slope" was a huge understatement. What she saw was a humongous cliff, tall and wide, extending almost as far as they could see. Karina finally understood why, on their first journey, they would have to walk around it. There was no way they would go down that thing. Cayla also looked worried, so no, this wasn't supposed to be easy, not even for the people there. Cayla turned around. "We have to tell them."

The girls raced back, then told the others what they'd seen. Ayanna was surprised, but Nia not so much. "I told you this was an impossible place to reach by land. Didn't you ever see a picture of the divide between rivers?"

"I saw a map," Cayla replied. "It doesn't show the height." She then turned to her sister. "Did you bring any more climbing equipment?"

"Just that rope."

"And what did Odell say?" Cayla asked. "He must have said something."

Ayanna looked down and shrugged. "He told me what I told you, to reach the top of the mountain then go down to the river and the castle. He didn't say anything else. Is the mountain that bad?"

Cayla had a grimace. "Yes. And it's all smooth. And even if it was easy, we don't have the equipment."

Nia looked distant and strangely silent.

Cayla asked her, "What do you think?"

She shrugged. "Well, Odell sent us here. He either wants us to reach Lylah's castle, or he wants us to be caught."

"No. No way," Cayla said.

Nia raised an eyebrow, as if annoyed, then continued, "Well, if he wants us to reach the castle, and if he didn't send us any equipment, there's a way down. If he wants us captured, someone will show up and we won't be able to do much."

Cayla seemed upset. "I'm absolutely sure Odell didn't send us here to be captured. He'd never do anything like that. Never."

"We'll find a way down tomorrow then," Nia said. "Nothing to worry about."

Karina remembered the possibility of being ambushed. More and more this possibility seemed likely. And this mountain looked like the perfect place for that. She wondered why Nia seemed so cool about it. "Aren't you worried?"

Nia sighed. "I'm tired. But perhaps we could keep watch." She looked at Cayla, who didn't seem to like the idea. "Just in case. We're close to Lylah's land, we have the king after us, it would be safer. I can go first, then you two." She pointed at Karina and Cayla.

Cayla pointed at her sister. "Why not her?"

Before Nia replied, Ayanna said, "I can watch. I want to. Please."

"Fine, all four of us will rotate," Nia said.

Karina envisioned another poor sleeping night, but she thought it would be better than risking being caught sleeping. Well, they would be caught awake then. She didn't want to think what the difference was. They sat and shared the last food they had, which wasn't enough to appease their hunger, at least not Karina's. For the first time in this world she felt a cool breeze, instead of the stuffy hot weather or the stagnant air from the tunnels.

Cayla looked around and seemed alarmed. "Wait."

"What's wrong?" Nia asked.

"Silence," Cayla said. "I can hear something."

Karina couldn't hear anything, but by this time she was so used to being incompetent in her senses that she wasn't surprised.

Nia looked around. "It's just the wind."

"No," Cayla whispered. "Someone's coming. We have to get back in the tunnel."

They all got up, but Nia held Cayla back. "Bad idea. If someone sees us getting in, we'll be trapped there."

Cayla closed her eyes, gestured for silence, pointed up and started climbing a tree.

At this point Karina had the impression that she did hear something, but it could be that she was influenced by Cayla. Nia didn't climb, but gestured to the others to move among some bushes. At least this was easier than going up the tree, and, since it was almost dark, perhaps they wouldn't be seen—if it was true that someone was coming.

CAYLA CLOSED her eyes and heard the world around her. There was wind, Nia, Ayanna's and Karina's breathing in the distance, lifts far away, the ocean at a great distance, jaguars in the valley —and someone walking carefully towards them. There was something familiar about those steps. Darian. It had to be him. But then, maybe not. The steps were heavier. She'd been wondering so much where he was that perhaps she was imagining she heard him. Only one person. It wasn't an ambush then, but it could be a scout. There could be people looking for them in all exits of the tunnels, and perhaps this person was one of them—and she wouldn't let them get away. She was lucky because the steps came in her direction. As the person walked below her, Cayla saw her chance and jumped, pinning the person to the ground face down. It was a man, back of his head covered by a hood, muscular back and arms, stronger than her. No way she could hold him down by force. But she still had skill.

She pulled his arm behind his back. "Move and I'll snap it."

He mumbled something, and she loosened the pressure over his head, just to hear what he'd say.

"It's me."

The voice she knew so well. But it didn't make sense. She had hugged him before. He should have been soft like his voice, the way he'd always been. Cayla moved away from him and got up. He got up and removed a hood that covered his hair and half his face.

"What's wrong?" Darian asked.

Cayla was still trying to match the person she'd held down to Darian. Even if she'd seen him two days before, somehow her memory was still of the boy she'd met almost two years before. "Sorry. I didn't know it was you."

"Do you, now? Cause you don't look like you recognize me."

"Well, you are different."

"Not at all."

As he said this, he wrapped his arms around her and pulled her close to him, hugging her really tight. He felt her head against his shoulder and wrapped her arms around his neck. She'd been longing for this hug for what felt like an eternity. It was Darian as she'd known.

He whispered, "Do you recognize me now?"

She squeezed him tighter and looked at him. "Uh-huh."

Their eyes met. Their faces were so close. Cayla didn't care what anyone would think—she wanted to kiss him.

But he let go of her and stepped back. "Sorry, I..." He shook his head. "I almost forgot."

He meant what she'd asked him. Not to kiss her. She almost regretted it now, but she could never forget the day she heard they wanted to kill him, and she'd never want to be responsible for that again. At least he had some sense, because she had none. "It's fine."

He smiled, then looked at the tree and back at her. "Wow, you had me there. How did you get so good at this?"

Cayla shrugged. "I don't know. Practice?"

"I thought you stopped wrestling." He raised an eyebrow. "Who have you been practicing with?"

"Nobody. Just... doing exercises on my own."

She felt a light in her direction. It was Nia, looking stern, staring at both of them. Karina was right behind her. Nia stepped closer to them, held up a light crystal and illuminated his face. "What's this? Cayla, how can you do this to us?"

Darian raised his hands, showing the palms. "I came here on my own. I'm not representing anyone. I know the King's after you, and I came to help."

He sounded so concerned, so honest, but Nia narrowed her eyes. "The king? Only the king? Aren't you going to mention General Keen? Protecting your family?"

Cayla wanted to protest, but Darian was faster, "This has nothing to do with my father." His voice was calm and soft. "I know I'm his son and I can't change that. But he knows nothing about this. I'm just here to help Cayla."

Nia hadn't changed her expression. "And pray, tell me, how did you find us?"

He pointed at Cayla. "She told me. Like I said, I came cause she asked."

The woman still didn't look convinced. "How could she have told you?"

He pulled his necklace. "This. Because we're friends."

Cayla had to catch some breath. She couldn't believe he'd just revealed one of their biggest secrets. Like that. And she couldn't even make a face, kick him, or tell him anything, or it would only make everything worse.

Nia turned to her. "Is that true?"

All Cayla could do was look down and mumble, "Yes."

Nia was still angry. "But he's in the army. Who knows who could've followed him?"

Again Darian showed the palms of his hands and shook

them. "I came alone, by boat, nobody knows where I am." He looked at Cayla. "My flying partner has been dismissed from the army." Cayla couldn't repress a little smile. Darian continued, "I had nobody checking where I was."

Nia stared at Cayla. "You should have told us." She turned to Darian. "I hope this doesn't cause us problems."

He shook his head. "No. I'd never—"

Nia sighed. "I hope so."

Cayla wanted to change the subject, and asked him, "How did you get here?"

"Very tough climb. I don't understand where you plan to go from here."

"Isn't there a way down?"

"As far as I know only lifts come here. Or very experienced climbers."

Cayla laughed. "Since when you're an experienced climber?"

"Since you asked me to meet you at this almost impossible to reach peak."

Right. *I'll find you.* He'd meant it. Cayla looked down, thought for a moment, then said, "But if you could do it, I can do it as well."

"No doubt," he said. "But I came up. I'm not sure I can climb down."

"Are we trapped up here then?" Nia asked.

He shook his head. "I don't know. Maybe we can come up with a solution. But the good thing about this summit is that nobody will come looking for you."

Ayanna came out of the bushes where she was hiding.

Darian seemed surprised. "I didn't know your sister was also here." He turned to Ayanna. "Hello, I'm Darian, Cayla's friend."

Her sister just stared at him.

He also noticed Karina. "Good to see you again too. I'm sorry for what happened. I made a mistake and I would like to apologize."

Karina shrugged. "It's fine." It didn't sound she meant it.

"Thank you," he said, then looked at everyone. "How are you doing with supplies? I brought some food."

Cayla smiled. "How did you know we'd be out of food?"

"I didn't." He then returned the smile. "But I thought, why not?"

Ayanna had a big smile. "Thank you. I was starving."

Nia stared at her. "You said you had enough."

The girl looked down. "Cause I wanted to leave some for you."

Darian laughed. "Good thing I came then."

They went to their camping site and sat on their blankets. Cayla tried to avoid looking at him too much, but she couldn't help sitting beside him. The few times their eyes met all she felt was calm complicity and security. They understood each other now, and it made all the difference. It was just a matter of time for their infinite kisses.

KARINA CHEWED the same bland tasteless dry things, but hunger had improved their taste. Pleasant night sky, nature, all they needed was a fire, except they obviously couldn't have one without drawing attention, which reminded Karina that this wasn't a camping expedition. Nia asked Darian how he'd kept in touch with Cayla. The girl looked down and seemed embarrassed. From their conversation, Karina gathered that he had left the castle over a year before, when he gave Cayla the necklace. He also said he knew the kingdom was under rebel threat but that he had no idea people so close to him would be involved. This last explanation didn't convince Karina very much, but, hey, he'd brought food, and for that she was willing to accept lame excuses.

At least he looked happy and relaxed, unlike the last time

she'd seen him. Cayla was also at ease around him. Karina was usually terrible at noticing lovey-dovey stuff, but these two, with their bright eyes, had a virtual billboard saying, "we're in love and we know it." She smiled, happy that they'd solved whatever problem they had before.

Nia and the girls were tired, and soon they got ready to sleep. Darian had a tent, but Nia thought it would be better for them all to sleep outside, so as not to split the group. Nia still insisted they should keep watch and volunteered to be first. Darian volunteered as well, but Nia insisted it should be her.

This place had grass! It felt so soft and comfortable that Karina soon fell asleep. She woke up with a voice, "You're in danger."

15

ABOUT THE REBELS

Karina sat up and saw only Ayanna and Cayla sleeping. She didn't see Nia or Darian, but she heard soft voices a little further down, and went in that direction, where she saw them.

Nia seemed angry, and spoke to Darian, "You are going to tell me everything, because I didn't believe half the stories you told. I want the truth."

"Fine," he then noticed Karina, "but I'm not gonna talk in front of her."

Nia turned to Karina. "It's great you're here." She turned to Darian. "You. You owe her an explanation, remember? I doubt she believed your lousy excuses, because you're a terrible liar. Are you going to explain yourself, or do you want her to discuss her worries with Cayla?"

Karina almost defended herself explaining she had no intention to discuss anything with anyone when she understood Nia was only arguing for Karina's inclusion in their conversation.

Darian looked upset. "I don't even know who she is. You can't expect me to—"

"Hey," Karina cut him off, "thanks to you I was captured, tied, imprisoned. I would appreciate an explanation. And I didn't really believe what you told us."

Nia added, "She's Cayla's friend; I think you'll want her on your side."

Darian took a deep breath. "Fine. She might as well listen." He stared at Karina. "But I'll talk to Cayla personally. If she hears any of this from anyone but me, I'll—"

"Hey," Nia interrupted. "You're not in a position to be threatening anyone. Now, if you want us to help you and keep your secret, you'll want to explain yourself first."

He looked down, stroked an imaginary beard, looked away, then finally faced Nia. "So, unlike I said earlier, I knew people close to me were part of the insurgent movement, and... I'm also part of that movement."

Karina had guessed something like that, but maybe not that much. Nia took a step back.

Darian continued, "I know it sounds bad. But you need to know that I grew up in a village that was threatened by the king. I was sent to the castle, to my father, and all it did was confirm everything I suspected. And I got in the army and, remember I was sent far South," he pointed to Nia, "where you came from. Well, once you're there, you start to see things, and... They are doing everything they can to wipe out anyone who might oppose the king, or any community that appears to have the slightest chance of opposing him. Or anyone who yields magic. Or seems to do so. The definition of magic is quite fuzzy, though. Anyways, the first thing I did was to bring this up to my father." He looked down and closed his eyes, as if in pain, then snorted. "But guess who's responsible for all that repression? Guess who wants to enforce these laws with violence?" He shook his head. "My father. I realized I would never change his mind. I considered deserting, at the risk of being executed, unless my father intervened, which would put me in a very uncomfortable position. Then I thought there should be another way, and I found it. Other people also found it. The insurgents stopped deserting the army only to be found and killed. Instead, we became the army, or at least a good part of it."

"You've been conspiring against the king," Nia said.

Darian looked down and nodded. "Cayla's father. I had no way to tell her. I never had the occasion to see her or talk to her. But," he looked at Nia, "I know that the king's after you. I thought perhaps you'd side with me, you'd understand."

"We're all running from him," Nia said.

"I know. I'm in the army, remember?" He laughed. "By the way, they think you're highly dangerous, Nia. But for the others, the order is to return them to the castle alive." He looked down. "But Cayla didn't seem very concerned about her own safety. She said she had some problems with her father, that all she had to do was finish her interrupted mission and everything would be fine. That her father was upset that she failed or something."

Nia rolled her eyes.

The mention of their failed expedition made Karina ask a question, "Who were those people who imprisoned us and wanted to cut our hands?"

Darian raised his eyebrows. "Hands? No, they said something about fingers, but that it was just a threat."

"They later decided on fingers, but it wasn't a threat. They were even preparing the equipment."

His face paled. "I'm sorry. Really sorry. Well, Rose's group, they are not in the army. There are many scattered independent groups, and hers is one of them. I was good friends with her sister, Zayra." He looked at Karina. "You met her. Like me, she supports the insurgency, but I would never think she would back-stab me like that. Also, Rose's group, they were not supposed to make decisions on their own. Still, I'm sorry for my part in it. But

I did tell Cayla it wasn't safe to go wandering on her own. I offered to go with her, but no."

"There were six or eight people," Karina said, "I don't think you would have made much difference."

He looked down. "I didn't mean like that. Anyways, I left her and I thought no harm would come to her, or you, because if anything happened I'd be the first to know."

Nia raised an eyebrow. "The first?"

He looked down and around. "I, I deal with communication. And since I dropped her off, I was paying attention to that area."

"Wow, lots of attention," Karina said. "Thank you so much."

He raised his shoulders. "They never reported, never contacted anyone. They did it on purpose. They betrayed me."

"Fair enough," Nia said as if to end the subject. "And what does this insurgence of yours plan to do?"

"We have to depose the king."

Nia narrowed her eyes and stared at him as if trying to see something. "Then Cayla would no longer be a princess."

Darian shrugged. "I don't mind. In fact—"

"She does," Nia interrupted. "The thing she most wants is to succeed her father."

He stroked his imaginary beard. "Well, I could make her queen."

Nia's eyes widened. "What?"

"I mean, there's a lot of discussion on who should take power in case we succeed. It could, uh, somehow, eventually be her."

"I think she would love the idea," Nia said, "until the other people who also want to take the power start showing up with part of the army. It would be chaos."

He shook his head. "If you knew what was happening, you wouldn't fear chaos. But yes, her life could be in danger. That's why I'm not a supporter of Cayla as a ruler, at least not until everything is stable."

"Who would rule then?"

"We'll decide among the leaders."

Nia snorted. "Sure, whoever gets the biggest chunk of the army is king."

"No, not like that. We'll establish a council. That's what we do anyways, no single leadership."

Nia rolled her eyes. "That's cute and sweet and idealistic." She became serious. "Until there's power to be split. And what about Lylah?"

He took a deep breath. "We haven't seen or heard from her in years. Nobody can enter that castle of hers. I don't even know if she's alive and if she is willing and capable of governing anything."

Karina had to correct him. "I saw her. She's alive, or at least she was, until, uh, a few days ago."

"She's very much alive, and that's where we are going," Nia added with a strange certainty.

Darian grimaced. "Even if she is alive, you'll never get there. Not from here."

"Odell sent us here," Nia said, "and I think he wants us to go there for some reason."

"But that could be dangerous," Darian said.

"Do you have another alternative?" Nia asked.

Again he took a deep breath. "That's part of what I meant to tell you. Since you're all safe here, and we have a good part of the army... we could take the castle. Then—"

"No. My son's there."

Darian looked down and bit his lip.

Nia stared at him. "You can't. You can't attack the castle. Cayla would never forgive you. There's my son, there's her father, there's your father."

Darian closed his eyes. "I was willing to make this sacrifice."

Nia became the furious scary woman Karina had seen once. "Sacrifice? You want power!"

Darian was still calm but shook his head. "No, no way."

Nia was definitely furious. "Is that why you're all over Cayla? To be king?"

He squinted and answered in a calm but dry voice. "Both your suggestions are offensive."

"We'll see. Now, has this attack been planned? How much influence do you have?"

He raised his arms, showing the palms of his hands. "No, no. Nothing's been planned. It was just something that came up to me now, seeing all of you here and safe. Sorry if I forgot about Cayla's little brother. I was just going to say it was safe now. Other people, not me, have planned an attack before. We've been having a good part of the army for some time, but I always told them it wasn't safe to take the castle. I can access top information, through my father, so I get a say on that. But I've been lying. We do have enough power to take down the castle, and I thought now I could tell them the truth."

Nia pointed her index finger to him. "If there's an attack planned, you have to halt it."

"Nothing's been planned." He spoke in a soft voice, as if to soothe her. "Nothing. It was something I wanted to suggest. If your son's there, we'll think of something else. We'll find another solution. We'll—"

He stopped suddenly and looked behind Nia. Karina also looked. Cayla was walking towards them. She stepped closer, rubbing her eyes.

"What attack? What's happening?" She then looked up, and opened her eyes wide, looking scared. "Why didn't you wake me up?"

They all looked where she looked. A roundish silver thing stood almost above them. It definitely looked like a flying saucer from below. But, in their context, it was scarier: a lift.

Darian said, "Hide. I'll deal with them."

Nia shook her head. "I think they saw us."

"Now. Hide," the boy repeated.

He sounded so insistent that Karina turned around and ran to the place where Ayanna was, to wake her up. She noticed Cayla and Nia were beside her. In fact, Nia was the first to reach the younger sister and pull her up. "Get up. Come."

Ayanna seemed sleepy and confused, but she did as she was told. They moved to the bushes where they had first hidden.

Nia then pulled Cayla's hand, as if to prevent her from climbing or running farther away. "We have to stay together."

Cayla grimaced, but she also hid in the same place.

"What's happening?" Ayanna asked.

"They're coming for us," Nia replied.

"Who's coming?" the girl asked.

"I don't know. Let's be quiet."

They could not see what was happening beyond the bushes and closest trees, but they saw the gleam of a bright light.

A man or boy spoke loud enough to be heard from that distance. "You know what we're here for."

"Well, hello, Jax," Darian replied. "It's good to see you. I don't actually know. Sorry. Why don't you tell me?" He sounded calm and friendly.

"I think you're the one who has something to tell," Jax said. "Do you have an explanation for this?" His tone of voice was a sharp contrast to Darian's, as he sounded anything but friendly.

"I'm pretty sure I can explain anything you want, as long as you ask. I can't read thoughts, though, unfortunately. Let's sit and talk." His voice was soft and smooth.

"Darian, we're not against you," a girl said, "just let us take the princesses. I'm sure you know it's for the best. We won't harm them, I'll make sure of that this time. And we know they're here."

"Zayra, I thought we had agreed on this..."

At the mention of this name, Cayla got up, but Nia held her. "No. Wait."

"We can fight," Cayla replied.

"Try to listen," Nia whispered.

Cayla sat down, looking cross. Karina could only hear the last part of what Darian was saying.

"... understand my position."

"Diplomatic ties," Jax replied. "I'm willing to accept that. Now, make use of them and help our cause. We can win this."

"We can," Darian replied. "But the princesses won't help us. They are running away from the king. Why do you think they are here? They'd be useless as hostages. Trying to use them for bargain would only expose us."

"We'd rather take our chances," Jax said. "Unless you care to convince us."

Nia looked worried. "They're trying to gain time. I think there are more people coming from behind us. We need to move." She then turned to Karina. "Please. You have to try."

Teleporting, she meant. Karina had a fraction of a second to weigh the possibilities in front of her. Her conclusion was terrible, but it was better than wasting time trying to do the impossible. "I can't. I won't be able to do it. I have no idea how. Even if I did, we're four people, and I can't guarantee we'd all go."

That was an uncomfortable confession, not only because it meant they were in real trouble, but also because she felt bad to have to admit she didn't know something. Nia shook her head.

Cayla didn't seem upset. "We can still fight and take their lift. Before the others come."

Nia closed her eyes, as if thinking. "Assuming your friend is on our side."

"It's our only chance," Cayla pleaded.

Nia sighed, then looked at Karina and Ayanna. "You two, stay here. When we yell, make a run for the lift. Understood?"

Karina nodded. Nia turned to Cayla. "On the count of three. One, two—"

Cayla started running and Nia followed. The girl grabbed a

twig, and the woman held her dagger. Karina wondered if her two companions would be able to win their fight, and what would happen if they lost. From beyond the bushes, she heard grunts and yells, and much sooner than expected, Nia's voice; "Girls, come."

Karina was startled, but she got up and ran, until she felt someone pushing her. She fell. She tried to get up, but then someone held her and put a hood on her. She tried to get away from the person holding her, or at least remove the hood, but she was being held so tight she could barely move. Soon she heard steps and grunts, felt that the person let her go, and found her opportunity to remove the hood. Cayla was trying to fight two people at once. Nia stood close, beside someone on the ground. Ayanna was getting up, her face dirty. Nia walked closer to one of the people Cayla was fighting. Nia tried to stab them. The person fell to the ground as if hit by something. Nia then stabbed the air close to Cayla's second opponent, who also fell. Her dagger seemed capable of affecting a person from a close distance, which was really weird.

"Run," Nia yelled, as she moved towards the lift.

Karina ran as fast as she could, then she heard a loud sound like an explosion, and the floor a few meters in front of her caught fire. She considered jumping or skirting it, but she heard more explosions and more places catching fire between them and the lift.

"They're throwing fireballs," Cayla said.

"We keep going," Nia replied.

The woman ran in the front and fanned the fire with her dagger, which only caused more smoke to rise. Meanwhile, Cayla turned around and threw a few stones. The smoke was so thick that the fire no longer could be seen.

"Come," Nia yelled. "They won't hit us."

Cayla and her sister ran towards that smoke, so Karina did the same, hearing more sounds of explosions behind them, and seeing fire all around them except in the place with the high smoke, where Nia had fanned the fire. Karina crossed the smoke and saw the lift, its back door open, bright light coming from the inside, illuminating the grass and bushes. Four people lay on the floor. One of them started sitting up. It was Darian, with a cut on his temple, looking confused.

"Get up," Nia told him. "You have to come with us."

"No!" Cayla yelled. "He's a traitor."

"But we need him," Nia said.

"We don't," the girl insisted, stepping inside the lift.

Karina assumed the girl knew how to pilot the ship, so she also ran inside, eager to get away from that summit and those people.

"Cayla, wait," Darian murmured, still sitting, his voice weak.

Nia was the last one to step inside, and stared at Cayla. "Can you fly this thing?"

"It can't be hard," she replied as she pushed something by the door that made it close.

More sounds of explosions were heard from outside, and when the door was almost shut, someone put a hand, as if trying to prevent it from closing. Cayla kicked it, and the door continued its movement until it was shut. Karina moved to the cockpit and tried to guess what was necessary to make that thing fly, but she had no idea. She turned to Cayla. "How does this work?"

The girl passed her hands through the panel. "I'm looking. Wait."

Nia seemed angry. "You're looking? Now it's too late to let him in."

"That's the idea," Cayla replied, still looking at the panel.

"You know? They might hurt him," Nia said.

"That's the idea."

"He's your friend!" Nia said.

Cayla turned and faced Nia. "No. He's with them. He defended her. And it's his fault these people are after us."

"Your fault," Nia corrected. "You're the one who contacted him. And either way, what are we going to do with a lift we can't fly? I thought you knew at least a little."

Cayla only stared at the panel. More and more sounds of explosions were heard. Karina stopped trying to figure out the panel and looked outside. The fire surrounding them was getting higher and higher. She imagined that thing exploding with them inside.

"What material is this lift made out of?" Karina asked.

"Oh. It won't catch fire, if that's what you're worried," Nia said. "But if we don't take off it might get hot. Too hot for us. Soon."

"And won't it explode?" Karina asked, wondering if the top had a combustible gas.

Nia had a puzzled face. "Explode? No."

Karina figured that despite the similar appearance the lifts were not anything like balloons or zeppelins. She would be really curious as to how exactly they worked, if she weren't more worried about her own life.

"Shouldn't we get out?" Ayanna asked. They all stared at her. The girl tried again. "Surrender?"

Nia shook her head. "No. We have to figure a way out."

"The only way out is through the door," Ayanna replied.

Karina thought they could still try to escape. "Maybe we could still get out and bring in someone who can guide this ship."

"No," Cayla replied, seeming horrified.

"I agree with you," Nia said to Karina, "I really do. But they're too many. No way we'll get out and back in again. If only," she stared at Cayla, "we had brought in a pilot when we could."

"Who knows where he'd take us!" Cayla defended herself. "You heard it. He's with them."

"Yes," Nia replied. "We're so much better without him."

The place indeed started to get warmer, and Karina hoped it was just an impression, fear, and increased heart rate, although, by its looks, the lift was becoming a pan.

"Who are they?" Ayanna asked.

"Insurgents. It's a long story," Nia said.

"Why are they after us?" Ayanna asked.

"Probably to take us as hostages."

Ayanna looked down, then asked, "They wouldn't kill me, would they?"

"They could harm you," Nia warned.

"I'm getting out," the girl said, walking to the door.

Karina admired the resolution in the little girl, and apparently so did Nia and her sister, who stared wide-eyed.

"Wait," Nia stepped in front of her. "Perhaps you're right. But we need a plan. Maybe try to capture and bring someone in, force them—"

"We're gonna get burned," Ayanna said.

Nia sighed. "I can't go back to the castle now."

Karina had a similar feeling, but she couldn't think of any other alternative, and she was feeling hot. "Maybe we can talk to them."

Nia took a deep breath. "Let's go out and hope for the best."

"I'm not going out," Cayla protested. "I'll fight until the end."

"The end doesn't need to be now," Nia said. "Sometimes it takes courage to quit. We'll have another opportunity." She looked down. "Hopefully." This last part was barely audible.

Cayla had tears in her eyes. "I don't want to face them. I don't want to see him."

"It's starting to burn my feet," Ayanna complained. She walked to the door, but she didn't know how to open it.

Cayla dried her tears and asked, "Does it look like I cried?"

Karina shook her head, lying, "No. Not at all."

Cayla touched a button near the door, which started to descend slowly. Granted, perhaps she couldn't take that thing out of the ground, but at least she knew how to get them out of that thing. Karina expected someone would come in as the door started to open, that they'd jump in and grab them, but nobody did. When the door was low enough, she saw that there were about fifteen people in a semi-circle around the door, some ten meters from them, pointing what looked like some kind of guns. The three girls and Nia stepped out. In the middle, a person who sent shivers down Karina's spine.

16

BACKSTABBING

"Drop the knife and raise your hands," Rose said. "Drop the knife."

See? Karina wasn't the only one who called it a knife. Nia threw her prized object—dagger—on the floor. Nobody took it, which was odd. Perhaps their fear of Nia's weapon explained their distance. Karina looked around for Darian, wondering on which side he really was, and if he would perhaps help them, but she didn't see him. She recognized some faces from when they had been first captured. Rose continued, "I don't want to see any fighting, I don't want to see any magic, and most of all, no attempt to escape."

"Or what?" Cayla provoked.

Rose smiled. "Jax, show them."

The boy, who had been behind Rose, stepped forward, holding a person with hands and feet tied and mouth covered; Darian. His head was down, and he didn't seem the least curious to glance up.

Rose continued, looking at Cayla, "Try anything, and you'll never see him again."

Cayla was pale, transfixed, staring at the scene in front of her.

After a short while, she seemed to realize Rose had addressed her, and chuckled. "Why should I care?" She sounded sincere.

For the first time, Darian glanced at her, but he looked relieved rather than hurt. Rose stepped beside him, holding a circular blade with a handle near his neck. "Oh, really?"

Karina thought it looked like a pizza wheel, and perhaps out of nervousness, she burst out laughing. When she stopped, she realized everyone stared at her as if she were an alien, which in a way she was, and she burst out laughing again. Rose now ran towards Karina, brandishing her pizza cutter. "What's so funny?"

The possibility of being cut into slices was definitely not funny. Rose advanced with fury, and Karina was about to run, when the strange circular weapon flew from Rose's hand. Nia then grabbed her, pointing her dagger to the woman's heart.

"Try anything and she dies," Nia said to the group, with a much more menacing voice than even Rose.

Karina covered her head in fear, because she thought someone would shoot them or at least try to fight them, but nothing happened, so perhaps Nia's trick worked.

"What for?" Jax asked, then gestured towards Darian. "Then he dies. We'll both run out of hostages. The difference is that we have more people. And more weapons."

"But you don't have a hostage!" Cayla said. "We're not on his side."

"And he is useful to you," Nia added. "Not a good deal."

"But he's our friend," Ayanna protested, for which she only received hard glances from her companions.

Nia pressed the knife on Rose's neck. "We're not your enemies. All we'll do is take her with us, and only because we need someone to pilot the lift."

Jax laughed. "Rose cannot pilot these either."

"Oh, but her sister can," Cayla said, then stared at Zayra. "So, will you have the pleasure of giving us a ride this time?"

Zayra looked down and didn't answer. She seemed to be crying.

"No!" Jax said, as if scared, addressing everyone, not just Zayra. "The lift is pulsing. Stay away."

Karina looked back and realized that indeed it was covered in flames. It reminded her of a marshmallow on a campfire. This time she didn't want to laugh. It wasn't funny to see what she thought was her way out as melted candy. And it seemed to be shaking or something, which explained the boy's fear.

"Everyone, run back," Jax ordered his companions.

Their agitation, together with the fear of an explosion, made Karina run faster than ever. Ayanna and Cayla also ran. Karina then heard the loudest noise behind her, and ducked to the ground, even though she wasn't sure if that was the right thing to do. Looking back, she saw that the lift had been blown into pieces. Nia was far behind them, standing, apparently unharmed, still holding Rose, who was in that weird open-eyed sleeping state.

"You said it didn't explode!" Karina yelled at her, upset.

"It never does. Never did. Until now at least," Nia said.

The rebels now ran back and encircled them. Karina ran towards Nia because the woman seemed capable of protecting them. Indeed she yelled, "Not one more step."

Her words produced the desired effect, as the people encircling them obeyed. She continued, "I'm warning you. I'll hurt her, unless you take us where we want to go."

"And where is that?" Jax asked.

"The valley below," she replied. "You won't gain anything by holding us."

"Can we stop this nonsense?" A voice was heard from beyond the circle. Darian stepped in, untied. "Why don't we just sit and talk?"

"You?" Jax was surprised. "You were our hostage. And we can't talk forever."

"We can't fight forever either," Darian replied. "Let's solve this."

"Fine," Jax replied. "Let's try it your way. For now." He stepped closer. The others watched from a distance.

Karina was surprised not only that Darian had freed himself, but that somehow, they listened to him.

Cayla was probably thinking something else, and yelled at her ex-friend or whatever, "You. False. Deceiving. Liar."

"I didn't mean to discuss your opinion of me," he replied, unfazed.

He didn't look or sound anything like the guy who had brought them food and sounded concerned on how to tell Cayla about his role in the rebellion. Karina wasn't sure where he stood. He'd been held as a hostage, so he couldn't have been responsible for their ambush, although they could all have pretended.

Darian addressed the other rebels, "I say the princesses come with us. As to the other two, they are no threat; we can let them go."

"You have to propose something I agree," Nia said.

"I'm not coming with you," Cayla told Darian.

"It's for your own good," Darian replied, addressing Cayla in a formal and cold way that was meant to be heard by everyone else. "We mean you no harm. Just comply, and we won't even touch a finger of yours."

Yikes. That finger part brought Karina bad memories. He must have said that on purpose.

"I'll never comply, so that's a terrible deal for me," Cayla said.

"That's the best we can propose," Darian replied. "You are outnumbered."

"I have her," Nia said, holding Rose.

"And while you hold her—or hurt her—you won't be able to fight," Darian replied.

"All I need is someone to take us to the valley," Nia said, still sounding menacing. "Then I'll let her go. And I want you to promise you won't harm any of us."

"As long as you don't oppose us we won't harm you," Darian said.

Now Jax intervened. "Wait. We didn't agree on that." He pointed at Nia. "She's dangerous."

"But she's not on the king's side," Darian replied.

"But she's with his daughters," Jax insisted.

Darian shook his head. "She's the former wife of the king. She had to flee. He's accusing her of being a witch."

Jax raised an eyebrow. "Wonder why."

"So what?" Nia yelled. "Lots of people have magical objects."

"What about the other one?" Jax pointed at Karina.

"Also running away. Same grounds. Harmless," Darian replied.

"Fine, then. We take only the princesses. And take these two to the valley." Jax then turned to Nia. "But you have to free Rose."

"No," Cayla yelled. "I'm not going with them."

"Cayla, please," Nia pleaded, then whispered. "I think he wants to keep you safe."

"I don't want to be kept by anyone," Cayla replied.

"I'll give you one minute to decide," Darian said.

Karina also thought that was a good proposal, but on the other hand knew that those people were capable of violence and cruelty, and she didn't really trust Darian. But she saw no other way. And plus, if Cayla didn't come with them, it would be much easier to negotiate with Lylah. She was about to plead with Cayla to accept their proposal when she heard a voice inside her head. "She has to come. It won't work without her." Karina then remembered that Cayla had the key to enter the castle, so they wouldn't be able to enter without her, unless, as they were going to negotiate, perhaps they could knock on the door? Or gate? But all she thought was that Cayla had to come with them.

"We have to stay together," Karina said. "I'm not leaving Cayla."

Nia stared at her, surprised.

"That means I'll take you three?" Darian asked.

"I'm not going," Cayla protested.

Darian ignored her and turned to Jax. "Well, we could leave her here. You know, there's no way out."

"How did they get here then?" Jax asked.

Darian only looked puzzled and shrugged.

"Take us four, then," Nia said. "But we have to go with him," she pointed to Darian, "because he was the one who promised we'd be safe."

"No way," Jax protested. "She'll go all evil on us with that dagger and free the princesses."

"That's not a bad proposal," Darian said.

"For a traitor," Jax replied. "You want to protect them, that's what you want. We should tie you again."

Darian offered his hands close together and shrugged. "If you think I'll be useful as a hostage, I don't mind."

Jax just crossed his arms.

Darian lowered his hands and said, "Look, your initial plan was to take the four of them. Here we go. We can take them. Without a fight."

Jax thought for a moment, then replied, "I guess you're right." He then turned to Nia. "Let Rose go."

"I'm not coming with you," Cayla protested, grabbing a twig from the floor. "You want me; you'll have to fight."

The girl didn't stand up, though, but rather fell on the floor. Nia had "air stabbed" her. Everyone looked surprised. Darian was still unfazed.

"Oh, she'll be up and fine in ten minutes," Nia said. "Let's go."

The rebels walked to the edge of the mountain, on the opposite side of where they had been, where three lifts were waiting for them. They agreed on having Karina and her friends on a lift with Darian, Jax, two other guys, two other girls Karina didn't know, and Zayra. At least Cayla was passed out and didn't know that she would have her as a travel companion. Travel. Where? This lift was even bigger than the previous one Karina had seen. Zayra went to the front, with the other girl. Karina and her friends were on the back with four people watching them. Or five, if one were to count Darian. Nia held Cayla, who leaned on her shoulder. None of their bags had been brought with them, as someone had decided to confiscate their things. A good thing the shoes were safe on Karina's waist. The lift took off.

Nia addressed everyone, "Listen, we are not on the king's side. You won't benefit from keeping us. Just leave us at the valley. We might even be able to help you."

"Why don't you two go," Darian said looking at Karina and Nia, "and leave them here?" He gestured towards Cayla and Ayanna.

"Are we going to change plans again?" Jax asked.

"If it's for the best, yes," Darian replied.

Nia whispered to Karina, "Why not?"

"Cayla needs to go too," Karina replied.

"Yes, it might be safer. But I thought you had a plan," Nia said, then looked at Darian's direction. "Or that he had a plan."

"I think his plan is to keep Cayla close by," Karina replied.

Nia looked down. "While they might take the castle." She then addressed Jax, "You're smart, you know?"

The comment was odd. He seemed surprised and was about to reply when Nia got up, pulled her dagger and air stabbed everyone except Darian, who looked astonished.

"What are you doing?"

"Going all evil with my dagger." She pointed to Jax. "It was his idea."

Darian seemed upset. "Stop it. You know I don't mean to hurt you. I'm even willing to help you go where you want to go. You know that."

Nia ignored him and banged on the door to the front. The noise called the girls' attention. Zayra opened the door and looked back. In less than a second, she and the other girl lay motionless.

"Great," Darian said. "Now I have to go to the front."

He carefully pushed Zayra out of her seat and sat there. Nia also went inside and sat in the middle. Karina and Ayanna stood at the door.

Nia turned to the younger girl. "Go back and hold your sister."

Ayanna looked disappointed but went to the back and sat by Cayla's side. Nia looked at Darian. "Now, will you take us to Lylah?"

The boy was exasperated. "Nia, I told you, that is reckless and useless, there's no point."

Nia pointed her dagger at him.

"That's stupid," he said. "Who's going to control this if I pass out?"

"I could just hurt you," Nia replied.

Darian didn't look upset. "I know you won't."

"Fine," Nia said, now holding her dagger close to Zayra, the way she had done to Rose. "What if I hurt her?"

"You wouldn't do that."

"I would. For my son," Nia replied.

"I'll do my best to make sure your son is unharmed," he said. "What's better than to check on me in person?"

"I still want to go to Lylah."

"As I said before, I'll take you there, or close to there."

Karina had to press her point. "Cayla needs to go too."

"No, she doesn't," he replied. "Why would she need to go on a pointless and dangerous mission?"

Nia pressed again her dagger on Zayra, who was unconscious. "I don't care about your opinion. I'll hurt her."

"Knock it off," he said. "You're not that kind of person."

"Let's see, then. And there are five more, in case I go too far."

She pressed her dagger on the girl's arm. A drop of blood dripped.

Darian looked upset. "Stop it."

"So she *is* important," Nia said.

"Just because I don't want her to be hurt?"

"And why did you defend her when we were fighting?"

"You just don't hit someone when they're already down," he said. "I understand Cayla was mad, but still."

"You know, you really have to make up your mind."

"What?" Darian seemed confused, then his eyes widened. "Stop it."

Nia narrowed her eyes. "Let's try something different. Cayla is about to wake up. Since you like to pretend to care about her—"

"Not pretend. We've been friends for a long time."

Nia sighed. "Well, since you care about her, why don't you try to take her side, and take her where she wants to go? This is your chance to redeem yourself."

"She's going to be upset either way. What's the difference? At least she won't be in danger." He looked down. "Like last time."

Karina was annoyed that the conversation wasn't leading anywhere, at least not anywhere near Lylah. But the mention of "last time" gave her an idea. She turned to Darian, "If you're only worried about Cayla's safety, why don't you come with us? That way you can protect her."

He listened.

Karina felt encouraged to continue. "So even if Cayla is upset at you, she'll know you never meant to betray her. And you'll get to spend time with her." Somehow that last part seemed to matter.

He looked down, thinking, then replied, "But they'll see we're straying from our regular path. We might bring attention to us. It could be someone still loyal to the king."

Karina thought that was just an excuse, and argued, "Perhaps you could leave your lift far away, or something, not to draw attention."

He stroked his non-existent beard, then looked back. "But then they'll know I protected her."

Nia rolled her eyes. "As if nobody noticed. But I'm sure you can come up with something. I take back what I said; you're an excellent liar."

He looked down, embarrassed, thinking, or both. The silence was the perfect opportunity for Karina to ask Nia a non-related question she was too curious to hold, "How do you know how long they'll sleep? Do you have a timer or something?"

Nia was surprised at the question. She thought for a moment, then answered, "No. I just, when I stab them, from a distance, I know. If I have to do it too fast, I only knock them out for a couple minutes, though."

Darian snorted. "Some magical object you have there. To bring down all the people you did, in a matter of seconds. Of course, it must take a lot of practice."

Nia looked down, which was odd for her. "No. I had never used it before. I didn't even know it could do this."

Karina was astonished. "What about the guards?"

Nia shook her head. "That was different."

Darian was also astonished. "You're saying you had no practice? Can you imagine what you could do with if you did?"

Nia snorted. "Maybe I don't want to imagine that." She faced Darian. "Now, will you take us to Lylah's castle?"

He sighed. "If that's what she wants..." He looked at his sleeping companions. "I'll leave them at the mountain, then we'll go. But I'm coming with you." He looked back where Cayla was. "Regardless of what she says."

Karina smiled. "Thank you."

The lift indeed changed course. Karina felt relieved, and happy that her idea had worked. Karina looked back and noticed that Cayla slept on the side couch, and so did Ayanna, who must have been tired, since they hadn't slept much.

Nia looked back, then turned to Darian. "She's going to wake up soon, and I have to ask you something." She then narrowed her eyes and observed him. "Why did you come to the mountain last night?"

"To help Cayla. And you all."

She still looked at him attentively. "It wasn't to lead the rebels then?"

"Why would I climb? I could have gotten there much faster."

"I have no proof you climbed," Nia said. "I don't mean to judge you, I understand this, uh, cause, means a lot to you. And that you think you can keep us all safe."

"No," he sounded offended. "I have no idea how they came, or how they knew where you were. I didn't tell anyone, and I took a lot of care not to be followed."

"How did they find us then?"

"I don't know." He stopped for a moment, then continued, "Unless, either someone heard me, but, I took a lot of care, or they put something on my things, to locate me. But again, I checked everything. Or else they knew how to locate you. I wasn't involved in any of this. Didn't you see I was tied? That Rose threatened to hurt me?"

Nia laughed. "That was fake, wasn't it?"

He shook his head. "It wasn't. Rose was furious."

"How did you escape then?"

He looked down, then glanced towards Zayra. "She untied me."

Nia narrowed her eyes looking at the girl, then at him.

Darian continued, "She was afraid they'd hurt me." As Nia kept her probing expression, he looked defensive. "It's not at all what you're thinking."

She looked puzzled. "You don't even know what I'm thinking.

But let me ask, then. So she freed you, then you just walked out telling everyone what to do?"

"You took down Rose. She was the problem. And I didn't tell anyone what to do, I just tried to mediate things, and luckily it worked out."

Nia rolled her eyes. "Listen, I can see you care and worry about Cayla. But, see, she's like a daughter to me—"

"I know, that's why I talked to you."

"Well, what if you're such a good friend to her, you know, just because of who she is?"

"Of course it's because of who she is."

Nia stared at him, jaw dropped.

He seemed puzzled for a second, then looked disgusted. "Oh, Nia please. You mean because she's her father's daughter? I didn't mean that, I meant the person she is. That has nothing to do with where she lives or who her parents are. You know, you're sounding just like her father. What are you going to do? Forbid me to ever see her?"

"No, but I can talk to her." Nia sat sideways, winked at Karina then said, "Still... Cayla, I love her, but she can be a little, uh, fierce, and, somewhat rough on the edges, if you know what I mean. And I don't see her treating you very well. So, well, I wonder why you care about her."

The boy seemed furious, and Karina wondered if, so close to landing, it was a good time to annoy him.

But Darian kept looking straight ahead as he replied, "Do you even know her? Really? If you did, you'd know her rough edges, as you're saying, are just on the outside. And what's wrong if she's fierce? What's the problem? I can deal with that. And you have no right to judge how she treats me, because you don't even know it."

Nia chuckled, which was weird.

Darian frowned. "I don't think I said anything funny."

Nia became serious. "No. Sorry. Just get us on the ground, then you can look behind you."

"What?" he said, then turned back.

Karina also looked. Cayla stood near the door, strangely silent, almost beside Karina. Darian was paralyzed for a moment.

"Watch out!" Nia yelled.

The lift hit the ground with a loud noise and tilted. Karina lost balance and almost fell. Why did Nia upset him right when they were about to reach the ground? Why?

Nia turned to Darian, "I told you not to look."

SIAN TURNED OFF THE COMM. Found him—his brother. Quite confusing account, frankly. Still, the girls were with his brother, on their way to the insurgents not-so-secret hideout. Trying to take the girls from the insurgents would be foolish—and needless. There were bigger pieces about to be moved. It was time to prepare for the final strike. His curiosity would have to wait.

17

TIME TO TURN AROUND

Cayla felt dizzy. From the crash, from having passed out, from so much information she didn't quite understand. Darian walked to the back to open the door and passed her without meeting her eyes.

Ayanna came to the front, rubbing her eyes. "What happened? Did we crash?"

"No. Just a bad landing," Nia replied.

Cayla asked Nia, "Where are we going?"

"To Lylah's castle," Nia replied.

Cayla exhaled in relief while looking at the sleeping bodies of the people who'd wanted to imprison them. Maybe she'd been wrong, and Darian had been on her side, but he seemed to be on their side as well.

She turned to Nia. "He'll drop us off?"

"He's coming with us."

Coming with us? No. That had not been the plan. Nia got up and went to the back, where Darian and Karina were carrying some people out. Cayla noticed a person on the pilot seat and all her anger against Darian boiled up again. Still, she helped them carry a couple people outside, landing them carefully on the grass, even if they didn't deserve any decent treatment.

Without any enemies on the lift, they were ready to take off.

Nia put her hand on her shoulder. "Cayla, go to the front, so you can learn a little how to pilot this. It could be useful."

Still somewhat dizzy and confused, Cayla found herself in the front compartment. Alone with Darian. The first time in such a long time. Her heart was racing and she had trouble breathing, but she tried not to think about it. He'd been with those people— on their side—and her stupid heart would have to shut up.

He looked at her as if waiting for a reaction. Afraid? Curious? Unsure?

She stepped away from him. "For the record, I changed my mind about what I told you last night." She looked away. "No infinite nothing."

He sighed. "I figured."

"I just wanted to make sure, you know? No misunderstanding."

He shook his head. "None."

So that was it? It wasn't as if he cared.

He said, "You need a hand."

"What?"

He pressed his hand on the right top corner of the panel. "For the lift to fly. You need someone authorized."

The panel lit up. It annoyed her to know that they would never have taken off without him.

He continued, "The person needs to be alive, but could be sleeping, and not everyone is authorized for every lift."

"How can you turn this one on?"

"I have authorization for every lift in the army." He looked down. "My father."

She sighed. "Darian, I need to know. Whose side are you on?"

"Your side."

"Are you saying you support my father? That you were just pretending?"

He looked away, sighed, then looked directly at her. "It's more complicated than that. I have to play both sides. But I always consider you. I do think about the wellbeing of the kingdom, Cayla, and your wellbeing as well. Always." His eyes had been locked in hers, open. He then stared ahead, while the lift took off, distancing itself from the summit.

His words and the way he'd said them put her at ease. She trusted him. But there was one thing still bothering her. "Why did you defend her?"

"Zayra? You were going to kick her face. She was already down."

"I wasn't. What do you think I am? And we were fighting."

"You're a better fighter, Cayla."

"So you had to protect her precious pretty face. Nice."

He glanced at her, then back ahead. He had a little smile on his face. A smile? Cayla wanted to punch him.

He glanced at her again. "Are you..." A pause. Another smile. "...jealous?"

Cayla looked away. "What a stupid question."

"Was that the problem that night?" Darian scoffed. "Were you jealous of Zayra?"

Laughing. He was laughing! A pity he was piloting because she really did want to punch him. "You're so hilarious."

Darian shook his head. "No, you are. That's the most ridiculous thing I've ever heard."

"You're the one who said it! No wonder it's ridiculous."

"Ridiculous and absurd."

"Absurd, right? It's not as if I had been locked in the castle, while you were flying around and living wonderful adventures with your pretty partner."

He frowned. "She's not pretty. What about you? Going to balls in the castle. Having a prince after you. I never, ever, ever thought anything about it. Ever."

"Well, the Arlenia prince is creepy and old, that's easy."

"He's nineteen. That's not old!"

"He's not like..." What was she even going to say? She lost her thought. And she was wasting time with stupid things when the most important mission in her life was ahead of her. "You're going to drop me off and let me do what I have to do, right?"

"Yes, but I'm coming with you."

That was terrible. He'd mess up everything. "Then I'll just ask Nia to make you sleep."

"I made a deal with her. She won't go back on her word."

"Make a deal with me then." Cayla pleaded. "If you care about what I think."

"I care more about your safety than your opinion." That tone again.

"Right. So you can tell me what to do."

"I'm not telling you what to do," he said. "I'm deciding what *I'm* going to do. It's different, you know?"

"But that's not what I want. I need to do this alone."

"Your sister, Nia, and the random girl there can go. What's the difference?"

Cayla was starting to feel impatient. "I can't explain it. You have to trust me. Don't you also have important stuff to do? For the kingdom? Well, me too!"

He stared at her, looked down, then looked away, as if thinking. "I can't let anything happen to you."

"You know I can defend myself, right?"

"That depends against how many."

She sighed. "It's not like you can take an army all by yourself either."

He shook his head. "Fighting, no. But I can talk to them."

Cayla rolled her eyes. "Impressive."

She looked away, decided to remain silent and distant. Maybe he'd get a clue. And then maybe not.

After some time, he said, "Lots of people are looking for you, rebel and loyal. That's why I can't just leave you."

"They want me as a hostage, Darian. If you're so good at talking, come and talk to them if I'm caught. You can't force your company when I don't want it."

He had a grimace. "I'm not *forcing...*"

Cayla stared.

He looked away, then back at her. "You'll need to promise you'll hide. And you'll contact me after you do whatever you want to do. And if it doesn't work, you'll hide in the woods."

"I don't need to promise anything, Darian. Stop doing that. I don't like it you when you try to tell me what to do. I trust you and you need to trust me—"

"But last time—"

"Was your fault. You exposed me to these insurgents, and you didn't tell me anything about them. You trusted someone you knew was conspiring against my father. You trusted her. Think about it. Let me take care of what I have to do, and take care of what you have to do."

"I should. You have no idea what I've..." He closed his eyes as if in pain. "You're right. There are things I put off for too long. Too long, Cayla. I need to fix this. But please—I'm asking—please contact me if you have any problem. And hide."

He sounded sweet again, and she felt bad for the way she'd spoken to him. She put her hand on his shoulder. "I know you worry because you care, but you can't cage me to protect me. Let me live my destiny, whatever it is."

He held her hand and closed his eyes, then opened them and looked at her. Her heart beat faster.

"I'll drop you off at the river." His tone was resigned and unhappy. He kissed her wrist, then let it go, and looked ahead.

Shivers ran down her spine as if his kiss had electricity. But the important thing was her task again. Cayla just smiled. "Thank you."

He smiled back, then looked ahead and focused, as if thoughtful. Other than glancing at her from time to time, it was as if he was concentrating before doing something difficult.

The lift stopped moving. Darian turned to her. "Please be safe."

He then opened the middle door and addressed everyone. "We're floating above the river. You'll all have to jump. Quickly, before anyone notices where I am."

Darian opened the hatch.

JUMP? Karina hadn't been prepared for that. She wondered how he had changed his mind. Or how Cayla had changed his mind. Although, now that she thought about it, perhaps she knew how. And indeed this was a lot safer than leaving the lift and walking near it.

Nia went first, then Ayanna. At least Karina wasn't afraid of falling since she was supposed to jump anyways. She made sure the shoes where well tied, gathered her courage, and jumped. The river was warm, but just warm enough that the water was still refreshing. The moon was now less than a semicircle down in the sky, about to hide behind mountains. Cayla jumped a few seconds afterwards, splashing Karina. The island with the castle was further up, and they started swimming. Hopefully Lylah would have some kind of expressway to take Karina back home, assuming of course that she would help her go home, assuming that they'd be able to get into her castle, that she would be alive and that she would even be helpful. But none of those thoughts made Karina ever question her need to go forward, for the simple reason that she had no other choice.

Even in the dark, they could see that the island had white

sand, not the color of sand, but rather white like salt or sugar, even shiny like them, very much like the castle itself. There were indeed no walls around it, and in fact no fortification of any kind. There was something strange about it. Even from such a close distance it didn't look real. Perhaps it was just a detail that Karina took a while to catch: it had no windows, and from the side they looked, no doors. Cayla swam ahead, and dove from time to time.

"What is she doing?" Nia asked Karina.

Only then she remembered that Nia didn't know everything about their plan. "There's an underwater passage," she explained.

Nia dove and came out. "It's too dark."

Beyond the farthest mountain the sky started to become blue, meaning that the sun would soon be up, and they'd soon be able to find what they were meant to find. But no. Karina remembered what Odell told them. "We were supposed to come to the river at night."

"Night?" Nia asked, thinking. "It must have some kind of light. We'll have to find the passage before the sun rises."

Karina looked at that beach and realized they were wasting time. "It's not here, but over there," she said, pointing to the other side of the island.

"Why are you saying that?" Cayla asked.

"The river is too shallow here. A passage would need a steeper slope."

"I'll look over there," Cayla said. She then started to swim around the island.

Nia and Ayanna followed her. Karina lagged behind because she was a lousy swimmer. When she reached the other side of the island, the others were diving. This side was indeed better suited for a passage as there were rocks instead of a beach.

"Nia, come here," Cayla said.

The woman swam in her direction and dove with her. As they came out of the water, Nia said, "She found it."

Time to face Lylah. Karina felt a knot in her stomach. Or was it hunger?

"Karina!" Cayla yelled, as if to hurry her.

Oh, she'd better hurry, or they'd leave her behind. Actually no, she still had the shoes, so they wouldn't go in without her. One thing she would certainly miss was the sense of importance.

When Karina reached the others, Cayla turned to Nia and Ayanna. "You wait here. I'll go in with Karina. She'll throw the shoes, and we'll be back."

Karina feared she would be forced to throw the shoes, and that wasn't exactly what she had been planning. Not that she had been planning much.

"No," Nia said. "You don't know what's waiting for us. We all go in." She glanced at Karina. "Then we'll see what we'll do."

"But—" Cayla started to protest.

Nia interrupted her, "If things go wrong, you may need me. Also, if I was supposed to guide you, I'll do it till the end."

Nia then dove as if meaning to enter the passage.

"Wait," Cayla said, then quickly turned to the others. "Follow me."

She dove fast, followed by her sister, then Karina. In those dark waters, she saw Ayanna entering a circle near the bottom which had a faint glimmer around it. It looked like it went down, not up, and that wasn't how she expected an underwater tunnel to go. She wondered how long it was and if she would be able to hold her breath for all its length, but she didn't have the opportunity to voice any of these concerns, because the girls had disappeared inside it and she didn't want to be left behind. The tunnel was circular, made out of that same shiny white material she'd seen around the stairs. It went down then curved and started going up, like a sink siphon. Karina almost ran out of air, but not quite, as she came out in a small artificial pond in a circular tall room in that same white stone. The others were already out of the water, and Karina followed. There was a fireplace lit at the back of the room. Now it would be time for the truth, as the girls would know she was siding with Lylah if she did not throw the shoes. The only piece of furniture was a very large square table with places for eight people. There was food at the table; fruit, some kind of bread and even scrambled eggs, or at least something that looked like it. Breakfast. At that moment, Karina thought she really liked Lylah.

Cayla approached Karina and whispered, "We need to find the fire."

"I know," she replied, because that was the only thing she could reply.

But that didn't make any sense. The fire was right in front of them. Could it be that Karina was the only one to see it? She wondered if anyone else would mention it. She turned back to glance at the water and didn't see anything. No pool, no opening of any kind. Was their exit blocked?

18

TRUTHS AND LIES

Would there be a door somewhere? Perhaps the food at the table meant they were prisoners. Not that again. Who would save them this time? But then, perhaps they could just go out the way they'd come, even though it wasn't visible.

"I'm hungry," Ayanna said.

Karina agreed, but she wasn't sure what to do.

Nia smiled. "Let's eat then."

Cayla stepped in front of her sister and squinted. "Are you crazy?"

"No. Hungry."

"It must be poisoned," Cayla protested.

Nia glanced at the table. "Too much trouble. There are much easier ways to kill someone. Trust me."

Her "trust me" was rather scary.

"Still, it has to be a trap," Cayla insisted.

"We're in her castle, with no way out."

"No." Cayla said, then turned around and pointed to the place where the little pool was. "Where is it?"

Nia shook her head. "It is gone. Now, if she wants us dead, there isn't much we can do. I'm eating with your sister."

She sat and so did Ayanna, who looked at her sister as if feeling guilty. Karina almost sat as well, but she didn't want to upset Cayla. The girl walked around as if searching for something before turning to Karina. "We have to do something."

The smell of food made Karina even hungrier. She looked around, seeing only smooth walls—and a fireplace. But she didn't want to think about that. "Do you see any door?"

Cayla shook her head, then said, "You might be able to do something. You have the key."

That didn't make sense. "No. You have the key."

"No," Cayla replied. "It was destroyed when the door opened. And I meant something different."

The girl glanced at Karina's waist. Of course. The shoes. But what could she do? Did the girl see the fire? It could not be, as she would have mentioned it. Nia and Ayanna were eating now, and none of them had dropped dead on the floor. All Karina could think was sitting with them and doing the same. Could it be dangerous? But that smell... And Nia seemed to know what she was talking about. Karina sighed. "I'm going to eat."

Cayla tried to hold her. "You can't. No. That's what she wants."

"I'm sorry."

Karina sat with Nia and Ayanna and filled a plate with bread and fruit. There was a jug with tea, but it was cold, and Karina filled a cup, because she was thirsty. When she drank it, she spat it out; it was water.

"It's from the river," Nia said. "It's brown but it's clean. It's just the plants."

Karina drank the water. Black River. Right.

Cayla still walked around touching the walls as if to look for a secret passage.

Nia noticed, then said, "Come eat. Forget it, there are no doors."

"I'm not eating. Who knows what's in this food? Maybe it'll make us obey her, turn against our against each other, sleep, or, who knows?"

"You should trust me. If I'm saying this food is safe, it's because it is."

Cayla sat at the table. "Why then? Why this? Why would she want us to eat?"

Nia shrugged. "Maybe she wants to be friendly?"

"Exactly," Cayla replied. "Then she'll convince us to give her whatever she wants from us. She's going to try to take... you know."

"And if we don't eat, she won't try to take anything back," Nia said.

Ayanna pointed at the food. "This is good. You should try it."

Cayla just looked sullen and glanced at the fruit from time to time. When the others were about finished, the girl plucked a few weird looking grapes and ate them. Karina looked around and realized that the place looked like her previous prison, except that it was white instead of yellow. She then thought that eating hadn't been the brightest idea, but that was easier said with a full belly.

"What now?" Cayla asked, plucking some pieces of bread without looking at them.

"We wait," Nia replied.

For what? Was Nia still considering siding with Lylah? Karina wondered if it had been a good idea not to tell the girls anything. Cayla never took a plate, she just plucked pieces of food and put in her mouth as if not looking at them could prevent any poisoning. At least, if there was something wrong with the food, they would be all doomed together. Having company in disgrace, that was a good consolation.

After they all ate, they remained sitting in silence for a short while, when they heard a voice coming from the direction where the little pool had been. "I hope it was to your taste."

They turned to look. There was Lylah, walking in their direction, as if she'd always been there. She looked as impressive as she had looked in Karina's room, with very shiny black hair, dressed in white. A shiver ran down Karina's spine, as she felt certain that the woman would ask for her shoes.

Cayla got up, but Nia held her by her arms. "You cannot fight her."

Cayla pulled her arm but sat down.

Lylah also sat down and looked at Nia. "Thank you." Then she addressed everyone. "I understand you had a tough journey here, and I congratulate you on your determination," she turned to Nia and Karina, "and sacrifices."

The woman's behavior was weird, as she seemed happy they were there. Perhaps this was indeed a trap. The question was for what.

The woman looked at them all. "I apologize if some of you had to be..." she paused and looked sideways before continuing. "Deceived. I had no other way to bring you here."

Cayla squinted. "Bring us here?"

"Listen," Nia whispered to her.

Karina was also wondering the same thing. Was it for the shoes? But then, why so much trouble? Was there a rule that they needed to be home delivered or something? Again she feared giving up her unique objects.

She hoped nobody else interrupted Lylah again, because she took a long time to continue talking. "You might be wondering then... why Odell sent you. Look at this place. This is not a castle, not a home."

Karina did look around, and then the woman confirmed her impression. "It's a prison. And a very strong one."

Great, so they were in fact all locked up.

Lylah continued, "Only two people can open it. Or their descendants."

"What do you want from us?" Cayla interrupted.

Lylah sat back in silence.

Cayla was impatient, and added, "You want something from us. I get that. Just tell us what it is." Then she whispered to Karina, "We can pretend to help her, then find a way to do it."

By "it" she probably meant destroy the shoes. Lylah stared at them for a long time. Maybe she wanted to annoy them.

The woman turned to the older princess. "Cayla, what do you know about your mother?"

"Less than you, I suppose."

Lylah nodded. "Very true. Do you understand that mothers sometimes have to make sacrifices? Look at Nia. You don't suppose she doesn't love her son, do you?"

"What do you care about my little brother?"

Cayla was fearless and provoking, and Karina wondered if that was a good way to address a witch in her own castle. Or prison, but still. The others were quiet. Ayanna seemed to pay a lot of attention to what was said.

Lylah sat back and closed her eyes. "I also have a little brother. I saw him grow up. I even took care of him. I love him almost like a son."

Cayla shrugged. "Why should I care about your brother?"

"Because you care."

Cayla seemed surprised at first, then thoughtful. "Do you mean... Darian?"

Lylah shook her head. "Not him."

"Then I don't know, and I don't care."

Lylah glanced at Nia, then said, "Your stepmother knows. "

Nia shook her head. "I'm not her stepmother. At least not anymore."

Cayla turned to Nia. "Who's her brother?"

Nia shrugged. "I don't know. It... it can't be."

"It's exactly who you're thinking," Lylah said.

Everyone looked at Nia. She looked unsure. "He's too old."

Lylah shook her head. "It's make-up. He pretends. He was a teenager when he joined the king."

"As a wise man?" Nia asked, incredulous.

Lylah nodded.

"Who is it?" Cayla asked.

"Odell," Nia replied.

Karina was stunned. She hadn't expected that, as much as she sometimes thought the bald man had been pretending.

"How come you never told us?" Cayla asked.

"I had no idea they were siblings," Nia said. "It occurred to me now. But I always told you he was working with her."

Cayla had tears in her eyes, and asked Nia, "Why did you come then? Why did you follow his directions?"

"Did I have a choice?"

Cayla looked down.

Lylah addressed Nia, "I know why you came, and I will do everything I can to protect your son. I'm grateful to you."

"We'd better move then," Nia said. "There is talk of an attack on the castle."

"Nia!" Cayla protested. "Are you going to turn against us?"

"I'm not against you," Nia replied. "One day you'll understand."

"I was hoping this would be the day," Lylah said, then turned to Cayla. "Have you ever considered that most of what you heard in your life were lies?"

"Now I'm hearing lies," Cayla said. "You're saying Odell's your brother, but that can't be. He's always helped us. I trust him. He'd never be against us."

"But he's not," Lylah said. "Why do you think he disguised himself for sixteen years?"

"It doesn't make any sense," Cayla replied.

"To protect you," Lylah said.

"You are lying."

Lylah was still calm. "Don't you trust Nia?"

"She's paranoid."

"Paranoid against your father, you mean," Lylah replied. "Could it be because he's threatened her with death? Have you ever wondered what happened to your sister's mother? Or your mother?"

Cayla got up and pointed her finger towards Lylah. "Don't you dare mention my mother."

Karina remembered what the girl had told her and felt guilty and sad.

Lylah closed her eyes and sighed. "Nia's right. Time's running out. I'll tell you what I want from you; then I'll explain why."

"We'll never help you!" Cayla said.

Nia grabbed the girl's arm, and sounded stern, "First you listen, then you say whatever you want to say."

Cayla pulled back her arm but remained quiet.

Lylah continued, "As you noticed, this is a prison, and the tunnel from where you came is gone. I need you to free me and free yourselves. There are two people who can free me. Either the person who built this castle, or the last person who locked it, and left me here, thinking he defeated me." Lylah looked down, took a deep breath, then continued, "I happen to be the one who built it, but I cannot free myself; I could only open the passage to other dimensions." She turned to Karina. "And that's how I came to your world." She then turned to everyone else, "And how I didn't die. The other person who can free me is the king. He locked me here. Unlike you might have heard, I have no army, and no assistants, except my brother. All I want is freedom, to be reunited with my family, and to help restore peace to the kingdom."

Cayla slammed her hand on the table. "You do want to take power!"

"Not necessarily. There are other people already fighting this war. I had to wait until you were old enough so that you'd come on your own free will." That last part seemed to be addressed at Cayla. "But now I can help them."

"You tricked us," Cayla protested. "You and Odell."

Lylah stared attentively at the girl. "Not really. You came to bring peace to your kingdom. That's what I plan to do."

"By force!"

"Listen," Lylah's voice was lower pitched, "I need either my daughter, or the daughter of the king, to open a door behind me. If you walk close to the wall, you will see it. This way we'll all be free."

Karina didn't see any door, but on the other hand, she was the only one to see the fire, so perhaps that prison offered a custom view for each of them.

"You're lying," Cayla said. "And I won't free you. I'd rather spend the rest of my life here."

Karina began to wonder how the rest of her life would be then. She hoped at least that Lylah would bring them some nice food from time to time. Not that it made up for losing her freedom, her life, her youth. Ugh, Karina didn't want to consider staying in that place.

But it was Nia who protested, "Cayla, my son!"

"Don't you see?" Cayla insisted. "He's safer if she's locked."

"You are the one who's not seeing it," Nia said. "Can't you see who she is? Because I can. Perhaps it's just that you can't look at yourself."

Cayla squinted. "What?"

To be fair, Karina had a similar mental reaction. Nia wasn't usually that enigmatic.

Lylah waited for a while, then continued to address Cayla, "In time, I'll tell you everything. For now, I need you to trust me. Cayla..." The woman paused mid-sentence, open mouthed, as if considering how to say something important. "Odell, you know how much he cares about you.

I hope you trust him, and you should, because of all he's done for you."

"He's a liar." Cayla sounded sad.

Lylah shook her head. "He only did what he did to protect you. Odell..." Lylah looked down and took a deep breath, then faced Cayla, "...is your uncle."

That was underwhelming. With all that suspense and emotion, Karina was expecting some big revelation, expecting perhaps Odell to be the girl's father or something more dramatic.

Cayla for her part laughed. "You just said he was your brother. Your lies don't even make sense anymore."

Lylah fell silent. Nia also looked down. How could Odell be Lylah's brother and Cayla's uncle at the same time? Then it hit her. Oh, it was obvious. The first time Karina saw Cayla, she'd reminded her of Lylah, and, now that the two were together, the similarity was there, although not obvious.

Lylah continued, "Cayla, all these years, I've been waiting to see you. I could not come to you, and I could not let you know anything that could endanger you, but I never forgot—"

"Forgot what? How you killed my mother?"

Karina covered her face with her hands. Lylah stared at the girl in silence.

Nia held Cayla's hand and said softly, "Cayla, dear." She pointed to Lylah. "She *is* your mother."

Karina had guessed as much. But still, to hear it like that was somewhat shocking.

Cayla was still upset, looking incredulous and hurt. Tears ran from her eyes and she said, "Even if it's true. You don't expect me to come here and simply free you. Now. After an entire life."

Lylah just looked in silence.

Nia addressed Cayla, "She couldn't. Don't you understand?"

Lylah looked nowhere while tears ran down her cheeks.

Ayanna walked close to her and asked, "And do you know what happened to my mother?"

More and more tears ran down Lylah's eyes. "I'm so sorry. I tried. Odell really tried. He could not save her. He was too late."

"What happened? I'd rather hear it," Ayanna said.

"She tried to run away. With you. But the king caught her. I'm sorry, I'm so sorry. My brother could never forgive himself. At least he tried to give you the love your mother couldn't give. I know it's not the same."

Ayanna shook her head. "I'm sure he did his best. He's always been there for us."

Lylah had a half smile.

The younger princess then asked, "You need the king's daughter to free you? Can that be me?"

Lylah seemed surprised, then nodded. "Yes, it could."

Ayanna pointed behind Lylah. "And all I have to do is open that door?"

Again Lylah nodded.

"Ayanna, don't!" Cayla pleaded.

Ayanna turned to her sister. "Sorry, but I'm not going to spend the rest of my life here."

Karina, who was following their conversation, still didn't see any door. And the shoes hadn't been mentioned yet. Karina felt safe to assume they had been forgotten, and she was thrilled. Somehow, she'd never felt comfortable about giving or destroying them.

Ayanna walked to the back of the room, right beside the fire. "This?"

"I can't see it," Lylah said. "But if you see a door, that must be it."

Cayla watched in silence. Her sister moved her arms, as if opening an invisible door, but no real door appeared. In fact, nothing happened.

Ayanna turned to Lylah. "And what now?"

Lylah looked puzzled. "It should... Unless..." She looked at Ayanna. "But you saw the door, right?"

"It was here," the girl replied, then pointed and looked. "But… not anymore."

Could it be that Lylah had made a mistake? That was what it seemed. Apparently, something should have happened when Ayanna "opened" the door, but it didn't. The woman's expression worried Karina more than anything. This time she feared they would be locked there forever. A thunderous rumbling put an end to her worries. Lylah looked relieved, but just for a second. Her expression became grim. The floor and walls trembled. At first, Karina feared the whole place would collapse on them, but since she didn't see anything falling, she decided to look. The place wasn't collapsing, but instead closing on them. Walls were getting closer together, the ceiling was coming down, and the floor was coming up. If that movement didn't stop, they would all be crushed in a minute. Maybe much less, but Karina didn't want to calculate that.

Lylah yelled something, but, with all the noise, Karina couldn't hear it. The woman had her arms spread out and gestured for the others to come under, as if she were to protect them, but she still looked troubled and afraid. Karina had known Lylah for a short while, but long enough to realize that she wouldn't be scared of something silly. Karina was about to run to the woman when she saw the fire. Instead of bigger, it got smaller and smaller even though the wall moved forward. It was about to disappear.

Nia came close to Karina and yelled, "The shoes, use them! Or give them to Lylah!"

Karina realized all their lives were in her hands. Or waist. Karina had to think faster than she had ever thought in her life. Did the shoes contain Lylah's power? If they did, why would their destruction harm her? If the shoes had any power, it would, in fact, be released. If Karina's logic made any sense. Karina then remembered Zoe's strange accident, and her own infatuation with the shoes. She also remembered Nia saying that the shoes would bind her. Karina had been bound for a long time. Too long. Lylah gestured for Karina. She wanted the shoes. The shoes. The power was in the shoes. Lylah's power. In a fraction of a second Karina made her decision. She untied the shoes from her waist, and instead of giving them to Lylah or trying to use them, she tossed them on the dwindling flame.

19

GOING SEPARATE WAYS

Something happened all right, because the noise increased, and the floor trembled even more. Karina fell down. The walls started to crack, and she thought they were about to crumble upon them for real this time. More than ever she regretted having left her bedroom and having to make decisions about things she didn't understand. What a terrible way to die: for a stupid mistake.

But soon Karina realized that although the ceiling was collapsing, no piece hit her. In fact, no part of the ceiling or wall reached the ground, as they disappeared mid-fall. As the ceiling opened, Karina could see the blue sky with a few clouds. After much trembling and noise, the castle, or rather, prison, disappeared. They all sat on muddy sand. Regular, beige sand, on the island in the river. The rest of the food lay on the floor, likely meaning that it had been real. Good to know that she hadn't eaten disappearing magical stuff. Everyone was alive, as they were moving, getting up from having fallen on the trembling floor.

Lylah walked to Karina and put a hand on her shoulder,

"How did you know? How did you know you had to throw the shoes?"

Karina was flushed. "It's just... I guess shoes should never be that important."

Lylah smiled. Karina was glad to have made the right decision. She was trembling, perhaps because she learned that the danger had in fact been real.

Cayla was getting up, when she said, "Something's coming."

Nia looked around, not seeming to have heard anything. "Should we hide?"

"No time," Lylah said, "but I doubt we'll see more than four lifts at once. I can handle them."

Either she was indeed all-powerful or she was quite presumptuous. Karina hoped for the first possibility.

"There are two lifts," Cayla said. "Maybe they are friends?"

A few seconds after, a lift appeared in the sky, above the mountains, then a second one. Something like a cannon pointed at them from the top of the first lift. Karina didn't remember lifts having weapons, or perhaps she simply didn't know. A huge ball of blue fire came in their direction. Her guess was that they weren't friendly. Karina considered jumping on the ground or the river, but before she did anything, the ball turned around, split in two, and hit both lifts, which fell on the valley.

"They'll survive," Lylah said.

One thing Karina noticed was that the lifts fell but didn't explode.

"More of them are coming," Lylah said. "We have to teleport somewhere away from here. I can do it, but only one at a time."

She turned to Ayanna, held her hand, then disappeared. In a matter of seconds Lylah was back alone. She then grabbed Karina's hand. The girl felt a now familiar feeling of falling, then found herself beside Ayanna, near the summit from the previous night, but beneath some trees. Lylah soon came with Nia, then disappeared. Some more time then passed, something like one or two minutes, before Lylah showed up with Cayla, who then sat on a rock and looked down. Lylah closed her eyes and kept them closed for a long time.

Karina didn't feel comfortable at that place, although it was unlikely that anyone would do anything to them with Nia and Lylah there. She felt a little sad and empty without the shoes, knowing that her mission was over and that she would no longer be important. At least she was still alive, so no regrets there.

Lylah looked down, thinking, then looked distraught, as if in pain. She looked at one of her bracelets. A red stone shone brightly.

"What's wrong?" Ayanna asked.

"Odell," Lylah replied. "He's in danger."

Nia grabbed the woman's hands. "My son. We have to go. Please take me there."

"It's not as simple," Lylah said.

"Please, just teleport me there. I know you can. Let me do something for my son. I've done a lot for Cayla."

Lylah closed her eyes for a moment, then said, "I'll come with you." She then turned to the girls. "Stay here and wait. I'll come back."

Nia looked worried. "Isn't it dangerous to leave them here?"

"No," Lylah replied. "And they can teleport if they are only two."

Karina didn't understand that, but maybe it had something to do with Cayla being her daughter.

"Actually, I'll take Ayanna as well," Lylah said. "I know a safe place for her. Come."

The dark-haired woman soon disappeared with Ayanna, then came back and disappeared with Nia, who still looked worried but did not protest. Karina wasn't upset at being left behind because she figured going to the castle would have been dangerous. Plus, that way she could keep Cayla company.

The girl sat down on the floor and plucked leaves of grass, looking sad.

Karina crouched beside her. "I know this may be difficult for you, but maybe you should give Lylah a chance. Just hear what she has to say. Maybe... talk to Odell. Perhaps, you know, you might see things differently."

Cayla shook her head. "It's not even that. I mean, it is, but... Either way you look at it, it's disturbing. Even if it's true that she's my mother, and that Odell is my uncle, it means I've been lied to my whole life. My whole life. It means there isn't a single person who hasn't been lying to me."

Karina looked down, then tried to come up with something to cheer her up. "I don't think Ayanna ever lied to you."

Cayla got up and gesticulated her arms. "Cause she's just a child! In the same situation as me. Or slightly better. You know, cause there's no chance her mother might be evil and take the kingdom. Because of me! It's all my fault. Trust me; I sure hope she isn't evil." She looked down. "But then, my father..."

Karina put her hand on her friend's shoulder. She had no idea what to say.

Cayla looked around. "I think we can see the castle from the other side. Let's look."

They walked to the other side of the summit. They could see an ocean of clouds, a valley with lakes, some hills, and, far away, a river. Karina couldn't see the castle, and it made sense, because it was so close to the hills by the river. But there was something she saw: fire near the river, like the fireballs and the fire that had consumed the lift the previous night. Karina remembered the attack Darian had mentioned. She felt sad that he hadn't kept his word, but on the other hand, she didn't know how much he could do.

Cayla looked shocked. "How is that? How can Lylah be doing that already?"

"Lylah has just teleported," Karina said. "I doubt she's responsible for the attack."

"Who is it then?"

Well, the rebels, of course. Karina looked at Cayla. "You know who's doing that."

"We have to do something. My father! Even if he's guilty, I don't want him to be killed."

Karina didn't think that was necessary. "Nobody said—"

"I need to make sure."

"And what do you want to do?"

"Go to the castle!" Cayla said as if it was rather obvious.

Karina didn't want to remind her that they'd been told to wait. By now, she understood Cayla was not good at following orders. For her part, she would much rather sit on the mountain and wait for all the trouble to stop. Either way, they were far from the castle. "How?"

Cayla pulled her necklace. "Darian. Darian." She sounded angry. Karina wondered how much she knew.

The stone, or rather, Darian, replied, "Cayla, are you alright?"

"I am."

"I see where you are. Please stay there and hide. I'll come for you as soon as I can. Right now, I can't... I'll explain everything when I see you again. Just stay safe now."

"Don't worry. I will." She sounded calm and complying.

"Really?" Karina asked.

Cayla grimaced. "Are you kidding me? Of course not! We're going to the castle. I mean, I'm going. You don't have to go."

Karina exhaled, relieved.

Cayla continued, "But I need to find a way to get there."

That sounded like a terrible idea. "Why don't you wait? It's dangerous going there. Especially alone."

Cayla shook her head. "It isn't. My father's army wouldn't harm me. I don't think these insurgents would harm me either. I mean, at least I'm sure they won't kill me."

Maybe she had a point. Karina then remembered what Lylah had told them. "Can't you teleport?"

"What? No."

"How come you came to my place then, and brought me?"

"There was a portal already opened. And I didn't do anything. Odell had it all set up. I mean," she snorted, "now that I know who actually did it, it makes a lot more sense."

"But Lylah just said we could teleport if we were just in two."

Cayla shrugged. "I have no idea what she meant. Maybe she forgot you threw the shoes or something."

It could be. Or maybe not. "But don't you, I mean, don't you have some power, considering who you are?"

"That's not something you're born with."

"But you know magic, right? I mean, you cast a light in my room—"

"Well, that... Fine, it was magic. Odell taught me a little. Just a little. The thing is, whenever you go to another dimension, you're more powerful, so I was testing."

"And what was the result?"

Cayla shrugged and snorted. "Some light. Not very useful." Cayla looked down at the horizon far away. "I think I know how to get there. Come, follow me."

She ran to the place where they had fought at night.

"What do you want to do?" Karina asked.

"They might have dropped something." She looked down to the floor. "Something we could use to communicate. Help me find it."

"What should it look like?"

"It's usually silver. But it could be different. If you find anything unusual, let me know."

Her tone was urgent. Cayla really believed she would find something. Karina tried to look. She wasn't sure if she wanted to find anything, though. The whole idea sounded dangerous.

Cayla looked behind Karina and smiled. "You can stop looking."

Karina looked at that direction and saw a lift coming in their direction. Great. "You think this is good?"

"Well, if it's the rebels, they'll take us to the castle. If it's the army, they'll take us to the castle. Easy, right?"

"Take you maybe. I'd rather hide."

"But you want to go home, right? You can only teleport from the blue tower, and you know where it is."

Karina shrugged. "I can wait."

"Fine. Wait then, but if it takes a month, don't blame me." Cayla crossed her arms, but then she got calmer. "There's something else you can do. Hide. See what happens. If they are friendly, you come with me. How's that?"

"And if they aren't?"

"You find a way to ask for help." Cayla sighed. "And, if by any chance, we don't see each other again, I want to—"

"Stop it." Karina was not ready for any goodbye. "Everything will be fine. I'm sure they are friendly and I'll come with you."

At least that was what Karina hoped. Cayla smiled. Still, Karina went to the middle of the bushes, while Cayla stood out in the open, waiting. Karina sat on the floor, and waited for some two or three minutes, until she heard the sound of a door opening. She ran to Cayla because she decided she didn't want to leave her alone, especially if the people were not friendly. There was a lift in front of Cayla. Two young men stepped out of it. One was very tall and thin, with wavy dark hair, and the other had average height and blond hair. The blond boy wore a similar uniform to the one he'd seen Darian and Zayra wearing. The tall boy wore civilian blown clothes, with leather-looking pants and a black shirt.

The taller boy glanced at Karina before turning to Cayla. "Hey, sis!"

Cayla crossed her arms. "Don't call me that."

"Fine, Princess Cayla." He gesticulated in an exaggerated way, while smirking. "I had no idea we were back to such formalities."

"Knock it off, Sian," Cayla said.

Sian seemed to know Cayla well, so it was safe to assume that they were not planning on imprisoning her or anything. He was a little weird, though.

"Hey, I came to help you," Sian said. He noticed Karina. "And may I have the pleasure of your name?"

"Karina. I'm Cayla's friend."

He stepped closer to her. "I'm Sian." He spread out his arms, then bowed. "At your service."

He was more than a little weird.

Sian then pointed to the blond boy. "This is Lee."

"Hey," Lee waved his hand.

Sian turned to Cayla, smug smirk on his face, "And to what do I owe the pleasure of coming to your rescue?"

"The castle. I need to go there."

He laughed. "You're kidding, right?" Sian stared at Cayla. "Nope, not kidding. That's too bad. As much as I'd love the honor of escorting you back to the castle, the place is, let's say, kind of messy right now. We wouldn't make it past the siege. Nobody could take you there, except... Have you tried my sweet little brother?"

Cayla stared at him in silence.

Sian frowned. "Oh, not even he'll take you. That's too bad. What's the problem, your beloved's too busy betraying your father?"

Cayla stepped close to Sian. "I asked you to knock it off. I did it nicely."

She raised her knee toward his groin. He blocked her and stepped back. Cayla tried to punch him and he blocked. At the same time, Lee stepped behind her and put a cloth on her face. This was all too fast, so Karina had no time to warn her friend. Cayla fainted. Maybe the boys weren't friendly after all. Lee advanced towards Karina, but Sian said, "Leave her. She's harmless."

Karina was somewhat relieved and wondered when and how tales of her lack of bravery had reached him.

Sian looked at Cayla on the floor. "Brat." He turned to Karina while pointing at Cayla. "What she did was attempted murder. She might have killed my future children." He shook his head. "No love for her future nephews and nieces."

Karina wasn't sure if he was serious or not, so she refrained from laughing.

Lee said, "More lifts might come. We need to take them somewhere safe."

"Of course," Sian said. He then got close to Lee and put a cloth in front of his nose and mouth. Lee fainted. Sian held him careful so that the boy would not fall on the floor, then said, "But I make the decisions."

2 0

ABOUT SIAN

Sian had just betrayed his companion. Karina's heart raced. She had no idea what to expect from him. He noticed and waved the gray cloth on his hand. "You want to take a nap too?"

Karina didn't reply.

"I wasn't serious," he said. "You should've laughed. Are my jokes that bad?"

Well, yes, but Karina wasn't going to say that. She just stared.

"You don't talk much, do you?" He smiled. "I like it! My favorite type of conversation partner. I can hear more of myself."

This was annoying. "What are you going to do to us?"

"Am I supposed to answer? Do you want to hear all my evil plans?"

"Yes, of course."

He grimaced. "This one doesn't work when you reply. There's no evil plan. I'll take you somewhere safe. Lee here has connections with the rebels. I don't trust him, that's why I had to do this."

That meant Sian was not with the rebels. Karina wondered why he'd make Cayla faint then. Was it because she'd tried to kick him?

"Let's go," Sian continued. "More lifts could come, although most of the rebels are around the castle now."

Sian then dragged Lee and Cayla to the lift. Karina followed, because she didn't want to leave her friend. This lift was entirely different from the other ones. It had no division, and it had what looked like one weapon on each side, like cannons or something. Karina sat by Cayla, on the back, where there were two rows of seats.

Sian went to the front, then turned back, "Hey, why don't you come sit by me? The view is great."

Karina preferred to stay in the back with Cayla. "Thanks, I'm good here."

She looked down at Cayla sleeping, wondering where they would be taken, and unsure on which side and for whom Sian was fighting. Karina then heard a sound and looked up to see Sian crouching in front of her.

"You don't understand, do you?" Sian said. "I'm only keeping you alive cause it's boring to make sarcastic remarks when there's nobody to hear them." He smiled as he said that.

Karina could also smirk when she wanted to. "Maybe I'd rather die."

He tilted his head, curious. "Some people would agree with you. You owe me your life, you know?"

"Really? How so?"

He shrugged and said matter-of-factly, "I didn't kill you."

Karina snorted. "Wow, am I supposed to be flattered or something?"

He became serious and looked down. "No." For the first time, he looked anything like Darian. "I'm sorry. I didn't mean that. I just want to talk to you."

His eyes were hazel with long eyelashes, and from that distance they were really beautiful, but Karina shouldn't be noticing that. She asked, "For what?"

His smirk was back, which was good, because then he looked

more annoying than anything. "We can exchange some information. How's that?"

Karina did want to learn where she was going and also wanted to figure out the mess she'd gotten into. She also wanted to check how those things moved. After a deep breath, she got up and sat in the front. His hands with long, thin fingers passed over the panel, and it became light blue, with black lines over it. Sian slid his hand over a strip of green light and the lift took off. They moved in a direction opposite of the meeting of the rivers. Karina saw lakes, the Black River, and even the ocean beyond the castle and the silver river. The view was indeed great.

Sian asked, "You've met my little brother Darian, haven't you?"

Karina remained silent, wondering where he wanted to take this conversation.

Sian laughed, "Oh, don't worry, I know you met him. I don't really need that kind of information from you. I know who the insurgents are, I know what they are planning, and I'm aware they are trying to take the castle right now."

"Good for you." She turned her face away from him and looked at the window.

"So, back to my sweet brother. I bet he never mentioned me, did he?"

Karina didn't reply.

"See? That's how much he cares about his family. But that's not my point. He thinks he got part of the army to follow him. I've been tracking all his steps. His rebellion will go nowhere."

Karina wasn't supposed to say anything, but she felt she had to. "He's not their leader."

"He convinced you of that? What did he say? No single leadership? People coming up with ideas on their own? He doesn't pose as their leader, but he gets them to do what he wants."

"He's too young."

"But that's the thing: young, idealistic. Quite catchy, you know?"

Karina wasn't sure if what he was saying was true or not, or even if he believed it.

Sian pointed to Cayla. "And that's why she's the perfect hostage. We'll ambush the insurgents once they are tired, but, if things go wrong, she might be useful. With her, we can get the king, and we can get Darian. It's just perfect. So you know why I'm doing this."

Karina felt a chill down her spine. She thought about Lylah. Cayla was too perfect as a hostage. But something he said didn't make sense. "The king? I thought you were protecting him."

Sian laughed. "The king is bonkers. That's another reason the rebels haven't been caught until now: they are doing the dirty work for my father. I, unlike my brother, care about family."

"You're doing this so that your father takes the kingdom?"

"No. Maybe I'm doing this because I think it's right. Whyland needs a better ruler." He smiled. "One with a charming older son. Who's better than Keen?"

Karina remembered escaping him, and then remembered what she'd heard from Darian and the rebels. "But he's cruel."

Sian waved his finger in the air. "You have to consider who told you this."

Maybe he had a point. But then maybe he didn't. Karina thought about Lylah and Nia. And how Sian didn't know about them. Lylah. Sian had no idea about her, and that could be the factor that changed everything. "Are you leading this ambush?" Karina asked.

"What do you want to hear? That no, I have nothing to do with it? Sorry but I'm not humble like my brother."

"Surrender then. Get your people to surrender, strike a deal, something. You can't win this."

He smiled. "Of course. I'll surrender just because you're

telling me so. You'll need a lot more than a sweet smile if you want to tell me what to do."

Karina thought it was better to be honest. "Lylah. We freed her. And Nia. They're powerful. You won't beat them."

"I think I can deal with two ladies. So Lylah was freed? And she was alive?" He laughed. "Thanks for the info, by the way."

"Use the information then. Cancel this attack, ambush, whatever."

He shook his head. "I don't think Lylah can make any difference."

"She brought down two lifts. I saw it."

He raised his eyebrows, puzzled or incredulous, then laughed. "If she does," he pointed at the back, "I still have the perfect hostage. Unlike my pathetic brother, I happen to know who Cayla's mother is."

Bummer. Karina tried to argue, "I don't think you're a bad person. Why are you doing this?"

He smiled and his eyes brightened. "You don't think I'm a bad person? That's a great start." He got serious again. "Now, you want to know why? For order, peace. This insurgence could lead us into chaos."

"You're doing this for power."

Sian smirked. "Same thing as my brother."

"He means well."

"I mean well too. I know you're not from here. I have no idea where you're from, but let me ask you something: how much do you know about Whyland?"

Uh, close to nothing? The question caught her. Maybe he had a point. But Karina remembered the rebels on the hill, and how they said that they were fighting brutality, she remembered what Darian had said, what Lylah had said. She knew that Sian was on the wrong side. She wasn't sure how much he knew, though, and whether his talk of taking power was real or some kind of joke.

Karina said, "I got to know people here, people who believe in what they are doing, and I believe in them."

"I also believe in what I'm doing! Get to know me! Did they give you a guide or anything? A book?"

"Well, no, but—"

"How sad. I'll get you a book. And you should believe me."

"Why do you care what I think?"

"Well isn't it obvious?"

"No."

"I'm just a guy trying to impress a pretty girl."

Karina hadn't expected that, but she tried not to show she was surprised, and looked around. "Where? I don't see any."

He looked at her intently. "Cause there's no mirror here."

Her face got hot. Was it some kind of joke? Anyways, he was just teasing and trying to get her confused. Maybe he thought she would get wobbly knees, feel out of air and stop thinking. Karina rolled her eyes. "I haven't brushed or washed my hair for five days."

"That explains the wild look."

She looked out the window.

He changed his tone. "I'll give you a better explanation, then." He pointed at Cayla. "She's a brat. I don't know how my brother can stand her. But somehow she trusts you. I don't know what's gonna happen, but of course I'll want a deal with my brother. Of course I want him by my side. That's where Cayla comes in. You might be able to help me."

"Strike a deal now. That's what I told you."

"See? We're coming to an understanding. If you knew me, you'd know I never fight when I can negotiate. But I need the upper hand."

"What do you want from me? Should I tell her that you mean well? That you're nice? You expect she'll listen? She doesn't listen to anyone."

He looked down. "I know."

"Why then?"

"I already told you, and now it's your turn to find an alternate explanation. Go on."

Karina didn't understand what he hoped to accomplish by treating her like that. She looked out the window.

He said, "So, I've told you all my secrets. What about you? What brings you to Whyland?"

Karina's story was so absurd she decided to tell it. "I came to bring a pair of shoes." He looked at her with an eyebrow raised. That was entertaining. She suppressed a smile and continued, "To Lylah." He looked at her in disbelief so she continued because she thought it was funny, "it was a pair of magical shoes. I thought they'd destroy Lylah, but they freed her."

If he lifted his right eyebrow any higher it would touch his hair. "Magical?"

"You guys are weird. You have interdimensional teleporting, but get all skeptical about magic?"

He frowned. "What do you mean interdimensional teleporting?"

"See? Weird."

"Tell me." All his smirking and attitude was gone. There was only curiosity and even some pleading. "I need to understand."

Guess who had the upper hand now? She smirked. "Halt the attack and I will."

He looked away, then looked at her, thoughtful. "Odell set it up. I mean, not the magic and everything, but having Cayla free Lylah."

Karina shrugged. "Maybe. If you want more information we'll have to strike a deal."

He shook his head. "It's fine. You don't have to tell me anything if you don't want to."

There was something soft and soothing about his voice. For a moment she wanted to tell him everything, for a moment she wished that all his talk about trying to impress her were real, she wished he really thought she was pretty, and then she wanted to slap herself to wake up and stop being stupid. He was obviously trying to manipulate her. She looked away and focused on her breathing. Air in, air out. The lift was descending into what looked like the crater of an inactive volcano. There were a bunch of lifts there. Probably ready to attack. Her heart beat faster and the whole breathing technique was gone. Some twenty or thirty. And they would take the castle by surprise. Maybe Lylah and Nia wouldn't make a difference after all. Karina worried about her friends. Darian and Lylah needed to know about this attack. She looked back at Cayla. Her necklace! The question was when she'd have an opportunity to use it. And plus, she didn't know how it worked. The lift landed.

Sian got up and said, "Listen, I would love to take you to the most beautiful place in Whyland, but that won't be now. You'll go to a prison with Cayla. Are you going to resist, or can you just walk by my side?"

That was a stupid question because even if Karina had a black belt in martial arts, she wouldn't be able to leave that place on her own. "I can walk."

He nodded, opened the door and got out. Karina followed. Sian made a gesture and four men entered their lift and carried Lee away.

Karina was worried. "Is he gonna get hurt?"

"For real?" Sian asked. "I talk to you all the way up here, tell you all my secrets, and you're worried about him?"

His tone and gesticulation were exaggerated. But Karina didn't think it was funny. "Is he gonna get hurt?"

"I wouldn't tell you, would I? But don't worry. He's one of us. It's just that right now he needs to be detained." He made a sad face. "Of course, it still breaks my heart to see you only care about him."

Karina didn't know when he was being serious or ironic and

was getting annoyed. Two young men carried Cayla and they all walked in a direction opposite to the one Lee was carried.

Sian turned to Karina. "I was joking. That was sweet."

More weirdness. "What?"

"Lee. You've met him for what? Twenty seconds? For all you know he would've attacked you if it wasn't for me. And yet you worry about him."

Karina shrugged. "I just don't want anyone to get hurt."

"Not even me I suppose."

Almost, cause now she thought Cayla's kick could have been deserved. But no more than that. "That's why I told you to surrender."

"Did you take a look around you? Still think we need to surrender?"

"Even if you don't need to, you can still strike a deal." Karina had no idea why she was pleading, but there she was. "Make peace. Assure nobody gets hurt."

"That's my plan. You should trust me."

They came to a prison cell, with a door made of iron bars.

Sian grimaced. "This place is ugly. I'm sorry, but Cayla needs to be kept somewhere safe. Hopefully you won't be here long. Do you want anything before I take the kingdom?"

Karina wasn't sure if he really meant that, but she decided to ask for something. "I don't want to be alone." Sian had a smile and his eyes brightened. Karina continued, "Could you... wake up Cayla? So she keeps me company?"

He looked down, making an exaggerated sad face. "I thought you meant me."

"Well, stay here then. Much more interesting than leading a stupid attack."

Sian laughed. "A lot more interesting!" He made a sad face again. "But what can I do? Duty calls me." He turned to the men carrying Cayla, and spoke in a neutral, serious tone, "Wake her up when she's inside. But careful. She's dangerous. Don't hurt either of them." He turned to Karina, "We'll catch up later." He turned around and left.

As Karina entered the cell watched as he walked away in sure steps, hair and overcoat flowing. He puzzled her. The guards entered and gave Cayla a shot. Her eyes opened. Karina wondered if the breathing cloth and the shot had any risk, and kind of regretted having asked for Cayla to be woken up.

The princess looked around. "Where are we?"

"We're in a military base, no idea where, while they are planning to attack the castle."

Cayla squinted, "Isn't the castle already being attacked?"

"By the rebels. These people are with General Keen."

"They're with my father then." Cayla squinted again. "Why are we in a prison?"

"Apparently Keen plans on betraying your father."

Cayla squinted even harder and tilted her head. "He's with the insurgents?" She sounded incredulous.

"No. He's with himself, I think. His plan is to let the rebels depose your father and then take power."

"How do you know all that?"

Karina looked down, embarrassed for some reason. "Sian told me."

Cayla had a puzzled face.

"I think he likes to talk," Karina added.

"He talks too much, that's what I think," Cayla said. She then looked around. "We have to get back to the castle."

Thanks, captain obvious. "No kidding, right? But there's something else you can do." She pointed to Cayla's necklace.

The princess raised her hands in despair. "How am I even supposed to know on which side he is?"

"He's with the rebels."

Cayla sighed, looked down, and closed her eyes. Yikes. Perhaps she shouldn't have received this information so suddenly. "You can't be sure."

"I can," Karina said. "Sian told me."

"It sounds like you guys became buddies or something. What else did he tell you?"

"Nothing." Karina looked down. "He wanted to explain why you were being held, that's all."

"How thoughtful of him."

Karina then pointed again at the necklace. "Are you going to try it?"

Cayla pointed at the guards. She didn't seem to want to contact him in front of them.

Karina then heard sounds of people moving. "What's happening?" she took a chance and asked one of the guards.

"The lifts are taking off."

Oh, no, they would attack now. The one upside was that at least Sian was kind of nice, so if they took the castle, they would hopefully allow her to go there, use the blue tower, and go home. But then, what about Nia, Lylah, Cayla, Ayanna? On the other hand, Lylah could maybe defeat them. Maybe.

"I can't believe we're here," Cayla said.

"Well, you're the one who thought they'd give us a ride to the castle."

"Come up with a better idea, then."

"Let's teleport!" Karina said, half joking.

"I told you. I can't do it."

Karina shrugged, "Well neither can—" An idea hit her, but she was not sure about it. "Wait. What did you say about magic?"

Cayla glanced at the guards. "That it's really evil and only witches use it?"

"Right. You also said that, uh, evil witches, when they go to another dimension, they get stronger. Does that work for anybody? Or do you have to have training?"

Cayla looked at Karina and seemed to understand. She whispered, "You. It was you. In the hill with the insurgents."

Karina wasn't sure. She still thought it could have been the shoes.

"You have to try it," Cayla said softly.

"How?"

One of the guards banged on the door. "Hey, no whispering."

Cayla held Karina's hand. "Close your eyes and see yourself there. In the blue tower."

Could it be that easy? Nia had said she needed an emotional spike. Karina thought about home, and how her way there would be through the blue tower, she thought about the friends she'd made, about Sian. The ground below her felt as if it was moving. She lost balance. She knew what it was, and it felt great.

Karina fell on the floor in a tall circular room surrounded by blue walls... The blue tower! She'd done it! She got up and looked around, almost waiting for some hostile soldiers to attack them, but nobody came. The emptiness and silence were more disturbing than some sound or movement, though. There were cracks in the wall that hadn't been there before. Or maybe she hadn't noticed them. And too late she realized that she'd brought them right to the middle of a conflict, like the eye of a storm, knowing nothing of what was really going on. But hey, getting entangled in stuff she knew nothing about was becoming Karina's specialty. The prison would have been safer, except that it would be annoying to stay there waiting for Sian to come back with a superior smirk.

"I know where we need to go," Cayla said. "Come."

They got out and Karina ran after her friend through a long corridor. The light from the ceiling was so obviously artificial now that she knew about it. They turned a corner—and were ambushed. Two soldiers appeared in front of them, with guns, whatever they were and whatever they did. The girls turned around to see two more behind them. Karina raised her hands, and Cayla did that as well.

21

THE FINAL BATTLES

"I'm princess Cayla." Her voice was calm and steady, and she was probably calm, if she didn't fear the insurgents or the royal guards. "I'm the King's daughter. Darian's friend as well."

A male voice came from behind them, "Friends don't let friends be sentenced to death, my darling." General Keen stepped from behind two soldiers, looking at Cayla. "I wanted you dead, but I guess you'll be useful alive—for now at least." He turned to the soldiers. "Shoot the younger girl."

What happened next felt unreal for Karina, as if it wasn't really happening to her. It was like seeing herself in a dream, facing the soldiers pointing their weapons, pressing their trigger, blue energy coming in her direction. She never made a decision to do anything, because there was no time to think. All she felt was the ground moving, and found herself alone in the blue tower. She felt bad for leaving Cayla, but there had been no time to reach for her hand. There had been no time for anything. And still there was no time to digest the shock of having almost been killed. The walls seemed to have even bigger cracks now, as if the tower was breaking. Karina was shaking in fear, but got out and ran in the opposite direction she'd run before, hoping she'd find someone friendly, someone who could help them, who could lead her to Lylah or Nia or someone who could free Cayla and stop the general. After many meters, she almost stopped and laughed. She could have gone home! And yet she didn't. She wanted to help clean the mess she'd gotten herself into, even if she wasn't really sure what the mess was. And she wouldn't leave Cayla. But where should she go? Those corridors were like an interminable maze, confusing her.

"Halt!"

Karina trembled. It was a woman's voice. She turned around and raised her hands, hoping it wasn't anyone planning on killing her. It was just a young woman with brown hair and eyes— pointing a gun. And wearing the army's uniform. This could turn out badly.

"Who are you?" The woman asked.

Karina chose to say a name that could work either way. "I'm a friend of Darian's."

"From which side?"

Right. Of course the woman also knew that Darian's name meant nothing. Karina risked the truth. "Not General Keen's." She held her breath, afraid of what would happen.

The woman lowered her weapon slightly. "With whom them? Cause you clearly don't know our code."

Of course. The rebels had a secret code Karina had no idea about and Darian never bothered informing them. But this was not the time to think about that. She decided to say the truth. "I need to talk to whoever is leading you. It's urgent and important."

The woman looked at Karina up and down. Her hesitation was annoying. At each second that passed Sian's lifts were getting closer to the castle, and who knows what was happening to Cayla?

Karina said, "You do realize I'm unarmed, right? And it's urgent."

The woman lowered her weapon. "Come."

Karina followed, uneasy because she feared meeting General Keen or someone loyal to him. They came to a wide auditorium. Lylah and Nia were there, as well as Darian, Jax and Zayra, and some twenty other people. That meant that the insurgents had won, and had help from Lylah. They were probably discussing the fate of the kingdom, unaware of the danger inside and outside the castle.

"Hey!" Karina yelled without waiting for an introduction or anything. "You're about to be attacked. Some twenty lifts are coming this way, for an ambush. They are armed. They are under General Keen, and he plans to take power."

Some murmur was heard in the room.

Darian said, "The army doesn't have that many more lifts."

"I saw them." Karina lowered her voice. "Your brother's there by the way." She hoped that would ensure they didn't hurt Sian.

Darian frowned, and many people spoke at the same time. Lylah's voice rose above the others. "I can hold them back."

And now it was time to give the other, more important news. "There's more," Karina yelled. The room fell silent. Her voice trembled as she looked at Lylah. "General Keen has Cayla. He wants to use her as a hostage."

Lylah fell back on her seat, but her voice was still calm. "Where is she?"

"I don't know." Karina looked down. "He wanted to kill me."

"I can find her," Darian yelled. "I'll deal with this."

Lylah got up, "I can—"

"With all due respect, miss," Darian said, "Cayla's none of your business."

Karina face palmed, but the situation was too intense for any clarification.

Lylah turned to Karina. "Was Keen alone?"

"No. He had four guards."

"What does it matter?" Darian asked. "She's a hostage. We

can't confront them. The fewer people the better. I'm still his son. I can talk to him." His voice became soft, smooth, almost relaxing. "I'm good at talking and I can solve this. Alone."

Lylah squinted. "You're Bianca's son." She said it as if she'd just recognized him, which was odd.

Darian raised his eyebrows. "So?"

"Go," Lylah said. She closed her eyes as if in pain. "I have an attack to halt."

Darian left.

Lylah turned to Karina. "Do you know where they are coming from?"

That was a tough question for Karina since she didn't know anything about the geography there, but she tried her best, "The place is near this river, but not in the direction where it meets with the Black River. The other. They were all gathered in a large place that looked like the crater of an inactive volcano."

Lylah nodded, then turned to Nia. "Help her go. Now. While the blue tower still stands."

Karina shuddered when she realized that it meant her. That it meant she would go home without knowing how everything ended. That she would go home without saying goodbye. Nia pulled her and Karina followed automatically, feeling sad and empty. But then, she wouldn't want to be stuck in this place that she still knew so little about.

They got to the tall blue room. Some pieces of the wall were falling, and the cracks were bigger. So it wasn't an impression. That tower was collapsing.

Nia held her hand. "Now close your eyes."

Karina figured closed eyes were necessary for interdimensional teleporting, wondering how many rules about it she would never have the opportunity to learn. The feeling of teleporting was in fact quite distinct from falling, and this time, she saw flashes of light through her closed eyelids. The lights didn't stop and Karina eventually opened her eyes, realizing that nobody held her hand anymore. It was day and she was in her room. This time she felt that she was in her room. So everything was back to normal. Sort of. How can anyone be normal after all that? She considered all the assumptions she had when she went to Whyland, and how each of them had been shattered. She even wondered whether Lylah and Darian were really on the good side, and if Sian was completely wrong. Well, he was. His father was indeed cruel and had almost killed Karina. But then maybe he was also under false impressions, and false assumptions. She wondered what made a person choose a side. Was it ideology, values, or just circumstance? Anyways, why was she thinking that? Was it about making excuses for the cheap flirter? Or was it just her mind going back and trying to understand how come nothing went as expected, and in the end it did? Karina helped save a kingdom—depending on one's definition of saving, of course. If the kingdom had been saved, because everything could still go wrong. But then, she remembered Sian saying he always negotiated when he could, and that thought put her mind at ease.

DARIAN LET his necklace guide him. He was shaking in anger. If only he'd answered when she called him. If only he'd turned around for her. If only. He only didn't punch himself because it wouldn't help. He needed to stay calm. Concentrate. And remain calm. He could do it. He had a gift for speaking, and this was his time to use it. Focused on his necklace, and where it guided him, he descended stairs he had never before been at. He came to an abandoned dungeon. The floor was wet and moldy, and mice scurried on the corners. Cayla was sitting on a chair. A large granite block hung above her, with a rope on a pulley and tied to a hook on the floor.

Keen had a hatchet, and said, "One step more and I'll cut the rope."

There were two guards with fireguns on each of her side. Darian wondered where the other two had gone. Cayla didn't seem scared. If anything, she looked annoyed or concentrated, maybe thinking about a way to escape. That would be foolish.

"It's me, father."

Cayla noticed him, and for the first time her eyes showed a hint of fear.

General Keen stood where he was. "Don't call me that. Is that how you pay me? After all I've done for you? After I've received you here and given you everything?"

Darian tried to calm himself down. He had to muster his calmest voice. "I was trying to be a good son. You wanted our family to stay in power, didn't you? That's how I infiltrated the insurgents. I have a good influence over them and no matter what happens our family will stay in power."

"Liar!"

His father moved his arm and Darian feared he'd cut the rope. Darian stepped forward, and the guards pointed their guns toward him.

But the general then stepped forward, away from the rope. "You conspired with them."

"I had to gain their trust."

General Keen looked at Darian as if he could see inside him. Darian looked at his father and didn't break eye contact. He knew he looked relaxed, calm, and truthful, and he hoped his father could be swayed.

Darian said, "Let's stop this. We can go to the main auditorium. They are revolting against the King. You can say you had nothing to do with this. I will support you. They listen to me, father."

General Keen laughed. "You know what's wrong in all that you're saying?"

Darian had no idea what his father meant.

"You never called me father. Not like that. You're like your mother. Never cared. You should pay for your treason, Darian, by watching the girl die." He stepped closer to the rope and touched it with the hatchet.

Darian had to remain calm. "I've never been the most loving son, no, but that doesn't change the fact that you won't gain anything by hurting the princess."

"Princess? She's no princess. Don't you know? The king is no more. It's going to be me. My true son is coming to take the power for those who really deserve it. Your silly plan to become king didn't work. It didn't work."

Darian glanced at Cayla. Their eyes met. She wasn't angry at him. She didn't believe the lies Keen was saying. Darian concentrated. Funny how sometimes he could do his convincing voice, but now it felt as if he was failing. "Let her go then. She's worthless as a hostage."

Keen laughed. "Oh, my innocent, stupid, ignorant, little son."

Cayla looked away. Darian had no idea what the laugh was about and he feared that it didn't matter because his father was losing his mind.

Darian tried to change his tactic. "Let her go, and I'll help you escape. In case your plans don't work."

"No."

"I told you I have good relations with the insurgents. Sian has good relations in the army. Our family can stay in power, no matter what happens. Let her go, and if the insurgents and Lylah win, I'll guarantee you'll still be general."

"And you think you can do that?"

"I'm good at convincing people."

"You're like your mother! Your unnatural magic, making people do what they don't want."

Darian had no idea that his father knew about his mother's special skill, and that he knew that it was considered a type of magic. Darian himself knew little about it. It was called spell-speaking, or whispering, depending on where you lived in

Whyland. Darian once heard that he had that skill as well, but sometimes he doubted it. It didn't seem to affect his father, though. And the worse is that he feared his father's mental state. Darian's heart beat faster as his confidence melted away. Still, he had to remain calm and try to negotiate.

"Yes, I'm good at convincing people. And I can convince them you can still be a general. It would be good. We could re-unify the army. Let her go and I give you my word, a binding word, like we say in my village, that I'll do everything I can to make sure you'll keep command of the army."

"Everything you can is not good enough. I'm going to be king, or else she dies."

Darian sighed. He was getting frustrated. Why Cayla? Was his father trying to hurt him because he'd betrayed him?

Keen stepped forward. "Do you want to help me? Get that witch here. I'll negotiate with her."

A loud shot startled Darian. His father fell forward. The two guards had their eyes closed, as if sleeping, and yet, they'd shot General Keen.

"I'm sorry." A woman's voice came from behind Darian.

Darian turned around and saw Lylah.

"I'm sorry for your father. There was no way to reach him," she said.

Darian looked at the guards. They had now fallen on the ground, as if sleeping, the same way Nia did with her dagger, except that Lylah had no magical object or weapon whatsoever. Darian didn't know how to feel about his father, but he knew how he felt about Cayla. He ran towards her and removed the gag around her mouth. She had red marks on her cheeks.

"How are you?" he asked.

"Fine." Cayla was stiff, and looked at Lylah's direction.

Darian looked at the woman as well. "Thank you for saving her."

Lylah shook her head. "I still wish I could have avoided his death. I wish, and I'm sorry, but I couldn't take chances. One day you'll understand. Well, I have an attack to halt." She turned around and left.

Darian had a lot of work untying Cayla's hands and feet. Darian glanced at his father's body. He wished his father had been different, he wished he didn't have to die, he wished they could have been a family. Now all that was left was his brother, and he didn't have great expectations from that side either. Cayla got up and looked around, at the guards, and at General Keen.

"You tried," she said. "It wasn't your fault."

"Let's get out of here. I'll send someone for the body and the guards."

He reached his hand for her.

Cayla shook her head. "Lylah."

Lylah had left, but for some reason she made Cayla nervous. Either way, this wasn't the time to argue why she wouldn't take his hand. With all that had happened, he wouldn't be surprised if Cayla refused to hold his hand for a long time. He left the room, and she followed him. Darian wanted to ask her how she'd gotten in the castle, why she didn't stay where she was, why she hadn't listened to him, but he knew he'd sound angry. Angry at Cayla. And he was angry with himself.

He asked something different, "Weren't you afraid?"

"If it had been my time to die, I'd accept it. I only hoped the block was heavy enough that it would be quick. But then I was afraid for you. Cause you'd be sad."

"Sad? I think I'd die." He wished he could hug her, but she was still distant. "I'm sorry," he said. "You called me, and I didn't..." he looked down. "I'm sorry."

Cayla sighed. "It's how things had to be. The only upside is that we learned about your brother's plans. From what I see Karina managed to tell Lylah about it."

Darian closed his eyes. "My brother."

"He was defending your father."

"He probably didn't know it all. He's not like my father, he isn't. I have to—"

"Go. I'll be fine."

Darian didn't want to leave her, but he didn't want to risk seeing his brother killed, even if he hadn't spoken to Sian in over a year, even with everything. He ran to the dock outside, decided to find a way at least to communicate with his brother.

Gone, they'd said. Gone. Sian tried to make sense of the message from Mouth Mountain. Nobody simply disappears from a cell. Maybe the guards had betrayed him, or had been bribed, and had let the girls go. But then, maybe they were telling the truth. And if that was the case, it changed everything. She'd said it. Apart from the glimmer in her eyes, she seemed to be telling the truth. Sian knew when people were lying, he knew it. Teleporting. Interdimensional teleporting. Magical shoes. And if all that was true, then his plans were based on a flawed logic. He couldn't win a game if he didn't know all the rules. It meant that his father's fear of magic wasn't nonsense, as Sian had always believed. Magic. It was real.

Sian took a deep breath and considered. He looked outside the window and saw a few lifts in the distance, flying towards the castle. Would their surprise be gone as well? He considered cancelling the attack. Maybe he'd need to rethink. He should have known, though. And what hurt more was that, in a way, he did know. From the moment he heard about Cayla stepping out of the castle on her own, with an unknown girl, he knew that something didn't add up. Even then, perhaps he hadn't under-stood how much.

A red light popped on his panel. Written communication this time, no sender, one of his sources within the insurgents: *Girl warned about your attack. Cayla taken by general Keen. Magic woman with us. Powerful. Lylah?*

Sian didn't have to read it twice. The girls had indeed teleported. And yes, the woman was Lylah. Karina had told him everything, and had warned him. *Cancel the attack, negotiate. Strike a deal.* Her plea was not for her friends, it was for him, as in "please don't attempt something you can't win, or please don't risk getting hurt", as if she cared. And yet she told the insurgents about his plans. His own fault. The first time in his entire life he'd done something stupid. Of course, had he taken into consideration teleporting to the castle, he'd have done everything different. So many things he hadn't taken into consideration.

What about Cayla taken by his father? He felt uneasy, since General Keen had wanted to kill her. Sian hated Cayla, but still... Then again, his father must have known by now that she was a valuable hostage. He'd use the annoying princess to find a safe way to escape. That's what Sian himself would have done.

Sian's mind went back to the war strategy classes. He liked those, and liked to wrap his head around all logical outcomes. The history of war wasn't as elaborate as it should have been, though. Most battles were quite straightforward. But one thing he learned, even if he had never imagined he'd need it; fighting is not only about knowing when to advance, but when to retreat. Her words came to his mind. *I saw her take down two lifts.* That hadn't made sense then. He'd thought it was a bluff. Again, it was a warning. *Strike a deal.* Sian had to make his decision. He always won, but that was because he knew when to act. This wasn't the time.

He opened the channel for all his troops. "Operation retreat. Spread out. Back up everyone, but don't return to Mouth Mountain."

He turned it off, and could almost hear the incredulous murmurs over the silence. A light came up. Liam.

"What's going on?" As Sian predicted, his friend sounded puzzled.

"I miscalculated. We'll have to surrender and negotiate. We need to blend in and support whatever new government they decide."

"What about your father?"

"He'll find a way to escape. His loyal soldiers in the castle have been imprisoned. Loyal troops are too far away to help us now. We'd plunge into a war we can't win. Not worth it. Our surprise element is gone as well."

"What's your new plan?"

Sian smiled. Liam knew that there was more to it than just surrendering. "I can't say right now. I'll be gone for a while. Could you lead the negotiations?"

"Wouldn't you—"

"Trust me. Contact my brother. He'll know how to get you to the insurgent chain of command. Tell them we were not supporting anyone, that it was just army's regular procedure, that we were an extra emergency force, answering a call from the castle."

"They won't believe me."

"No. But they'll be happy to pretend they do. They have the forces to take Whyland. The question is not whether they can win, but how easily. They'll take all the help they can."

"Why don't you stay then?"

"My precious ego can't stand bruises."

Liam laughed. "What about mine?"

"You didn't come up with the plan. No, I need time. I need to leave. I'll be in touch, though."

"Peace it is, then."

And like that, Sian dismantled one year of planning. Planning based on false premises, missing key points. He'd never again try to do anything before understanding more about magic. He'd have to understand what he'd always thought was nonsense, the nothingness his father fought against. But then, forbidding people to talk about something or pretending it doesn't exist didn't make it any less real. It was even worse, because it made people unprepared. Denial was stupid. The key was understanding. Sian was ready to revamp all his assumptions and beliefs. That was the only way he could ever reach his goals.

22

DARIAN AND CAYLA

Darian looked from the window in his temporary room in the Army tower in Siphoria. He could see a good part of the city, illuminated in its night-lights. Across the river stood the castle. He wondered what kind of place it would be. The leaders would meet the next day, and he wondered what would happen. Strange how he'd planned to depose the king and yet hadn't really planned about what would come after. It wasn't as he expected. Not at all. Not only he'd underestimated the forces loyal to his father, he had absolutely no idea about Lylah. He had always thought that he'd grown up surrounded by magic, or people who practiced so-called magic, but he had no idea that there was a type of magic that could manipulate elements, that could control people, that could help a single person take a castle in a matter of minutes. All of this was new, and all of this was something he had to think about and digest.

He hadn't been able to find his brother, but his brother had found him, for a weird goodbye with a book and a request, before disappearing, who knows where. At least he was alive. Darian didn't dare tell him how his father had died. The thought consumed him with guilt.

But his biggest worry was Cayla, as she was in the castle that was no longer her father's. Nia had been nominated guardian of the castle, but still... And he couldn't talk to her since her necklace didn't work there. He wondered how she was taking everything, and what would happen to her, now that her father was imprisoned. He also wondered how she felt about his part in deposing her father. He'd left a note for her, but wasn't sure whether she'd got it.

Staying in the tower and worrying wouldn't accomplish anything. He decided to go to the castle. It wasn't the safest place for Cayla right now. There was always the possibility of an offense by some remaining forces loyal to the deposed King. True that Lylah was in the castle, which should dissuade anyone from attacking it. She'd probably be nominated queen. That was what many people wanted. Darian had always thought that there could be a different way to rule Whyland, but then again, his plans hadn't included a transition to a different type of government, and hadn't taken Lylah into consideration. He'd spend so long thinking he had to depose the king that he'd forgotten to think what would come after. Maybe restoring the queen would be a good idea. Lylah. She'd killed his father, but saved Cayla.

The night was warm but not hot, and he felt a cool breeze as he crossed the bridge over the Silver River, book in his hand. In the castle, the guards at the door knew who Darian was, and allowed him to get in. He had no problems getting anywhere. In the maze of corridors, he was still able to sense the direction where Cayla was. Maybe the necklace did work a little in the castle. Or maybe he could feel where she was. Darian didn't doubt anything anymore. He came to her hallway. His heart started racing. Of course he was afraid. He was coming to her bedroom. He'd never knocked on her door before, and he wondered if it was too intrusive, too...

"Hello." A woman's voice startled him.

Lylah was there. What was she doing in that area of the

castle? Right. Royal quarters. Perhaps she would have more right to a room in that area than Cayla, but that was a day too early.

"Hello," he replied.

"Are you looking for someone?"

"I need to check how Cayla is."

She squinted. "At this time?"

Maybe Lylah could make someone shoot the person they were supposed to defend. Maybe, like some people said, she could even bring down lifts. She wasn't his enemy and didn't intimidate him.

"It was a long day." He pulled his necklace and held the now yellow stone. "You do know what this is, right?" Lylah had a look of recognition. Of course she knew. "Cayla has the other twin. So you know what we are."

She took a long deep look at him. "You're welcome to come back tomorrow."

"Cayla had a hard day and I need to talk to her. Tell me, do you plan on preventing me from seeing her?"

"I need to understand what you want."

Darian asked, "In her bedroom? I could name a couple things. None of them forbidden, based on everything people claim you believe. Or are they wrong? I'm just asking to check if you're like the previous king. Curiosity." Maybe he'd gone too far, but he had to know where this new, maybe-queen, stood. He had to. He hadn't gone through all this trouble to be forbidden to see Cayla again.

Lylah stared at him. Her eyes were calm, deep—and piercing, as if she could see his soul.

She spoke after a few long seconds. "I'm not forbidding anything. Her door is the third on the left."

"I know."

Lylah had a half smile then turned around and walked away. The interaction had been odd. Why was she asking those questions? Darian walked to Cayla's door and took a deep breath before knocking. Perhaps she would be angry, surprised, or annoyed. But he had to see her.

The door opened sooner than he'd expected. From surprise her face changed to worry. She pulled him inside and shut the door. "What are you doing here?"

"I needed to see you."

"Here? What if someone catches you?"

Darian looked down. How could he say it in a way that wouldn't be rude to her father? He tried, "I don't think anyone minds." This didn't sound good. "Anymore. Meaning someone who can make decisions." She didn't look happy. He added, "I'm sorry for your father."

"Don't lie," she snapped, then changed her tone. "How did you get in? Didn't anyone stop you?"

He didn't want to mention Lylah and didn't think it mattered. "Not really. I just had to see how you were. I'll leave. Or we can go somewhere else."

She looked at him and took a moment as if considering. "Isn't it dangerous out there?"

He took a deep breath. "Well..."

Cayla snorted, then pointed to a table and chairs. "Sit."

Darian sat down.

Cayla sat across him. "Talk. Wasn't that why you came?"

"I also wanted to know how you're feeling."

Cayla raised her arms in a grand gesture. "Amazing. Didn't you know? Every single person I trusted lied to me. Every single one. Including you."

"I didn't lie. I just... I never had the chance to explain."

"You could have explained it when you met me, before joining your traitor friend. You could have explained at the Apex. You could have told me when I asked you on which side you were. I asked you."

"I didn't think it was the right time. That was all, Cayla. I was waiting for the right time."

"The right time would be after my father was deposed, of course, because otherwise perhaps I'd ruin your plans. Tell me it isn't true."

That made sense, actually. Revealing his plans to Cayla could have been dangerous. Darian nodded. "It's part of the truth, yes."

Cayla closed her eyes. "At least you're getting better now. What about before you even left the castle? Before everything? You were never a great supporter of the King, were you? You didn't even support your father. You never mentioned any of that."

"Well, when we first met you didn't even mention you were the King's daughter!"

"I never denied it!"

He stared at her in silence for a moment. "I didn't want you to…"

"You know what the problem is? You never trusted me. You never bothered to share your plans with me, your thoughts, your hopes, your wishes. Why? Wasn't I worthy of knowing what you thought? Or was it that my opinion didn't matter? Tell me."

Darian looked down thinking, then looked in her eyes. "Maybe if I had more time, if I saw you more often, I would have told you, Cayla. I would have explained everything. But I only saw you briefly, when everything was already in motion. I'm sorry your father had to be deposed and imprisoned. I can take all the time in the world to explain the reasons why I was part of a movement against him. If you'll listen to me, I'll explain. But I didn't have all this time before."

Cayla shrugged. "That's something I have to come to terms on my own. Maybe I was blind to certain things. What hurts is not so much the truth, but the fact that nobody bothered telling me."

He did see her point. "I understand. I was wrong. If I tell you that from now on, I'll always trust you, and I'll never hide anything from you, would that make things better?"

"You're assuming that there will be a from now on."

Darian bit his lip. "I don't mean... it can be as friends. If you want. Other than that, I can't turn back time."

Cayla looked away, then looked at his book. "What's that?"

This was hardly the time to ask for a favor, and he felt awkward. "I... I was going to ask you to give this to someone. But it's fine, I'll figure another way."

"No, I can give it. Who is it for?"

"Your friend. Uh, Odell's niece."

Her eyes widened. "Who do you mean?"

"That girl. What was her name again? Ka..."

Cayla squinted. "Why do you want to give Karina a book?"

"My brother. He said he'd promised."

"You found Sian?"

Darian felt uneasy. "He disappeared again."

Cayla rolled her eyes. "Awesome. And now he wants me to do him an almost impossible favor."

"No. I mean, if you know how I can find her... Maybe it was foolish, but I promised him."

Cayla snorted. "Your brother played a trick on you. He's probably having a good laugh right now. Karina lives..." she paused. "Far. Very, very, far. I also have things to explain to you, once I can understand them myself. I don't even know who I am anymore. But you can leave the book with me."

Her confusion was understandable. Darian pushed the book across the table. He had something more serious to ask her.

"What are you going to do now? I mean, I know you're living in the castle but..."

"I'll see what happens tomorrow."

"If Lylah is proclaimed queen... I don't know if you are going to live here."

Cayla had an odd expression.

Darian continued, "If you want, and it can be, you know, as friends, or acquaintances, we could move up North. I could find my village—"

Cayla shook her head. "Acquaintances don't move together. And we're a little too young for that." She looked in his eyes and her expression softened. "I appreciate the offer, I do." She looked away. "But you don't need to worry about me."

"I'll always worry. And I'm here, if you need anything. I think it must be hard for you now that you're not princess anymore. Trust me, I thought about it a million times, and I'm sorry for my part in that."

She stared at him. "Are you really sorry, though? Doesn't a small part of you feel happy that I'm no longer princess? That you feel you have more power than I do? Tell me."

"I won't lie. I'm glad that I'm allowed to see you now. The rest doesn't matter."

She sighed. "Fair enough. Maybe you'd better go. Now that you can see me you can come back another time."

Darian got up. "You won't be upset if I come see you again?"

Cayla walked toward the door. "It depends. Come asking another impossible favor and I might snap."

He followed her. "I don't mind you snapping."

She smiled. Her first genuine smile since her father had been deposed. It illuminated all her face. Darian was partly glad she was finally smiling, and partly struck, because even though she was very beautiful, she looked ethereal when she smiled. It was hard to believe that she was even real.

Of course, it didn't last long. Cayla squinted. "What are you staring at?"

"I like your smile."

She rolled her eyes. "Right. You're going to start flattering me now."

"I promised I'd be honest, what can I do? By the way, I also like it when you squint. Or roll your eyes."

She stared at him. "You like it when I frown as well?"

"Love it. I also like it when you stare at me as if you meant to kill me."

Cayla laughed and then smiled. Again. "That's good to know. Cause, you know, I plan on doing that a lot."

Their eyes locked. There was something different about her. The coldness and distance were gone. Her expression was open, eager, as she stood close to him. So close. He was looking at her eyes one moment, the next he had his eyes closed and lips locked on hers, arms wrapped around her. Cayla was soft, loving, and willing, holding him tight. He'd always wondered when it would be the right time to kiss her, but the truth is that he didn't even notice how they started it, and wasn't even sure who'd initiated it. Probably both.

She kept hugging him but moved her face and whispered in his ear, "For the record, I'm still upset you didn't trust me."

Darian held her even tighter and kissed her forehead. "I'm upset at myself." But he had something else to say. He kept one hand on her waist, but took a step back and showed the stone of his necklace. "Do you see this?" Cayla nodded. He continued, "It was black before. Do you know why it's bright now? These are twin necklaces. They'll shine when the two people wearing them love each other. So every time you look at it—"

"Hold on." She broke away from his grip and put her hands on her hips. He didn't understand why she'd be upset that he was telling he loved her. She continued, "You mean to say you've known I loved you for more than one year? And never bothered telling me what it meant? While I was here, alone, wondering if you'd forgotten me, you never needed to have any doubts, because you had a freaking stone telling you so. Really?"

"I... I..." He was puzzled, surprised, and unsure what to say. "I thought it was obvious."

"Cause you told me how many times again?"

"You are the most beautiful girl in Whyland. Anyone who sees you—"

Cayla grimaced. "The most beautiful blablabla. Maybe you need your eyes checked."

He sighed. "I've waited for you for more than one year and a half. I never even looked at anyone else. And the stone doesn't lie."

She snorted. "Yeah, and I only know about it now. At least now I understand your presumption. Sometimes I thought you were full of yourself."

"I'm not. At some point I thought that I was mistaken, that maybe the stone was about a different kind of love—friendship or something."

Cayla rolled her eyes. "Friendship? You can't be serious. Now, other than this stone, what about the rest? All the other things you hid from me? Are you going to tell me?"

"Let's sit. Unless you want me to come tomorrow or another day."

Cayla shook her head. "I want to know now. Now. Everything. Tell me everything."

Darian sat. He told her about his childhood and his mother, how he had grown up in a village in the North, and how they were being threatened by the King's forces. He told her about how he hadn't known he had a brother until he got to the castle, how his brother seemed to hate him for that, and how his father had always been cold and distant. He spoke about his days away from the castle, when he started seeing the King's forces committing unjust violence against defenseless villagers. He told her how he'd protected some of them, how he formed alliances, and how he helped connect everyone who was in the army and didn't agree with what was happening. Cayla listened. Sometimes she asked questions for clarification, but she mostly heard. Her expression was one of understanding and complicity. Talking to her and telling him all the truths that had been hidden for so long felt as if a part of himself was healing, and he was becoming whole again.

"There's one last thing," he said. She listened. He continued, "My mother was great at speaking. When she spoke, it was as if a hypnotic energy took over. There was something almost magical about it. I've also seen how my brother charms people."

Cayla grimaced. "That depends on opinion, I guess."

"Fine, then, forget my brother. Sometimes I've noticed I have this skill, that I can talk to people, and convince them. Not always, though. Once I heard that I was called a whisperer, in the South, or spell speaker, in the North. As it's some kind of magic. But I've never again heard or learned anything about it."

Her eyes were calm. "There's a hidden library in the castle. We could look into it."

Darian nodded. "Thanks. But I have one fear. That perhaps, because of this skill, or power, maybe I made you fall in love with me."

Cayla laughed. "I'll ignore the presumption, now that I know about the ratting stone. Why would you think you bewitched me or something?"

Darian shrugged. "I was just a kid when we met. Scrawny even."

"You were sweet, though."

"Maybe. Still, sometimes I wonder."

"Let me test. Look at me and remain quiet for a second." He looked. Cayla tilted her head, looked at him up and down and examined his face. "You know what I think, it's your good looks. How dare you hypnotize me into liking you?"

He laughed. "At least we both need our eyes checked."

"Not me. Now seriously. You have the answer in your stone. I know a little about magic. Making someone fall in love with you would be evil and quite dangerous. Amplifying one's love or attraction is already dangerous enough that it could drive someone mad. Our twin necklaces would tell us that something was wrong."

Darian was puzzled. "How come you know about magic?"

"I have a lot to tell you. A lot. And I want to tell you, but let me come to terms with all of it first. Also... it's late. I don't want to sound like a prude, but I fear it might look, you know, if you spend that long in my bedroom."

"I understand." He was ready to leave, when he remembered his encounter with Lylah. *There are a couple things he could want in her bedroom.* In hindsight, that was inappropriate and disrespectful. He'd better tell Cayla. "I crossed Lylah when I was coming here—"

"Lylah?" She asked it as if he'd just told her the castle was about to explode. Maybe the woman still intimidated her.

Things were about to get worse, but he had to tell her the truth. "She asked me what I wanted with you, at this time. And maybe, I," his voice was trailing off and his throat was dry, but he made an effort to keep speaking "didn't really prevent her from, uh, making assumptions."

The color faded from Cayla's face. She shook her head as if in horror. "You didn't. You didn't. Do you know who she is?"

"Probably the future queen."

Cayla took a deep breath, as if trying to calm herself down. "Sit down. Now it's my turn to tell you a few things."

CAYLA WOKE up and realized she'd overslept. The sun was up. Memories of the previous night came to her. All the truths she'd finally shared with Darian, all their barriers melting away. She realized he was the person she most liked to talk to, and most liked to confide in. Not only was he the boy she loved, he was her best friend. His lies and the hidden truths had been an odd anomaly that had been solved in one night. Their talk had eased the difficult time she was going through. She felt closer to him than anyone else in the world. She got up and found him lying on the floor, over a blanket. Cayla wasn't sure how they'd made that sleeping arrangement or if she'd just had fallen asleep and he stayed. Cayla knelt beside him and brushed a strand of his hair away from his face.

He opened his eyes. "I'm sorry."

Cayla didn't understand what he meant.

He continued, "About your mother. That she thinks…"

Cayla laughed. "…we totally did it. If there was any doubt, now she'll be sure."

"I'm sorry."

"Look at the bright side. At least when the time comes, we know she won't mind."

His eyes brightened. "When the time comes?"

"I never said it was anytime soon."

"Neither did I. If it takes forever, it means I'll be forever with you."

"Haha, so sweet and romantic. Meanwhile, I'm sure you're thinking about… when the time comes."

Darian closed his eyes, held her hand and pulled it over his chest. "Uhm, I won't lie, the thought will give me some sleepless nights."

"Me too."

He opened his eyes and squeezed her hand. "You want to kill me from sleep deprivation."

"Maybe not. But first we have some kissing to catch up. For two years!"

Cayla leaned over and kissed him.

23

AFTER THE END

A good part of Karina's following morning was spent in the shower, using half a bottle of conditioner to untangle her hair. How come nobody had told her she looked like a cave woman? Wait, Sian had told her. Yikes. She wondered if he was okay, if Cayla, Ayanna, Darian, Nia and Lylah were okay, and if everyone had gotten out of the castle.

Other than questioning her long shower, her parents didn't notice anything wrong or strange. It was as if she'd never gone anywhere. Karina then visited Zoe. It was good to see her again and remember that she also had good friends in her own dimension. Zoe would be shocked if she'd seen Karina wearing the same clothes for days and going without a proper shower, though. Some different priorities. Karina was itching to tell her all about her adventure, but she never knew how to start. Every sentence she imagined, like "so, I went to a different dimension," or "I was visited by a nice woman, who then I learned was an evil which, then I learned was a nice woman," sounded crazy. Unlike Karina thought, Zoe had no clue that the shoes had any special power. In fact, the girl had completely forgotten them. Karina didn't miss them or regret having destroyed them, which was a little odd. Perhaps it was if they'd never existed.

As for her adventure, Karina regretted not having learned more about the different science, or how to travel to different dimensions. Her adventure seemed unreal, especially because she couldn't share it with anyone, but she knew it had been real, because of the amount of time that passed, and because she ate, and unlike in dreams, food tasted like food. True that most of it had been a little bland, but still. The only thing she still wanted to know was how everyone was doing.

Her doubts were answered one day, when she came home from school and found a visitor in her bedroom; Lylah. Karina felt so happy she would have hugged the woman had she felt more at ease around her.

Lylah stared at Karina and said, "You have questions for me."

"How's everyone? How did the attack end?"

Lylah smiled. "Everyone is fine."

Karina was itching with curiosity. "But what happened?"

"We won. The ambush you told us about never happened. They made a deal with us. There was still some conflict in distant areas of the kingdom, but soon it was all settled. We took prisoners, but in time many of them were released. They were just following orders."

Karina sighed in relief to learn that everyone had survived, even Lylah's enemies, because she didn't wish Sian any harm. And she was happy to hear that in the end he did what she'd asked, even if it obviously wasn't because she asked.

Lylah continued, "There were good people on all sides. We've been working on reuniting everyone, reuniting the kingdom." The woman then smiled, "If you hadn't warned us, they would have taken us by surprise. Perhaps we could still have won, but it would take longer. And people might have gotten hurt."

"But you said they struck a deal."

"The fact that they no longer had surprise on their side might have helped."

That was good news. At least Karina had helped, somehow.

"But you have more questions, don't you?" Lylah asked.

Well, yes. "The shoes. What were they? Did they have any power?"

"Well... They were magical objects. When people go to other dimensions, they have more power. It works for magical objects as well. That is why the shoes were so fascinating for you here, and you almost forgot about them when you got to our world. In my world, they worked differently. I used them to communicate with you. Don't you remember I spoke to you sometimes?"

Karina forced her memory, but nothing came. "Uh, no."

The woman nodded. "I see. That explains a lot. But at least I knew what was happening to you, and I was able to inform and make plans with my brother."

"So... you could hear us?"

"I had access to your thoughts."

Awkward. Karina had never felt her privacy so abused in her entire life.

Lylah then added, "Only in what concerned my daughter."

Still, that was a lot. Karina would never, ever, call her mom nosy again. "Wouldn't it be easier then for Cayla to carry the shoes?"

"No. They were too connected with me, and I was in a powerful prison. If Cayla touched them, she could be taken to the white castle, with no means to get out. Her sister would've had no problem, but that wasn't something that could be easily explained."

"I see." But there was something else Karina had to ask. She still couldn't really believe it. "But if the shoes had no power... Was it really me? I could teleport?"

"Everyone has some power. Not only did you teleport, you

almost teleported from the yellow tower. That was impressive, although dangerous. You also made a lift explode."

"What?" That didn't make sense, unless... "Wait. Do you mean the lift that we were going to use to escape? You are saying I did it?"

"Yes. Lifts don't explode by themselves."

"No, no, no. You are saying I had some kind of superpower, and I used it to blow the vehicle that could have helped me escape?"

Lylah stared for a moment. "I also thought the choice was odd."

Karina covered her face with her hands. "That's the worst misuse of talent ever!"

"I wouldn't say that. You are still young."

Was that some kind of encouragement? Karina shrugged. "Well, I won't ever have any magical power again, so I'm sure I won't misuse it."

"That depends on how you define magic. Or power."

Perhaps the woman meant scientific knowledge or something? Karina didn't want to waste that either, and didn't want to think about that. She then wondered what happened to Cayla and Darian. She was about to ask when she remembered the woman was the girl's mother, and Karina would be mortified if anyone talked to her mom about boys. She asked another question, "How's Cayla doing?"

"She is slowly accepting things... as they are. She told me to say hello, and to tell you that she is doing well. Darian's also fine."

Of course, if Lylah had accessed Karina's thoughts, she knew it all.

Karina then changed the subject. "Can you really grant wishes?"

The woman sat back, smiled, looked at Karina for a while, then said, "I don't think you could have asked anything you could not achieve for yourself anyways. So I wasn't lying. But, no, I wasn't planning on buying the shoes, if that's what you want to know."

Of course, Karina knew that, but it was still nice to know she had been right, although she felt a little silly remembering her enthusiasm about making a wish.

The woman then smiled and said, "Don't dismiss what you did. You helped my family, my kingdom and me. A lot. Someone had to carry the shoes. You never quit, never gave up, never returned."

That was not really true because the only reason Karina had not returned is that she hadn't been able to.

Lylah stared at her. "No, Karina, you could have returned, but you didn't try it. At least not enough. You were not really trying to get back home. With the exception of a few difficult moments, the rest of the time you were focused on going forward, on finishing your task."

Had she just read her thought? Better not think about it too much. Karina had a more important question. "Why me?"

"Why did you buy the shoes? Why did you agree to come? It could have been anyone, but it happened to be you."

"Oh, I..." Karina didn't finish the sentence, because she was embarrassed to admit she thought she had been some kind of "chosen one."

"You don't understand," the woman said. "There are many things anyone could do. Each person is faced with infinite possibilities. It doesn't matter why you choose one or the other, or why life draws you one way or another. What matters is not why, or what exactly, but your choices along the way. Perhaps any girl could have done it. But not all of them would have done it."

"But I mean... there was no special reason then?"

"Maybe. Have you considered that perhaps the shoes called you? Or that you sought them? You can either think that everything happens for a reason or that everything is random. Both conclusions are identical."

That didn't make sense. "No. They are complete opposites."

Lylah laughed a normal, happy laugh. "You can see it any way you want." When she stopped laughing she became serious and thoughtful, then said, "I have something for you." She had a large bag, from where she took a large book and gave it to Karina.

It had a green cover in leather, and some maps and pictures inside it. Karina opened it, and recognized a map. It was Whyland. Everything in images. "Is it so that I remember my adventure?"

"I think so. Darian sent it to you. He says it's from his brother."

Karina was surprised to hear that. Sian remembered her? Her stupid heart beat faster. But maybe it was just that she was glad for the brothers. "So they're getting along now?"

Lylah shook her head "I'm afraid not. Sian has disappeared." She looked at Karina. "He wouldn't have faced any serious accusations. But now he's gone."

Karina hoped he was all right. But something didn't make sense. "How could he send the book then?"

"To be honest, I didn't ask. He must have met his brother before leaving."

Karina looked down. "Now I can know more about Whyland, but..." She looked at Lylah, as a sadness suddenly filled her chest. "Am I ever going to visit it again?"

"It would be hard."

As Karina feared. She felt sad.

Lylah continued, "The time difference is changing, and soon it will be reversed. The flowing tower was destroyed because it was connected to the white castle. But at least you won't forget the places you visited and the friends you made."

At least that was something. Karina had a sad smile. "I won't."

"I have to go now," Lylah said.

"Wait," Karina said. She wanted to change her mood, so she asked one last silly question, "How come you speak English?"

"Tu préfères français?"

That was odd. "No. I mean..."

Karina could not really word it. She was sure they would speak a different language in a different world. Or almost sure. Whatever.

"You understand things the way you understand them," Lylah said. "That doesn't mean that's what they are. Interdimensional travel warps the logic you know. Thank you for helping me save my kingdom. Goodbye Karina."

Lylah then disappeared, leaving only sparkly dust behind her. Karina was sure the dust wasn't from blinking. It was real. She opened the book. Maybe it would be a good idea to learn about the place she visited. On the other hand, maybe it would be an even better idea to learn more about her own dimension. Whyland didn't have to be her last adventure. There were so many places, so many countries she didn't know. Of course, she wouldn't be a hero again, but maybe all she needed was to do the little she could, and to make good choices along the way. True that the one problem with going to different places was missing the people she met. She held the book against her chest. It was better than not meeting them. At least their memory would be with her forever.

～

Prologue
15 months before - Siphoria - Whyland

DARIAN TASTED VICTORY ALL RIGHT, except that he could never before have imagined what its real taste was. There was something bitter and sour, perhaps incomplete. Yes, his insurgency had won. A new era was about to start in Whyland. And yet, his father... Gone forever. Gone was the chance to find any reconciliation, anything human in him. His brother had disappeared. Cayla... He'd have to talk to her.

Darian opened his bag and arranged his belongings. His future was uncertain, but this would be his new home for now; a room in Siphoria's military complex, close to Whyland's castle.

A sound at the window interrupted his thoughts. This room was on the seventh floor of the complex tower, so there shouldn't be anyone or anything at the window, but it would be unwise to dismiss the disruption as wind. It had to be an intruder, and a very skilled one, to have climbed to that height.

Darian could rush to the window, but the intruder probably expected that. Instead, he hid behind the bed and listened. As expected, someone entered his room. Before the intruder did anything, Darian jumped on the person and dropped him or her on the floor. It was a guy, based on his height and build, but before Darian could immobilize him, the intruder pulled Darian's arm and rolled on top of him. It was Darian who ended up pinned on the floor. With his foot, Darian reached for a knife but soon realized that it wouldn't be necessary, as he noticed familiar gleaming brown eyes in a face framed with wavy dark hair.

It was his older brother Sian, grinning. "Little brother, I'm happy you're finally showing me some love."

One would think Sian was on top of the world and had just won a war, not that all his plans had failed and that he was on the run. But at that moment, Darian was simply glad to see his brother alive and well. "You disappeared. I was worried."

Sian raised an eyebrow. "Worried you couldn't arrest me?"

"Worried about you. Can you let me go now?"

Sian tilted his head. "You don't like your brother's hug? Not surprising." He laughed and got up.

Darian also got up. "Stop being funny. Or trying to. Do you know how many people are looking for you?"

"Well, that's the point, isn't it? Not being caught. But I'm here because I wanted to talk to you."

Relief took over Darian's chest. "Listen, I'm sure the insurgents will forgive you. I know them well. I could—"

"No chance, brother," Sian interrupted. "Too long I've lived by my father's shadow. I'm not gonna live under yours."

"That's not at all what I was saying. What I mean is—" Darian sighed. "You don't need to run away."

Sian glared at him. "I don't run away. I retreat. Regroup. Rethink." He pointed at his head, then looked down,, a bitter grin on his face. "I would have beaten you. I would have conquered the kingdom. But I didn't expect magic to make such a difference. My mistake, I recognize." He stared at Darian with fiery fierce eyes. "But I learn from my mistakes."

"And you hope me to just let you go?"

"I don't hope. I'm sure you will. There's certainly a bit of love buried deep within that chest." Behind his brother's impenetrable grin there was something soft, real.

"It's not buried. You'd do much better by my side, Sian. Think about it. With your knowledge, and your leadership—"

"By your side is the part where it all sours." Sian grimaced. "Not interested. Thank you, though. I guess." He smirked then became serious. "But if you want to help me, there's something you can do. You're close to the princess, Cayla."

Darian was taken aback. He couldn't imagine what his brother would want with her.

Before Darian said anything, Sian continued, "She traveled with a girl, Karina. I promised I'd give her a book, and I'm counting on your fraternal love to fulfill my promise." He took a large green book from a bag he had tied to his back.

That was an odd request. "Why don't you give it in person?"

"Not possible. I have to go." Sian then spoke with an overly dramatic and hurt tone: "Are you going to refuse your brother's last wish?"

"You're not dying."

Sian shrugged. "You don't know if you'll ever see me alive again."

"What's this about?"

"A promise. I keep my word." He smiled and looked up with an exaggerated dreamy expression. "Especially to pretty girls, you know? If you can, send it with all my love."

Darian rolled his eyes. "If you didn't flirt with every girl you meet, you'd have a girlfriend by now."

"You assume too much, little brother. I'm just a loving person with a broad definition of love. Maybe one day, if I ever decide to get a girlfriend, I'll do like you and obey her like a puppy while she ignores me."

Darian clenched his fists. But no. Sian had meant to offend him. That's what he wanted. He wouldn't give his brother that pleasure. Darian shrugged and put up his best smug smile. "Well, what can I say? At least it works."

Sian laughed. "Works wonders. I bet even you still haven't realized how lucky you got. Well done." He patted Darian's back, then became serious and distant. "But that's not what I want right now. I still keep my word, though. My broad definition of love has nothing to do with it."

Darian took the book. He could ask Cayla, he didn't see much into it. In fact, that would be an excellent excuse to talk to her.

Sian stared in his eyes. "Can you give me your word? That you'll make sure Cayla's friend gets the book?"

Darian scoffed. "Sure. You come here, offend me, while you're on the run, and I'm supposed to arrest you. Now I have to give you my word. Why again?"

"I didn't offend you. But I apologize if you felt that way. I just want to make sure the book reaches its destination."

It wasn't a big deal, really. "I also keep my word. I said I'd give it; I will. The book. Not the empty words that come with it."

Sian waved a hand. "Oh, please, I sure don't want you sending anyone any love."

Darian still wished he could convince his brother to stay. "Where are you going?"

Sian raised his eyebrows and smiled. "I'm on the run, right? Why should I tell you?"

"You can't go anywhere from here. You'll need to go downstairs, and—"

Sian walked to the window. Of course, he wasn't going to walk out the door.

"By the time you climb down, I'll have you surrounded." He

didn't want to threaten his brother, but he would have to do something if given no choice.

Sian laughed. "Your guards are lighting fast, then. I'll be impressed." He climbed on the windowsill.

"Wait," Darian pleaded.

Sian stood up on the window and let his body fall. Cold emptiness was what was left in Darian's chest. He ran and looked down.

Instead of the body of his injured brother, he saw a flying machine, a lift, coming up, with his brother on top of it, climbing down to enter. Sian had planned to jump and to escape. How a private lift had gotten so close to the military tower, he had no idea. Darian wished his brother could have stayed, that they could have become friends, allies, but it wouldn't be this time.

He looked at the book. At least one bit of brotherly trust. There was still something there that could be salvaged between them. As much as it was no big deal, it meant a step towards reconciliation with his brother.

The story continues in Kissing Magic.

Karina needs to return to Whyland. This time it's not to save the kingdom, but to save Sian. Can she save herself, though?

Get more info at

dayleitao.com/books/kissing-magic

ABOUT THE AUTHOR

Originally from Brazil, Day Leitao lives in Montreal, Canada, with her son. She likes to imagine worlds and characters.

To learn more, visit her at dayleitao.com

Also, don't forget to sign up for my newsletter to receive news, freebies, reading suggestions, and more!

BB bookbub.com/profile/day-leitao

a amazon.com/author/day-leitao

AFTERWORD

Thanks very much for reading this book. I hope you enjoyed it. You can write to me at day@sparklywave.com if you have comments.

I'd also like to thank everyone who helped me with this book by beta reading it, editing it, or just giving me advice and encouragement.

Super thanks for everyone in my mailing list, who encouraged me and gave me suggestions and support.

Many, many thanks to all the wonderful reviewers who help readers decide if this is a book they'd like to read or not, and who helped spread the word about Portals to Whyland.